Please God **bald and fat.**

Kate held her breath as her ex-husband walked down the hall behind her. She recognized David's step, but more than that, after twenty years, she'd know that scent in the dark. Without turning, she said in what she hoped was a conversational tone, "Hello, David."

"Hello, Kate." That voice definitely hadn't grown fat and bald. David's full baritone still eddied around her like warm clover honey.

She knew she had to turn around and face this man who had betrayed her in the most devastating way a man could betray a woman. She was glad she'd changed from her jeans to her Chanel. Her suit screamed success. She wished she had sweated off the ten pounds she'd gained in the past couple of years, but she was still twenty pounds lighter than she'd been when he'd last seen her.

She could do this. She shoved away from the wall, took a deep breath and turned around.

Despite her good intentions she had to close her eyes a moment against the impact of him. Not fat and bald.

Not fair.

Dear Reader,

I remember watching my friends fall in love, and wondering whether lightning would ever strike me. I wasn't sure I'd recognize love if it jumped up and bit me. When it did, it was like an earthquake—you may not have been through one before, but when it hits, nobody has to tell you what's happening.

Many of us leave our first loves for some reason, and lose track of them. In our secret hearts, we hope they are miserable without us, no matter who dumped whom. No matter how happy we are now, every once in a while we all wonder whatever happened to the guy who... If we met, would the sparks still fly? Could I bear to have him see I've put on forty pounds? Do I really want to know whether he's kept his hair and his waistline? Am I proud of the woman I've become in the intervening years?

Well, this is a story of a woman who finds herself face-to-face with the man who loved her and betrayed her, the man she longs to roast over a slow fire. The man who suddenly needs her desperately. She can have her revenge simply by walking away. But can she live with herself if she does?

Carolyn McSparren

Books by Carolyn McSparren

HARLEQUIN SUPERROMANCE

FATHERS AND SONS
Carolyn McSparren

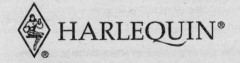

HARLEQUIN®

TORONTO • NEW YORK • LONDON
AMSTERDAM • PARIS • SYDNEY • HAMBURG
STOCKHOLM • ATHENS • TOKYO • MILAN • MADRID
PRAGUE • WARSAW • BUDAPEST • AUCKLAND

ISBN 0-373-70829-7

FATHERS AND SONS

For Beverly Williams and Lottie Garner, who advised me on Mississippi jurisprudence; for Phyllis Appleby, who can always spot the holes in my plots; for Patricia Potter, a true romantic, a great writer and a dear friend.

For Sidney Eckerly, who gave me the name for the plantation. Finally, for my flamboyant actress mother, who never saw my first book. She used to say that being happy took an effort of will—and a lot of hard work.

CHAPTER ONE

A TELEPHONE CALL at thirty thousand feet over Oklahoma meant only one thing—disaster.

"You can take it up there, Mrs. Mulholland," the flight attendant whispered and pointed toward the cubby at the front of the first-class seating. The sleeping man across the aisle grunted and turned his back on her.

Kate Mulholland laid the blue legal folders on the seat beside her and walked forward to pick up the telephone. "Mulholland," she said. She could hear the pounding of her heart over the grumble of the 747.

"Kate!" the voice on the other end of the phone sounded elated. "I just—"

"Arnold? Oh, God, who died?"

"Hold on a minute. You worry too much. You did good. I thought you deserved to be congratulated."

"At—" she glanced at her watch "—seven-thirty in the morning and halfway up into the ionosphere? You couldn't wait until I got to Atlanta?"

"I'm not in Atlanta."

"Where are you? And why?"

"Besides, you definitely deserve congratulations," he said, ignoring the question. "You played against the big boys and won."

"Yeah, I did, didn't I?" Kate rubbed her eyes and wished she'd waited for a morning flight out of LAX. "At least Sunny Borland will be able to raise her kids decently on the judgment we got her, but I know she'd rather have Pete Borland alive.'' Her eyes felt like hot lava rocks, but her heart had settled.

''A five-mil settlement is five mil. Nice chunk of change for the firm as well.''

''Pete Borland died from a lousy gallbladder operation because his anesthesiologist was high on coke. That doctor should have gone to jail for murder.''

''Hey, Kate, we do what we can do.'' There was a moment's hesitation.

''All right, Arnold. You're not calling just to make nice. What do you want?''

''Kate, I need your help.''

''No you do not. I'm going home to Atlanta, spend six hours in the whirlpool and sleep for a week.''

''Now, Kate, this is important. A Mississippi planter has just hired us to defend his nineteen-year-old son against a murder charge. Hired *you,* that is.''

''Me? You keep trying to con me back into doing criminal stuff. Won't work. I like civil litigation. *My* clients deserve to win.''

Arnold laughed. ''*All* our clients are innocent, you know that. This one is accused, however, of raping and murdering his girlfriend, one Waneath Talley, a former homecoming queen and third runner-up to Miss Mississippi last year. Small southern town, prominent families, explosive situation.'' He hesitated. ''Humongous retainer.''

''Why does he want me?''

''Because you're old enough to be the kid's mother? Because you're a woman? Because juries love you? Because you have a rep for only defending people you believe in? Maybe because if you believe he's innocent, the jury will too.''

"I have never been a mother. Do I look motherly to you? Besides, what if I don't believe him?"

"Make certain you do. Listen, this is costing a fortune. Don't go on to Atlanta. Get off the plane in Memphis and make 'em get your luggage off the plane. I'll have a car waiting to drive you down here..."

"Where's here?"

Her answer came in garbled words and static. "Arnold? Arnold, you're breaking up."

More static. If Arnold Selig were not her dearest friend as well as the best lawyer she knew, she would have called him a few unprintable names. But what was the use? She'd save her guns for a face-to-face encounter. He owed her big for this, and she'd make darned sure he knew it.

FOUR HOURS LATER she kissed the air to the right of Arnold Selig's thin cheek and dropped her briefcase onto the table in the center of the dingy jail interview room. "I will get you for this."

He spread his hands with an apologetic grin. "So what else have you got to do?"

"Arnold, I have just spent a month living in a hotel room in California fighting the biggest malpractice suit of my career. My Thanksgiving turkey came from room service. I ate it alone. The jury got the holiday off, but I sure as heck didn't."

"They brought in a guilty verdict the minute they got back, didn't they? You won."

"What I won was the seat on the red-eye you dragged me off. What I deserve is my own bed in my own apartment and about three days' uninterrupted sleep. Definitely not this."

She wrinkled her nose. She had tried to forget the odor of human sweat and urine that pervaded every jail in which

she'd ever interviewed a client. In the last six months she'd
been meeting her civil-case clients around palatial conference tables with plenty of fresh coffee and the occasional
pastry. "Place smells like a sewer."

She moved her foot and heard a pop. "This floor has
something repellently sticky on it." She checked the seat
of the plain wooden chair. It seemed clean. She sat and
eased her feet under the table. "So, where's my client and
how soon can we get him out of this hellhole?"

"The D.A.'s opposing bail. Says the kid's grandfather is
perfectly capable of spiriting the boy off to Brazil on a
private jet."

"Is he?"

"You bet, but we don't want the judge to believe that.
Ah, the client arrives." He made a grand gesture toward
the heavy wooden door at the far side of the room.

It opened, and a uniformed guard the size of at least two
Alabama point guards stood aside. Kate turned for her first
look at her client. Her heart stopped. She gulped and
grabbed at her briefcase. Anything to keep her hands from
shaking.

"Kate, this is..."

"David Canfield," Kate whispered.

The young man narrowed his eyes and said truculently,
"I'm Jason. David's my daddy."

Kate shoved her chair back and bolted for the hall. A
moment later she heard Arnold's apologetic murmur to the
men in the room, then he came out to stand beside her. She
knew it was Arnold because she recognized his shoes—all
of him she could see from her position with her fists
clenched into her stomach and her head bent halfway to her
knees.

"The smell wasn't that bad. You gonna throw up?" Arnold asked solicitously.

He kneaded her shoulder gently.

Her voice sounded to her as though it came from the bottom of a well. "I can't do this. Even if I could, you don't want me to."

"The kid's father knows you haven't been doing criminal cases lately. He's okay with that."

She shook her head violently, and waves of nausea coursed through her. She rose, leaned her head against the bilious yellow painted wall and closed her eyes.

"Kate? Katherine?"

He never called her Katherine. She heard the panic in his voice. He must think she was having a heart attack. In a sense, she was.

She waved a hand toward the room from which Arnold had just come. "I'm not that boy's mother, but I could have been. A lifetime ago I spent a year married to his father."

"You what?"

"No way you could know, Arnold. I was married once before I married Alec Mulholland. Christmas vacation my senior year in college, I married David Canfield, that boy's father."

"Damn!" Arnold whispered. He pulled her around to face him.

She kept the shoulder he didn't have his hand on against the wall so that she wouldn't slide down to sprawl on that nasty floor like a rag doll. She felt a giggle start somewhere deep within her at the thought of what the grunge on that wall was probably doing to her sky blue Chanel suit.

"Open your eyes, look at me," Arnold said.

She saw Arnold through a mist of unshed tears that threatened to spill over to run down her cheeks. She blinked them back. No way would she cry now. Not visibly, at any rate. She'd long since learned to shed her tears inside.

"It was not, I take it, an amicable divorce?" Arnold asked. "Your first marriage did not die a natural death?"

"It was murdered." She chopped her hand down hard. "Guillotined, stabbed, shot, bludgeoned to death with a blunt instrument, strangled, poisoned, drawn and quartered and sawed in half."

She began to shake as the laughter she'd held at bay got out of hand. Arnold stared at her in alarm. He did not deal well with emotion of any kind. Hysterics in a law partner would terrify him.

"Surely this guy couldn't have hired you without knowing who you are, could he? I mean, you have a different name now."

"How on earth should I know? I didn't even know David had a son, much less that he was growing up in some godforsaken wide place in the road in the middle of the Mississippi delta where he was learning the fine art of murder."

DAVID HAD NEVER MANAGED to convince Kate she was beautiful. Not in two years as his live-in girlfriend at college, nor in a year as his wife in New York. He had, however, managed to convince her—and himself—of his talent and discipline and desire to be a great star. But she'd thought she was big and awkward, that her hair was too thin and her thighs too fat. She'd believed in her fierce intellect, but could never see the fire in her soul that gave her an even more fierce beauty.

Maybe Alec Mulholland had convinced her of that beauty. David felt his stomach churn. The man had been dead nearly a year now. A man David had never met. From all reports, a great lawyer. Possibly a great human being. But every time David thought of Mulholland in bed with Kate he got heartburn. His Kate.

He wondered what she looked like after twenty years. He

had a drawer full of clippings and letters about her, but no photos. He prayed she was the size of a truck and as bald as an egg.

Who was he kidding? To him she'd be the most beautiful bald-headed eighteen-wheeler in the universe.

He had sweated bullets before he decided to call her. One part of him longed to see her again. The other part wished she was in Siberia buried under a glacier.

Dub had made up his mind for him. Jason's grandfather was treating the boy's arrest as though it were at best a huge joke, at worst a minor misunderstanding. The old man agreed Jason should have a lawyer, all right, but he'd wanted to use his own attorney, Jack Slaydon, whose closest involvement with a criminal case had been a DUI he'd defended Dub against twenty years ago. And lost.

The man wrote wills, for God's sake. Handled real-estate closings.

Jason's arrest was no joke. Even if the boy and Dub didn't understand the seriousness of Jason's position, David did. And the best criminal-defense attorney he knew was Kate Mulholland.

Hell, she was the only criminal-defense lawyer he knew.

And he did know her, even if he hadn't seen her for twenty years. He knew when she passed the bar, moved to Atlanta, become a partner, married Alec Mulholland.

He had followed her career—the civil and criminal cases she won against battering husbands and for abused children, against employers who harassed and hospitals that killed or maimed. He knew about the innocent clients who were walking around free because she'd defended them. She fought for underdogs. And more often than not she won.

He'd had a conduit straight into her life ever since she kicked him out.

If she ever discovered how he'd managed to stay aware

of everything going on in her life, Kate would be mad enough to commit murder.

He caught his breath. How casually everybody spoke of murder! After this, he'd never be able to watch one of those crime shows on television again. This was real, and it was damn scary.

David pulled into a parking slot that had miraculously opened up within a block of the county courthouse, turned off the ignition, but made no attempt to get out of the car. He dropped his head onto the steering wheel.

He must have been crazy to mortgage his house to hire her firm to save Jason's butt. At three hundred bucks an hour, that fat retainer would be eaten up in a heartbeat. Dub was still mad that David had pulled an end run on him by hiring Kate. But these days he and Dub seldom agreed about anything. In his present frame of mind, the old man wouldn't offer one thin dime to help pay the lawyer's bills.

David climbed out of the car and locked it, then started to walk the block to the yellow brick building in the center of the square.

"'Afternoon, Canfield,'" a man spoke in passing.

David looked up and nodded. The man walked on without stopping to chat. In Athena, Mississippi, most meetings gave an excuse to stop and chat. David felt a cold breath on his neck, and not from the November wind.

A good many people had already taken sides—the pro-Jason side and the anti-Jason side. Apparently, the rest were keeping their heads down and trying to appear neutral until they saw which way the wind blew.

Of course, Dub had made many enemies through the years with his wealth and power. For many of Athena's townspeople, Jason's trouble meant payback time. People like Big Bill Talley, Waneath's father, resented Dub's old-money wealth and life-style. No matter how much money men like Big Bill made, the size of the mansions they built, the clubs they ran, they never attained the comfortable acceptance Dub took for granted. As a result, justice for Jason might be very hard to come by in Athena.

David dug his hands into the pockets of his windbreaker and walked on with his shoulders back and his eyes front. No one else spoke to him. He was left with his own thoughts.

Kate would probably take one look at him and try to run a stake through his heart. He had to convince her to stay and to take Jason's case. Appealing to their common history sure as hell wouldn't do it.

She might be willing to take the case to show David how well she was doing without him. Thumb her nose at him. Fine. Whatever worked.

Because he needed her.

He started up the courthouse steps, made his way across the hall, and downstairs to the jail area in the basement. A deputy whom he knew by sight but not by name stood aside and watched him curiously. David could feel the man's eyes on his back as he pulled open the door and walked down the hall to the interrogation rooms.

When he'd seen Jason's white face as the boy had been driven away in the back of Sheriff Tait's squad car, David had wondered whether this was his final penance. To lose Jason, the one truly blessed thing to come out of all the mistakes he'd made in his life.

No God could be that cruel. If David had to face Kate's wrath, her recriminations, her hatred, then for the sake of his child he'd do precisely that. He'd offer no excuses and no explanations. She probably wouldn't listen anyway.

He had trusted only two women in his life—his mother, who'd believed everything she'd ever told him, and Kate, who had never lied to him about anything. And she'd always stood up for what she believed.

Now he needed to persuade her to fight for Jason. David hadn't done any serious acting in twenty years, but he hoped he hadn't lost his touch.

If he wanted Kate to stay, he'd have to convince her he believed Jason was innocent...when he was desperately afraid his son was guilty.

KATE CAUGHT her breath. David was walking down the hall behind her. She knew his step, but more than that, after twenty years she'd recognize that scent in the dark. Her eyes still on Arnold's face, she said in what she hoped was a conversational tone, "Hello, David." *Please God,* she thought. *Let him be bald and fat.*

"Hello, Kate," he said. "Jason didn't murder anyone."

That voice definitely hadn't grown fat and bald. David's full baritone still eddied around her like warm clover honey.

She kept her panicked eyes on Arnold's face and fought to keep her voice steady. "Really?"

She knew she had to turn around, to face this man who had betrayed her in the most devastating way a man could betray a woman. She was glad she'd changed from jeans to her Chanel in the bathroom at the airport. Her suit screamed success.

She wished she had sweated off that ten pounds she'd gained in the last couple of years, but she was still twenty pounds lighter than she'd been when she and David lived in that godawful flat on the Lower East Side in Manhattan. These days she ran and she worked out. Her buns might not be steel exactly, but they were definitely aluminum. Her haircut had cost a packet in Beverly Hills and looked it.

She could do this. She shoved away from the wall, took a deep breath and turned around.

"How did you know it was me?" he asked.

Despite her good intentions she had to close her eyes a moment against the impact of him. Not fat and bald. Not fair.

He held out his hand. She ignored it. "You still use that expensive sandalwood soap." She curled her lip. "No doubt you can afford it—now. I suppose you could say I smelled you."

He nodded.

Oh, damn, damn, damn. Why did men have to get better as they aged while women got worse? He seemed even taller, although that couldn't be. Maybe he was wearing those high-heeled cowboy boots. His shoulders seemed broader, more muscular in his plaid shirt. There was gray in his sandy hair, but while most people got dull bits of gray straggling all over, David's lay in neat silver wings over his ears. His face was tan, his body lean and taut, and the incipient crow's-feet around his eyes seemed like arrows pointing to the blue of his eyes.

Crazy eyes. Plenty of people wore contact lenses to turn their eyes that blue, but David had been born with them. Never saw a man with eyes that dark blue. Like the Blue Grotto in Capri or the Hope Diamond. Killer diamond. Better analogy. Definitely killer eyes.

The David she remembered was a combination of Brad Pitt and his namesake *David* by Michelangelo. This man was Harrison Ford and Richard Gere and Sean Connery and...

And she hated him.

He dropped his hand as though he hadn't really expected her to shake it.

"Are you responsible for getting me down here for your son?" she asked, waving toward the door behind which his no-doubt bewildered son still sat with his huge baby-sitter.

"Yes."

"Oh, David, what possessed you? My Lord, even if I were F. Lee Bailey and Johnnie Cochran rolled into one I wouldn't handle this case. And if you know enough about me to find me as Kate Mulholland, you must know I'm not a criminal litigator any longer. I don't do murderers."

"He's not a murderer. He's innocent."

"He could be as innocent as the angels and I still wouldn't be the right lawyer to defend him. If you're dead set on using the firm, we've got a crack team of guys who will use every trick in the book to get him free. We call them 'the murder twins.' Say the word *murder* and they point like bird dogs and begin to drool."

"I want you."

"Then you're crazy. Besides, Jason may not want me. Does he know who I am? Who I was?"

"Nobody does. Nobody has to. So far as Athena is concerned, you're here because you're a great lawyer."

"And so far as you're concerned?"

"Because you're a great lawyer and because I would trust you with my life. More to the point, I would trust you with my son's life."

She shook her head. "We'll return your check."

"Um," Arnold said, "I'm afraid it's been deposited."

She waved a hand at him. "Call the office and tell them to cut one to David for the same amount."

"I refuse to accept it," David said. "I am paying for your services, and I will accept no one and nothing less."

Kate wondered if fear for his son was enough motivation to put that strength in him, or whether he'd actually grown stronger through the years. Even as Macbeth his senior year in college, he'd never truly caught the timbre of command she heard in his voice now. He'd always been too amiable.

He hated making enemies. Maybe making an enemy of Kate had taught him the knack.

"Your check entitles you to the services of the firm. And that's what you'll get."

"When? Tomorrow? The next day? When somebody else can manage to get down here?" He reached out a large brown hand. She shrank away—the thought of any molecule from his body touching any molecule of hers appalled her.

"We can't wait that long. Jason can't spend another night in this place. He's innocent, for God's sake. Forget he's my son and think of him as a terrified nineteen-year-old kid stuck in a situation he doesn't understand."

"What do you want me to do about it? Break him out?"

"Can't you get him out on bail?"

"This afternoon?" She glanced at Arnold. "Is there a judge in this place we can see this afternoon?"

"Bail hearing tentatively set for four," Arnold told her. "I still have to confirm, but I think we can manage it."

Kate sighed. "One of these days you're going to go too far, Arnold, dear."

"Hey. It's my job to smooth your path, right?"

"You've sandbagged me is what you've done."

"So you'll handle the bail hearing?" David asked. Kate heard the hope in his voice. "And then come on out to the house later and meet Dub?"

"Dub?"

"His real name is Douglas Mays. He's my father-in-law and the biggest planter in this part of the state. Hear us out. Hear Jason out. Then make up your mind whether to take the case or not." He ran his hand down his face, and when he removed it, the steel was gone. "Maybe you're right that this is a bad idea, but please, Kate, do this one thing for me."

"For you? I thought it was for your son." She turned away. "It is always and forever about *you,* isn't it? Come on, Arnold, let's go talk to our client."

"THIS IS CRAZY."

Jason sat slumped on his side of the table in his orange prison jumpsuit. His fingers played five-finger piano exercises on the table in front of him. He walked them thumb to little finger and back again. He watched them as though if he concentrated long and hard enough, he'd be able to hear Mozart. Or, more likely in his case, some new hard-rock group with a creepy name.

Arnold pulled a pack of cigarettes out of his pocket and shoved it across the table. Jason looked up at him with a sneer. "Don't smoke."

"Neither do I," Arnold said, retrieved the packet and stuck it back in his briefcase. "I keep them for nervous clients."

Jason glanced up at the guard. "I don't smoke cigarettes or anything stronger. No dope. You hear me, Otis?" The guard, who leaned against the wall looking half-asleep, didn't acknowledge the remark.

"I think it's time we had a little privacy, isn't it, Otis?" Kate asked sweetly. "And I assume there's no one behind that." She gestured to a broad two-way mirror along one wall. "That would be terribly naughty. Lawyers speak to their clients in total privacy. Rather like the confessional." She smiled again. "Oh, and unlock his ankles and wrists on your way out, please."

"Can't do it."

"Of course you can, Otis. As a matter of fact, I insist on it. And so, incidentally, does the Constitution of the United States, if you'd care to check. We'll be happy to wait."

Grumbling, Otis unlocked the chains and pulled them away from Jason's body. "I'll be right outside."

"Thank you so much. We'll call you when we're finished."

Jason's head stayed bent. His fingers hesitated only momentarily and then went back to their Czerny exercises, but Kate caught the edge of a grin on his face and winked at Arnold.

"So, what happened?" Kate asked.

"Huh?" This time Jason looked at her directly.

Kate caught her breath. Michelangelo would have fainted dead away with lust at the sight of the boy. He was, if anything, more beautiful than David had been at that age. No, David had been ruggedly handsome. Jason looked like David, but with a fine-boned elegance that was only heightened by the tension in his body. Those fine bones came, no doubt, from his mother, good old Melba, she of the size-two dresses and the size-nothing shoes. But he had his father's sapphire eyes. Suddenly Kate wanted to reach across the table and hug him.

She was so startled by her impulse that she dropped her pen under the table in all the muck and had to bend over to get it. Under the table, Jason's feet in their expensive running shoes—without either socks or laces for fear of a suicide attempt in his cell—were drumming in tiny dance patterns.

When she had rearranged herself, she said, "All right, Jason, let's get down to it. I'm asking you what happened. You're sitting in jail without your shoelaces and obviously without a shower and accused of rape and murder. Unless this is an everyday occurrence in your life, I imagine you'd be anxious to tell me why you're here."

"I didn't do it."

No fear. Jason Canfield was stunned and angry, but he wasn't afraid.

"Okay. So who did?"

He jerked in his chair and looked away. "How the hell should I know?"

"All right," Arnold said soothingly. "Since you have refused to give a statement to the authorities—good thinking, by the way…"

"I watch 'Homicide' and 'N.Y.P.D. Blue,'" Jason said. "I know I'm not supposed to say squat to anybody without my lawyer."

"Thank God for television," Arnold breathed. "We are, however, your lawyers, and we are now here. So take it from the top. What happened?"

"I don't know."

"All right," Arnold said smoothly. "But according to witnesses, you did have a date with Waneath Talley Saturday night."

"Sure. I mean I'm home on Thanksgiving vacation, right? And Waneath and I have been dating since high school, right? So why wouldn't I have a date with her? What's the biggie?"

"No biggie," Kate said, "except that you had a screaming fight in front of some juke joint that was overheard by half the town. Then you drove off together still fighting, and nobody saw Waneath until her body was discovered by the side of the road the following morning."

"Well, somebody sure saw her after I did."

"Did you have sex?"

"That's none of your business."

Kate leaned back in her chair. She was becoming deeply ticked off at her client. Scratch that—her firm's client. Stubborn as a mule. Just like his daddy. Must be something in the genes.

At the thought of David, who was probably storming up and down the hall outside, she felt a flutter in her stomach. Sooner or later she'd have to face him again. Probably after she'd failed to secure bail for this truculent little jerk in front of her. She had a history of failure when it came to David. History did tend to repeat itself.

"All right," she said quietly. "I assume this means that you really want to spend the next twenty-five years of your life in Parchman Penitentiary which, from everything I hear, is the garden spot of the universe. Assuming they don't execute you, that is."

"I didn't do anything!" Jason wailed. And now there was fear. His face broke out in a sheen of sweat. His hands stopped playing Mozart and clenched tight to keep them from trembling. "She was alive when I left her."

"After you'd made love?"

"Yes. Okay, yes."

"Where?"

"In the back seat of my car, where else?" He'd recovered some of his truculence, but now Kate knew that it was an act. He really was a scared kid. With David's eyes.

"Always worked for me," Arnold said.

Kate glanced over at him in surprise. She couldn't conceive of an Arnold young enough and wild enough to make love in the back seat of a car. He caught her glance, shrugged and grinned.

"The D.A. is saying you raped her."

"Get real. I mean, we'd been messing around since the tenth grade. Why would I suddenly have to rape her? They got semen?"

"You leave any?"

"Nah. Always use a condom. Listen, I go to Pepperdine."

"Malibu?"

"Right. I always practice safe sex. In California you'd be crazy not to." He clammed up suddenly.

"With your girlfriend at Pepperdine."

"I never said I had a girlfriend at Pepperdine."

"But you do, don't you? More than one, maybe? Was that what the argument with Waneath was about? Another girl?"

He looked up and then to his right. "Yeah."

You're lying, Kate thought. Whatever they had fought about, that wasn't it. Or not all of it, at any rate.

Pulling information from him was like dentistry with fence pliers.

At the end of twenty minutes, Kate leaned back and rubbed the muscles along the tops of her shoulders.

"All right. Now, your story is that you had an argument over a possible girlfriend or girlfriends at Pepperdine, and moved it to your car, where, in the course of the rest of the evening, you made up. You then moved to the back seat where you had sex—dutifully protected by a condom. Then she began to make demands that you dump the girlfriends in California, which you refused to do. So she got out of the car and began walking home. By that time you were half-smashed on the beer you had brought along—a lovely DUI to add to the charges, by the way, both dangerous and nitwitted—and you were mad at her. So you drove off and left her to walk home alone."

"Hey, I came back, didn't I?"

"So you say. You say you drove around, parked until you were semisober, then realized you couldn't leave Waneath walking along a back road after midnight, no matter how you felt about her, so you drove to where you'd left her."

"But she was gone. I drove up and down a couple of

times and called her name. I figured she'd hitched a ride with somebody.''

"So you went home to your grandfather's house and went to bed without bothering to call her house to find out whether or not she'd gotten home safely. Quite the little gentleman.''

"Hey, her daddy would have skinned me alive if I'd called at one in the morning. I mean, nothing ever happens around here. I wasn't worried.''

"Not until they dragged you out of bed at your grandfather's and arrested you for her murder.''

"I keep telling you. I didn't do it.''

Suddenly Kate had had enough. "Fine. We're trying to set up a bail hearing for you this afternoon.''

"I'm going home?''

"I have no idea. They're going to try like crazy to keep you. In the meantime, I'll get the guards to let you shower and shave.''

"In this place?'' Jason curled his lip. "I'll wait until I get home. I might drop the soap.'' He grinned at her with an attempt at insouciance that didn't quite conceal the terror he obviously felt. "I'm already being screwed over this murder stuff. Once is enough.''

After Otis had taken Jason back to his cell, Arnold turned to Kate.

"You've got to face him, you know. And I'm not talking about Jason.''

"We need to talk to the district attorney or whoever passes for one in this godforsaken place,'' she said as they left the interview room and went into the hallway.

"You need some lunch.''

"Not with David.''

"I don't know where to eat in this town. He does.''

"Then not alone. You come too.''

At the far end of the hall, David stood silhouetted with his hands in his pockets. He stared up through the grimy window at the increasingly gray November skies. The little light that filtered through struck his hair like a nimbus.

"Always find the hot spot," Kate breathed.

"Huh?" Arnold asked.

"David would find a spotlight to stand under in the Black Hole of Calcutta."

"Cut the man a little slack, Kate. He's in big trouble with this kid of his."

"And after twenty years, he's still looking at me to bail him out of it. Well, David, as they say down here in Mississippi, that hound won't hunt."

CHAPTER TWO

"YOU SEE?" David said the moment he turned and saw them. "I told you Jason was innocent."

"He's lying through his teeth," Kate said.

She saw the deep flush even under David's tan.

"Jason's not a liar, and he's not a killer."

"Maybe not a killer, but a liar? Oh, yeah."

David turned and thrust his hands in his pockets. "Maybe this wasn't such a good idea, after all. Obviously you intend to take out whatever you feel about me on Jason."

"How dare you," Kate said softly. "You drag me down here on false pretenses to save your son's precious hide, and then when I don't think he's Little Lord Fauntleroy the way you do, you accuse me of using him to get revenge on you? If I'd wanted revenge, I wouldn't have waited twenty years for it."

"Revenge is a dish best eaten cold. Didn't somebody say that?"

"Somebody else said living well is the best revenge. I've already got my revenge, David. In case it's escaped your attention, I am living extremely well without you. Come on, Arnold, we're outa here."

As she brushed past him, David caught her arm. Even after twenty years she'd have known the feel of his fingers against her body in a dark cavern. His touch awakened memories so powerful that she stumbled and almost fell.

She righted herself with a hand against that filthy wall and yanked her arm out of his grasp.

"You promised to stay through the bail hearing," he said. "I'm sorry if I upset you, but you must realize I'm going crazy over this."

"And when you're crazy, everybody around you goes nuts trying to make sure you don't suffer."

"Jason's the one who's suffering."

"He's not the one using emotional blackmail."

"Is that what you think I'm doing?" David asked.

"Yes. If I walk away, I'm supposed to feel guilty because I'm taking out my feelings for you on your innocent kid—isn't that the way you phrased it? If I stay and don't get a reasonable bail, then I'm not doing my job. Again because of you. It's always because of you. You expect the Archangel Gabriel to ask if sounding the last trumpet on Tuesday will be quite convenient for you, or should he maybe wait until Thursday."

Arnold intervened before David could reply. "Kate," he said, "go get some lunch. It's almost one and you haven't had a bite since you got off the red-eye. Starvation does tend to turn you a bit testy."

"Damn right I'm testy."

"I don't give a damn what you think about me," David said. "The fact is that you're a lawyer, you're on retainer, and you're here. You're supposed to be good at what you do. So get my kid out on bail. Then we'll talk about the rest of it."

Kate stared at him with narrowed eyes for a moment. Then she relaxed. "Fair enough. I am very good at what I do, and I will do the bail hearing this afternoon. If you don't like the outcome, blame the situation, the crime, the district attorney and the judge, not necessarily in that order.

But don't you ever accuse me of doing less than my best. The bail could be astronomical.''

"Thank you.'' His shoulders sagged. "We'll worry about the amount when we know what it is. At the moment, the important thing is to get Jason home.''

"After lunch,'' Arnold said. "Kate'll pass out if she doesn't get something to eat.''

"Later, Arnold,'' Kate said. "Right now I need to see the district attorney, find out what they've got on Jason, what I can use to bolster his character, review the forensics…'' She realized she was talking as though she'd already taken the case.

David sighed in relief.

Trapped. "Okay,'' Kate said. "We're hired and we're here. But get this straight. I agree to stay through the bail hearing, period. Whatever happens, we get somebody else to take over after that.''

"I've already set up an interim affiliation with Whitman, Tarber and McDonough in Jackson,'' Arnold said. "They're the biggest law firm in Mississippi. I'm sure they'll have someone who can represent you if you decide to go with a criminal lawyer closer to home.''

"I know Pinkney Tarber,'' David said. "Seems like a good man. But he's not who I want to represent Jason.'' He turned to Kate. "I want you.''

"No can do.''

"We'll discuss that over lunch.''

"I just told you—''

Arnold intervened. "I'll go deal with the sheriff and the district attorney. Keep your cell phone on, Kate. I'll let you know for certain if and when we go before the judge today. Don't count on it. Could fall through.'' He turned to David. "She's right, you know, the kid's lying about something.

Don't be an ass. Feed the lady. You need her. She does not need you.''

"Arnold," Kate said menacingly. "You are going to join us for lunch, remember?"

He smiled at her blandly. "I had a late breakfast, and one of us has to do some work." He shoved her gently in David's direction. "It won't kill you to have a simple little lunch. Go in health."

As David propelled her toward the front door, she glowered at Arnold over her shoulder and mouthed, "That's two you owe me."

He wiggled his fingers at her.

Down the steps of the courthouse, across the street and past a block of grubby shops, Kate and David walked without a word to each other. She noticed several people staring at them as they passed, but nobody spoke. It was obvious that several people knew David and were deliberately avoiding meeting his eyes. She glanced at him. His jaw was set, his broad shoulders back, his fists clenched at his sides. He stared straight ahead.

She felt a pang of sympathy. Being Jason's father was already causing him a lot of grief. She owed him grief, but not this kind.

He held open the passenger door of a shiny new navy blue Navigator. It was an expensive car with leather upholstery and all the bells and whistles. So David was living well too. Perhaps the car belonged to his father-in-law.

As David pulled out of the parking space, she glanced at his hands.

"I'm surprised Melba doesn't make you wear a wedding ring," she said.

He flushed but said nothing.

"Where is she, by the way? Hiding at home from her son's little peccadillo?"

"She's dead."

Kate gulped. "Oh."

He glanced at her. "You had no way of knowing. She died three years ago. Congestive heart failure. Runs in the family. Her mother died young."

"I didn't know. Is Jason's health all right?"

David nodded. "He's fine. Runs on the female side, apparently. Melba never fully recovered from carrying him."

"I'm sorry. Truly."

"So we've both lost our spouses."

"You know about Alec's death?" She was surprised. "I wasn't even certain you and Melba were still married, much less where you lived or what you did."

"You've developed a fairly high profile. I hear things from time to time."

HE HEARD EVERYTHING about her life, but he wasn't about to clue her in on his source. Not now, certainly. Probably not ever.

And then there were the friends from their old theater crowd at college he kept up with. Funny, David thought, that he should have been the one to keep up with them. They'd always been more her friends than his, but after the divorce she'd cut herself off from everyone who knew them as a couple. Maybe she thought they'd take his side. Fat chance. They all thought he was crazy for losing her. He couldn't agree more.

Maybe she thought they'd known about his infidelity all along and had kept it from her. True, a couple of them had done just that, but only because guys did not rat on their married male friends even when they were tomcatting around on the perfect wife. And it had lasted less than a week—the affair, that is, if that's what you could call it. Terminal idiocy is what he called it.

He'd been paying the price for his momentary madness for twenty years. Just as he had finally decided he'd paid enough—Jason was now in college—and could see his way clear to getting on with the next phase of his life, this murder charge popped up. Seemed as if he'd been given a life sentence without possibility of parole. And no chance of escape. "There's a Sonic out by the highway," he said.

"I don't like drive-ins," she answered. "Don't you have a decent restaurant in this town?"

"Not a restaurant where everybody won't gawk and gossip and try to overhear our conversation."

"I noticed we were drawing attention on our way to the car."

"Yeah. Plenty of people are taking sides—loud sides, at that. They're basing their opinions not on whether Jason is guilty or innocent, but on how they feel about Dub and his kin. It's old South versus new, Katie. I may not be Athena born and bred, but Dub and his family have been here since before the war."

NOBODY ELSE HAD EVER *called her Katie.* David had only called her that on rare occasions, usually after they'd made love and were lying sated in each other's arms. She felt hot tears start and blinked them back. Alec had always called her Katherine, even when they made love, which, given his heart condition and their conflicting schedules, they had not done very often, and even less during the last three years of his life. For a moment she felt a physical ache to turn back the clock, to become once more "Katie," twenty-two and in love with the next Laurence Olivier.

Not possible. Her life had been chopped into three parts—B. D., before David; W. D., with David; and A. D., after David. She could barely remember B. D., and she fought every day of her life to forget W. D. A. D. ached like a tooth that never hurts quite badly enough to require a root canal.

"At least if we eat in the car we can have some privacy," David continued.

"Fine. Whatever."

David pulled under the awning at the Sonic, cut the engine and turned to her. "Do you still like your cheeseburgers with everything?"

"I can't go before a judge with onions on my breath."

"Except onions, then? And with large fries?"

"No fries." Then she said, "Oh, heck, after this morning I deserve comfort food. Yes, large fries. And iced tea."

He gave the order to the small two-way radio beside the car and a bored female voice confirmed it. "Oh, and could you bring us a bottle of steak sauce?" he asked and turned to her. "You still eat steak sauce on your cheeseburgers and fries?"

"You remember?"

"I remember everything about us," he said softly.

She couldn't bear to look into those eyes of his. *God help me, so do I*, she thought. She turned away to avoid his gaze and to get her breathing back under control.

"Kate, I—"

"So, how're your parents doing?" she asked brightly.

After a pause in which he visibly changed gears, he said, "Okay. Since Dad's retired, he spends all his time with his roses. He's winning prizes. Says my farming genes must have come from his side of the family because my mother can kill dirt."

"I remember. That was about the only trait she and I had in common." She pointed to the driver's-side window.

David turned and rolled down the window so that the waitress could set the tray on the edge of the car. David pulled out his wallet, paid the bill and watched her walk away. "That girl went to school with Jason. She's been out to Long Pond to pool parties a dozen times. She acts as though she's never seen me before in her life."

"Jason's bccn arrested for raping and murdering one of her friends."

"She can't possibly believe it."

"One thing I've learned, David, is that almost everyone assumes a person is arrested because he or she is guilty. Everyone's embarrassed for you. Nobody knows what to say so they look right through you."

"They know Jason wouldn't do something like this."

"Do they?" David was learning a hard truth. He was suddenly alone among people who had been his friends since he came down here to marry Melba.

David kept getting hit in the face with life's lessons long after most people had assimilated them and moved on. Like chicken pox, the older you were when the disease hit, the worse the case. And the deeper the scars that remained.

"You've got to eat," she urged.

"Tastes like cardboard."

"Do it anyway. Try the fries."

He bit into one and closed his eyes as though he'd forgotten how to swallow. After a moment he asked, "How's your mother?"

"You knew my father died?"

"Yeah."

"Testicular cancer. Ironic given his history of rampant infidelity. Six weeks later my mother sold the house in Mount View, bought a condo in Saint Petersburg and is blossoming like one of your daddy's roses. She says it's a relief not to have to act as though she doesn't recognize Daddy's latest mistress in the supermarket or the reception line at the faculty tea."

She heard the bitterness in her voice and knew that David

would recognize her tone. Well, let him. She wadded up the paper from her cheeseburger and handed it to David. He'd eaten practically nothing, but he added his detritus to hers on the tray, set it into the holder beside the car and rolled up the window.

"We'd better get back," he said.

As if in answer, her cell phone shrilled. She heard Arnold's voice.

"I'm still trying to confirm that bail hearing this afternoon at four," he told her. "So far I haven't heard one way or the other. But we have an appointment with the sheriff and the D.A."

"You have the arrest reports?"

"Yeah. And the sheriff is supposed to give us a copy of the autopsy."

"Fine. We're on our way back." She turned to David. "Is there a motel in this place?"

"Dub may want you to stay at Long Pond."

"No way."

"There are five guest rooms. I don't live there, Kate."

"That has nothing to do with it. Arnold and I want our own space. I'll only be here one night anyway. So, is there a motel?"

"Yeah, but hardly four star. The Paradise out on the bypass."

She passed on the information to Arnold. "Call them and get us a couple of adjoining rooms if possible." Out of the corner of her eye she caught the quick turn of David's head toward her. She glanced at him and saw the speculation in his eyes. He was obviously wondering whether she and Arnold had a relationship that went deeper than business. Let him wonder.

David's parking karma was not so hot this time. The courthouse square was full of cars.

"Let me out please, David. Then go home. There's nothing you can do until the bail hearing."

"How does that work?" He pulled into a loading zone under the watchful eye of a deputy sheriff.

"If the judge grants bail, then you have to hand over ten percent of the total amount to a licensed bail bondsman along with collateral for the rest in case Jason runs away. He gives surety to the court, and Jason is released pending his court appearance."

"I don't know whether we even have a bail bondsman in Athena."

"Bound to. It's the county seat. Look in the telephone book and make some calls. But be prepared for a hefty sum. Do you have a house you can mortgage?"

"I already mortgaged it to pay your retainer."

"I see. Land?"

He shook his head. "Not possible. Not your problem. You concentrate on getting any kind of bail. We'll come up with the money somehow."

"I'll try to get it as low as I can. That young man in the police uniform over there is getting antsy. Let me out. Go home. Make those calls, then try to get some rest. See you at four." She felt an incredible impulse to lean across the car and kiss him goodbye as she'd done a zillion times before. She caught herself, opened the door and bolted up the marble courthouse steps as fast as her high-heeled pumps would take her.

THE ROOM IN WHICH the bail hearing took place was smaller than the average corporate conference room. A dozen scratched, gray, metal folding chairs sat in rows across the back. At the front, four of the same chairs stood behind a pair of six-foot deal tables, one on either side of a center aisle. In front of them at a similar table sat the judge beside his clerk. A court reporter was behind him and to his left, her fingers poised over the keys of her machine, ready to record the proceedings.

When Otis brought Jason in to sit between Kate and Arnold at the defense table, she realized he'd cleaned himself up. Maybe he'd even risked that shower after all, but he still wore shackles and handcuffs and prison orange.

After the preliminaries, the prosecuting attorney, an intense man in an ill-fitting blue suit, outlined the charges against Jason and inveighed against granting bail in any amount.

Whether Jason was guilty or not, Kate and Arnold had recognized five minutes into their meeting with Athena County district attorney James Roy Allenby that he viewed this case as a stepping stone to a bigger pond. He obviously realized the case had what lawyers called ''legs.'' Beauty queen murdered, possibly raped. Suspect from a prominent old family. Victim's family newly rich. And a pair of hotshot Atlanta attorneys.

Kate listened as James Roy spent ten minutes playing poor little good ole boy from the sticks up against the powerful Delta elite. Kate recognized immediately that the judge was unimpressed. Fortunately, there was no jury to play to. If this case went to trial, her Beverly Hills haircut might become a liability. The Chanel suit would definitely have to go. The last thing she needed was to come across as the ''pro from Dover'' willing to use any big-city trick to get a guilty rich kid off a jail sentence he richly deserved.

She'd have to try for the motherly look. Difficult since she had so few good role models. Her stepchildren had been grown before she'd ever married Alec; her own mother had spent years as Queen of Denial, and David's mother made Clytemnestra look like Mother Goose.

She realized she'd been wool-gathering and hoped that

Arnold had been taking good notes, although Allenby merely seemed to be going over the same territory again and again. Finally, after an interminable harangue that nearly made her eyes cross, he sat down with a satisfied smirk in her direction.

She heard the door behind her open and close as she stood to address the judge, but she didn't turn around to see who had come in. She assumed that David had returned, possibly with Dub. For a moment she felt a flutter of disquiet, but quelled it. David had never seen her in action in a courtroom. She longed to impress him, but knew she'd have to forget all about him if she expected to perform adequately. Given the short notice she'd been given to prepare, all she could hope to be was adequate. With luck that would be enough.

The judge was close to retirement age—possibly past it— but from the button-bright black eyes he turned on her, she didn't make the mistake of underestimating his intelligence or his knowledge of the law. She had caught his exasperation at Allenby's emotional tactics. The best thing to do would be to lay out the facts—or lack of them. If she lost here, she'd appeal his decision. Somewhere up the line she'd probably win bail, but in the meantime Jason would be stuck in the Athena jail, and David would be even more frantic than he was at the moment.

"Your Honor, this is hardly the time to argue the merits of the case against my client, although the evidence is tenuous. It basically amounts to arresting the handiest suspect without bothering to do much investigating."

"Counselor," the judge said, "don't tell me what you're *not* going to tell me and then proceed to tell me." But there was a slight upward tic to his dewlaps when he said it.

"Yes, sir. My client has ties to the community that go back over a century. He has no intention of leaving Athena.

He wants his name cleared. He doesn't even have an outstanding parking ticket. He's never been in any trouble. He was an A student all during school. He was on the honor roll and in the Beta Society in high school. He was a finalist for a national merit scholarship—''

''All right, Counselor, I get the picture.''

''Your Honor,'' Allenby interrupted, ''I'm sure he has both a passport and the money to use to leave the country.''

''We'll surrender his passport,'' Kate said. ''Immediately. He's already under a hardship because he's going to college in California and won't be able to go back to school...'' Beside her, she heard Jason shift and an irritable sound issue from his throat. She glanced down at him. Surely he didn't dream they'd let him fly back to Malibu? Assuming Pepperdine would even let him in the doors under the present circumstances.

''We do want a speedy trial, Your Honor, in the event that the charges aren't dropped for lack of evidence. This young man is functioning under a cloud. He has the complete support of a very close-knit family. He just wants to get this over and move on with his life without suspicion hanging over him. We ask for bail in the amount of twenty thousand dollars.'' David should be able to come up with two thou—not that the judge was likely to agree to that. Kate heard the disgusted snort from Allenby and sat down beside David.

Jason leaned over and whispered, ''I can't miss school.''

''Shut up,'' Kate said out of the corner of her mouth.

''But—''

''Shut up.'' She smiled at the judge.

His eyes swept the room behind her. He rubbed his hand down his jaw and Kate heard a scritch as though he hadn't bothered to shave this morning.

''Well, y'all,'' he said, ''I can see both your points. But

this is not a capital murder case—nobody's asking for the death penalty here. So I pretty much got to set bail, but just to make sure I got everybody's attention—'' he glanced at Jason with a raised eyebrow ''—I'm setting it a tad higher than defense counsel's request.'' The gavel fell. ''Bail is set at five hundred thousand dollars.'' The judge stood and turned to leave the room. Everyone but Jason scrambled to their feet and stood as he prepared to leave the room.

Otis reached over, grabbed Jason by the collar of his jumpsuit and hauled him to his feet.

''Five...'' Jason sputtered. ''Jeez. We'll never be able to come up with that.''

From over her right shoulder Kate heard a booming bass voice, ''Hey, Pete, y'all take a personal check in this place?''

The judge stopped with his hand on the door, turned back and grinned at the man behind Kate. ''You wouldn't try to kite a rubber check on the people of the sovereign state of Mississippi, would you, Dub?''

''Hell, no, y'all'd catch me. Never did like jail ever since you and me got busted running beer from Memphis down to Oxford that time and our daddies had to come get us out the next morning.''

The judge laughed, shook his head and shut the door to his chambers behind him.

''Granddaddy.'' Jason sighed. It was as though the arch-angel had finally showed up just as the lions started nibbling Daniel's toes.

''Miz Mulholland, I'm Dub Mays,'' the man said and stuck out his hand. ''Damn foolishness dragging y'all down here for something this silly.''

She blinked. Rape and murder silly? She took her first good look at him.

How on earth had tiny Melba Mays ever come from this

tall, elegant man with his hawk nose and mass of shining white hair? He wore the Delta farmer's universal uniform, but slicked up for the occasion. He had on immaculate chinos with a crease that would probably slice butter, a starched plaid logger's shirt, and when Kate glanced down at his feet she saw that someone had spit-shined his brown engineer's boots. His face was the color and consistency of tanned leather, and the palm of the hand he offered her felt as though he'd lined it with rhinoceros horn.

"I never expected bail quite this high," she said.

He waved a hand. "Shoot, just to be on the safe side, I set up a million five with Acme Bail Bonds out of Jackson yesterday." He grinned. "Good thing this happened in November. Most Delta farmers say they are solvent one day of the year—that's the day between the time they pay off last year's crop loans and sign the papers for this year's. That day generally comes along about November." For the first time he looked at Jason. "You all right, boy?" he asked. Kate heard the love behind the gruffness.

"Yessir."

"He's fine, Dub," Otis said. "I been looking after him."

Dub nodded and shook Otis's hand. "Thank you, Otis."

"We got to take him back down and get him processed," the guard said. "You take care of the bail with Harry in the office."

"You did bring his passport?" Arnold asked.

Dub nodded and handed the passport to Arnold. "Foolishness. This is all a damn-fool misunderstanding." He grinned at his grandson. "Ain't it, boy?"

Jason nodded as though his grandfather's words could hypnotize him into believing it really was all foolishness.

"Arnold, why don't you and Mr. Mays…" Kate began.

"Call me Dub, sugar, everybody does."

Sugar? "Fine, Dub. You and Arnold take care of the bail.

I'll go down to the jail and wait for Jason to get his things on. Arnold, where'd you park the rental car?''

"Dave's waiting by the jail in my Cadillac," Dub said. "He'll drive you all. Mr. Selig can drive me back to Long Pond in his car.''

"Long Pond?''

"Our homeplace.''

"Mr. Mays—Dub—I'd really like to check into my motel," she said.

"Motel? Heck fire, woman, you got any idea what that motel is like? Shoot, half the time they rent rooms by the hour. Y'all can stay at Long Pond. Besides, we got to have us a council of war about this foolishness.''

She started to protest, then realized she was too tired to fight. "We'll discuss it later." As he turned away, she said, "If David's waiting outside, you must have had a good deal of faith that I'd manage to secure bail.''

He grinned. "With ole Pete on the bench? Shoot, he'd never deny any kin of mine bail.''

CHAPTER THREE

KATE LEFT Arnold and Dub settling up with the clerk of the court for Jason's release and walked down the ancient marble steps to the foyer, then down one more flight to the cells. The jail area had its own door that opened onto an alley where she assumed David waited in Dub's Cadillac.

Good thing. They didn't need to parade through the main square of Athena with Jason in tow.

She was stuck riding with David once more, but this time Jason's presence would keep them from talking about anything personal.

David had already given hints that he wanted to rehash old times. The last thing she wanted was to wallow in memories of his defection—the worst personal defeat of her life.

No, she didn't need to hear David's apologia for cheating on her and getting Melba Mays pregnant. That was self-explanatory. And absolutely, totally, and completely unacceptable.

She'd watched her mother ignore her father's infidelities ever since she was old enough to recognize sexual betrayal. She had sworn that no man would ever betray her that way and get away with it.

When she'd finally told her mother why she had kicked David out, her mother had tried to convince her that any dog gets one bite. Despite her own anger, she'd wanted Kate to forgive and forget.

Yeah. Right. Kate could have put up with almost anything else from David, so, of course, that was what he had done. It was downright biblical—that which she had greatly feared had come upon her.

On the other hand, she'd never dreamed that Alec would die on her. Not at fifty-six. He'd had one mild heart attack before she met him, but during their marriage his cholesterol had been perfect, he'd worked out four times a week in the company gym in the basement of their offices. He'd jogged and eaten right and kept his weight down.

He'd been on medication to keep his blood thin and his pressure down. That tended to make erection difficult for him, but they'd managed. Even if she had felt physically deprived, she would never have taken Alec's impotence as carte blanche to take a lover.

But men felt differently about sex. She'd never known what she'd been unable to provide David sexually, what had sent him careening into Melba's arms the first time she showed up in New York. So far as she was concerned, their sex life had been great. More than great. David took her places she'd only read about. Of course, since she'd come to his bed her junior year in college as a virgin, she didn't have any frame of reference, but she'd loved making love with him. He always seemed satisfied and content afterward. Still, she'd failed somewhere. Otherwise he'd never have turned to Melba.

Locks clanged and voices murmured from the cells.

As she waited for the door to open and Jason to emerge, she heard the click of heels coming down the stairs behind her, and an instant later a woman's voice. "Are you that lawyer from Atlanta?"

She turned to see a plump partridge of a woman wearing too much makeup, and with dyed blond hair that looked as though it had been set with concrete. The woman's red-rimmed eyes seemed crazed, and her too-red lipstick was smeared at the corners of her mouth.

"I'm Kate Mulholland," she said warily.

"How do you live with yourself?" The woman's voice sounded as though she were running it through a cheese grater. She took a step toward Kate, who backed up instinctively.

"I beg your pardon?"

"You got that little demon out, didn't you?"

Kate saw that the woman was on the verge of tears.

"The judge granted bail, yes."

"So that, that…killer—" she spat the word "—goes home to his fancy house and sleeps in a soft bed. Do you know where my little girl is sleeping?"

Kate gulped. Waneath's mother.

The woman pointed over her shoulder, "She's over there naked on a steel table."

"Mrs. Talley, I'm so sorry for your loss." It was the standard response, and Kate knew how weak it sounded, but she didn't know what else to say.

"You *should* be sorry. You're going to get him off, aren't you? You and your fancy clothes and Dub's big money. Those people think they can get away with anything. He killed my baby! He deserves to die like she did."

"I know you're upset—"

"Upset?" The woman's mouth twisted. "Oh, yes, I am definitely upset. Are you a mother?" She peered into Kate's face. "No, you're not. I can see that. If you were a mother you'd know. You wouldn't get him off."

The door behind Mrs. Talley opened, and Otis stepped through. Behind him stood Jason wearing his own clothes, free of shackles. Kate prayed that Waneath's mother wouldn't hear the sound, wouldn't see Jason standing there.

"Mrs. Talley, do you have anyone with you? Anyone

who's looking after you?'' she asked, and realized how patronizing she sounded as the words left her mouth.

''You think I'm crazy? I'm not the one who's setting a killer free. I hope you rot in hell!''

Kate caught the movement out of the corner of her eye only a second before Mrs. Talley slapped her across the face with enough force to snap her head against the wall behind her. The sound reverberated down the narrow hall.

For a moment Mrs. Talley stared at Kate openmouthed, as though she'd been struck dumb by the force of her anger. Then she spun and ran toward the alley door just as David opened it. Her hands covered her face, and Kate could hear her sobs. She wasn't even aware that the man who held the door for her was Jason's father.

''Mrs. Talley?'' he said to her retreating back, and turned toward the tableau in front of him. ''Kate? What's going on?''

Otis shoved Jason ahead of him and came to her. ''You want to file charges, Mrs. Mulholland? She assaulted you.''

Kate's cheek stung. She tasted her own blood where her teeth had been forced against her lips. She blinked back tears of pain and shook her head. ''No, Otis, no. Forget it.''

''But ma'am…''

''That's the last thing we need. Is Jason free to go?''

''Yes'm, if you're sure.''

''I am. Come on, Jason, let's get you out of here.''

His eyes were wide and frightened, but he came.

''Jason.'' His father reached out to embrace him, but Jason glanced at him with a look of such loathing that he stepped back in confusion.

''You coming?'' Jason said over his shoulder to Kate. ''Before the lynch mob shows up?''

Outside in the alley Kate shoved Jason into the back seat

and ran around to the passenger side. David climbed into the driver's seat and started the engine.

In the back seat Jason slumped down as though he didn't want anyone to see him. Kate heard the electronic locks click. Fortunately the car's windows were tinted, so nobody could see in.

"What happened in there?" David asked.

"Nothing," Kate replied. "Mrs. Talley was upset about Jason's bail. She thinks Dub is buying his freedom."

"She's had Jason and Waneath engaged for three years. Every time I saw the woman in church I could almost see her figuring out the decorations for the wedding in her head. And now even *she* thinks he killed Waneath?"

"Yeah. Man, you find out who your friends are real quick when you get arrested for murder, am I right?" Jason said.

"You are righter than you know," Kate said, swiveling to look at him. "So you are going to keep a very low profile. You're not to leave the house, not go out to dinner, call your friends, anything, until we see how the wind blows."

"So you're saying I'm still a prisoner, right?"

"In a sense, yes. Waneath hasn't been buried yet. You want to run into the entire football team from the high school after they've had a few beers?"

"Man, I can't believe this."

"Maybe it's time to tell us the truth," David said quickly.

Too quickly. Kate glanced over at him and realized he was looking at his son in the rearview mirror. She remembered that set of his jaw—it signified either real anger or real fear. Maybe both. So he wasn't as certain of his son's innocence as he'd tried to convince her he was.

Kate twisted around in time to catch the sullen expression

in Jason's eyes as he looked daggers at the back of his father's head. "I didn't do anything, you know."

"Until we can persuade a jury of that, people are always going to think you did," Kate said. "So why don't you tell me what really happened?"

Jason stared at her. "I thought my lawyer was supposed to believe me."

"The first rule you learn in law school is that clients always lie. Sometimes they do it just to make themselves look better, and sometimes because they're guilty, and sometimes when they don't know they're doing it, but they lie. Just the way you lied to me this morning."

"The hell I did."

"Jason," his father said in a warning tone. "Watch your language. Mrs. Mulholland is trying to help you."

"Oh, sure, by calling me a liar. Listen, I'm sick and tired of all this. I'm going to take a nap. Wake me when we get to Long Pond." With those words, he keeled over onto the leather seat, wrapped his arms around his body and closed his eyes.

"So that's it for now." Kate sighed.

"Kate, what did I miss in there?"

"Waneath's mother is understandably very upset. That's par for the course, although I'd like to know how she got down there without somebody stopping her. I think if she'd had a gun she'd have used it on me, Otis, Jason, you and God knows who else."

"You're serious."

"Indeed I am. As it was, she made do with her hand. She slapped me."

"She what?"

"Keep your eyes on the road. Those ditches we're driving between look as though they might be full of alligators. God, this country is flat!"

"So that's what Otis meant when he asked if you wanted to press charges?"

"Yeah. A good coating of makeup should cover her handprint on my cheek. I don't think I'm going to have a black eye, although—" she ran her tongue over her teeth "—the inside of my lip is cut."

"Sweet heaven, Kate, if I'd thought I was putting you in any danger, I'd never have brought you down here."

"I know that." Without thinking she laid her palm on his forearm. The car shimmied and then righted itself. She snatched her hand away.

How could the electricity between them have lasted twenty years?

They drove in silence along back roads, narrow and lined with stubby trees. On either side stretched flat fields, already plowed or still covered in the stubble of this year's soybeans and cotton. Suddenly David pulled over to the side of the road and leaned across her. "That's Long Pond," he said, pointing across the field.

The house was large and luminously white, with a Palladian colonnaded front porch and second-floor balcony. It loomed up no more than a mile across the fields as though it were a giant riverboat riding seas of mud and dirt. A few immense old trees in the yard swayed leafless in the late-November breeze.

"My Lord," Kate whispered.

David started the car again. Several miles down the road he turned right, and after another couple of miles or so turned again between gleaming white board fences into a gravel driveway that ran past barns, silos and outbuildings to a turnaround at the front steps of the house.

Now Kate saw that the lawn was small for such a big house. Land must be too precious to waste on luxuries like grass. The house was surrounded by big azaleas that would bloom gloriously come spring.

Arnold's rental car stood in the parking area under a broad naked pin oak. David stopped at the front steps and reached around to shake Jason's shoulder. "Wake up, son, you're home."

Jason grumbled, sat up and opened the car door.

"I'll put the car in the garage. Dub is very particular about his automobiles," David said.

Jason half stumbled up the front stairs and across the porch with Kate following. As he reached the double front doors, they opened, and a tiny woman, like an elderly wren, flew out.

"Jason!" She threw her arms around him and dragged him inside. "You go right upstairs now and scrub that jail-house stink right off you and put on some clean clothes. I laid 'em out for you on your bed."

"Yes, ma'am," Jason said. He said over his shoulder, "I'm going to sleep for a week. Don't call me for dinner."

The woman turned and held out her hands to Kate. "You must be Miz Mulholland. I'm Neva Hardin, Dub's house-keeper." She took both of Kate's hands and pulled her into the front hall. "Thank you for bringing my boy back home."

Kate had no idea how old the woman was. Her face was as wrinkled as an apple doll, but her spine was straight, and she moved with the grace and speed of a young woman.

Kate smiled down at the woman, but looked up when she heard Dub's booming bass. "Get yourself on up to your room, boy," Dub said. "Then when you look halfway human, come and join us on the back porch for a little afternoon libation."

"I just wanna sleep, Granddaddy," Jason said as he

passed his grandfather and Arnold Selig, who stood just behind him.

"You got to eat."

"I'll fix myself something later." He disappeared down the broad hall at the head of the staircase.

Dub watched him a moment anxiously, then turned to Kate with a broad grin. "Well, come on in," Dub boomed. As he descended the broad peach marble staircase, he held tightly to the curving banister.

"This is an incredible house," Kate said.

"It's just your basic old southern dogtrot house," Dub said.

"Dogtrot for mastiffs and elephants, maybe."

"Built right after the war."

"Civil?" Kate asked.

Dub grinned. "Second World. Whenever my daddy got really mad he'd accuse my momma of having set fire to the old house just so she could get her a fancy new one. The old one was a dogtrot too, just not so fancy."

"Excuse me," Arnold said quietly. "What, precisely, is a dogtrot house? I am, as Kate will recall, born and bred on Long Island."

Dub slipped his hand under Kate's arm and began to guide her to the right of the stairs toward the back of the house. She saw the glint of water from what must be a swimming pool or an ornamental pond of some sort.

"Well, son, originally it meant a cabin that was built in two parts—one on each side of a big open central hall. Sleeping rooms on one side, parlor on the other. The center stayed open so…"

"The dogs could trot through unimpeded." Kate finished.

"So now any house built with a big old central hall front to back is called a dogtrot house, at least down here."

"Thank you," Arnold said.

"But Momma had to have it both ways," Dub said. "She was bound and determined to have a center staircase right out of Ashley Wilkes's house in *Gone with the Wind.*"

"I don't remember that his was this broad," Kate said. "Or this…"

Kate watched Arnold search for the appropriate words and grinned at him.

"Or this, um…marble," he said finally.

Dub glanced at the staircase with chagrin. "Momma wanted what she wanted, and cotton prices were high right about then." He shrugged. "Not like now."

From behind them, Mrs. Hardin said, "Now that Jason's home, I'm leaving, Dub."

"Yes, fine, Neva," he said absently.

"The country captain's in the warming oven, salad's in the refrigerator, the table's laid and the cobbler's in the microwave. All you got to do is heat it up for dessert."

Dub seemed to be ignoring the woman. She gave an exasperated sigh and turned to Kate. "Since this happened he's been in another world. Did you get all that?"

"I'm not much of a cook."

"Huh, anything's better than that man. He's hopeless." Neva Hardin shrugged into a windbreaker, picked up a leather handbag from what looked to be an original Sheraton chair beside the front door and walked out. "I'll be here tomorrow before lunch," she said over her shoulder.

"Yes, fine." Dub said to the closing door. Then to Kate and Arnold, "Come on out onto the back porch."

"Um, isn't it a bit chilly?" Arnold asked as he followed Dub toward the back of the house. Then, as he entered the glass-enclosed room, he said, "Oh. Of course."

The room resembled an old-fashioned Victorian solarium complete with tropical plants that Kate could not begin to identify. Through the back windows she saw that she had been correct. Stairs led down to a large rectangular swimming pool above which a haze of mist drifted lazily. The pool must be heated. It would probably be usable until January if the weather continued to be as warm as it had been today.

Beyond the pool stood a low but substantial house with its own colonnade. "That's where David had his office until he got uppity and built him a new house after Melba died," Dub said.

"Now, Dub, it wasn't like that," David's voice said amiably.

Kate turned to see David lounging against a bar built into the side of the room. His voice sent shivers down her spine, even when he wasn't speaking to her. She caught Arnold's raised eyebrows. She'd have to watch herself. Arnold knew her entirely too well.

David handed Kate a glass of white wine. "Still like Chardonnay, or have you moved up to martinis?"

"Chardonnay is fine, thank you."

"Mr. Selig?"

"Gin and tonic, please. Light. I'm driving us back to that ghastly motel."

"What?" Dub said. "Thought I told you, you two are staying right here at Long Pond. David'll take you on up to your rooms right this minute if you want to freshen up."

"I don't think so, Dub." Kate said. "We need privacy. So, we'll have our drink and a strategy session, then we'll go to town and find someplace to have dinner."

"Hell no!" Dub said. "You think Neva Hardin leaves me country captain and cobbler every night? That dinner's for *you*. And the boy, when he wakes up."

"Pardon my ignorance again, but what is country captain? Sounds positively cannibalistic."

"Shoot, son. Chicken with rice and raisins and things. Hot rolls too, if I remember to put 'em in the oven. Neva Hardin thinks she's perfect, but she damn well forgot to mention the rolls, didn't she?" He seemed inordinately pleased at her omission. "She always makes rolls for company."

Kate glanced at David, who merely shrugged and raised a glass of what looked like cola at her in silent salute. "We'll stay for dinner," she said. "But we will not spend the night."

"We'll see." Dub said and rubbed his hands together as though he'd won a victory. "Got to thank you properly for bringing my boy home to me," he said.

"You did that already."

"Well, I'm doing it again. How quick can you all get the charges dropped?"

Kate blew out a breath. "I haven't done any criminal-defense work in well over six months. I agreed to try to secure bail for Jason, then Arnold and I are heading back to Atlanta."

"Leaving us in the lurch? No way."

"The firm has an excellent team of criminal litigators."

"Hunh. Cost more'n Long Pond's worth, probably." Dub was growing agitated. His fingers drummed on the side of his glass. "Didn't want to bring you in the first place. David said my lawyer, Jack Slaydon, wasn't good enough. Shoot, he's good enough to deal with a piece of foolishness like this."

Watching him, Kate remembered Jason's five-finger exercises in the interrogation room and wondered whether nervous tics could be passed along in the gene pool.

"Whatever you may want to think, this is a far cry from foolishness," she said. "The district attorney is planning to convene a special grand jury in January."

"Can he do that?"

"Absolutely. And if it's like most grand juries, they'll do as they are told and return a true bill against Jason."

"Well, shoot, you got to stop 'em." Dub stood and began to pace. "Jason's not guilty of a damn thing except being young and getting mixed up with a woman who wasn't half good enough for him."

"And fathering her baby."

"What?" David asked. He walked around the edge of the wicker sofa on which Arnold perched uncomfortably, sat and leaned toward Kate. "She was pregnant?" He shook his head. "It's not Jason's."

"How can you be so sure?" Kate said.

"Because he always uses a condom." David flushed and looked away. "I taught him that."

"Yes, that's a lesson you're qualified to teach," Kate whispered.

Dub looked from one to the other with his eyes narrowed, but he said nothing.

Kate finished her wine and set the glass down on the table. "Perhaps I'd better see what we need to do for dinner, if you'll point me at the kitchen."

"Lord, no," Dub said. "You're company."

"Mrs. Hardin says you're hopeless in the kitchen, Dub. I can at least turn on an oven and start a microwave. Let me do it, please. You all sit here and finish your drinks."

"I'll show you," David said.

Trapped again.

She followed him out a door in the side of the room and into a large and extremely modern kitchen with a center island and a steel-fronted stove and refrigerator. "I assume those rolls Dub wants baked are in the refrigerator," she said cheerfully.

"Kate, stop it." David curled his hand around her upper arm as she passed him. "Brittle never became you."

She froze and stood, passive, refusing to acknowledge his power by trying to shake him off.

"I remember you were a great believer in justice even twenty years ago," he said softly. "Is it justice to punish Jason for something that I did to you? To us? My God, Kate, look at him. He could be our son, yours and mine."

She yanked her arm away and turned a furious face to him. "Wrong button to push, Mr. Canfield. If you remember, you and I discussed having a baby, and decided we couldn't afford for me to quit supporting us until you starting getting decent parts."

"I remember."

"Has the old gang informed you that I don't have any children?" She opened the refrigerator, pulled out a large crystal bowl of salad covered securely in plastic wrap and then found a pan of raised rolls ready for the oven. She banged the pan onto the counter and leaned over it. "When I married Alec, he had two grown children and a ten-year-old vasectomy. We tried twice to reverse it, but it was no good. So Jason is the son I never had, never will have. The son you had because you couldn't stay out of bed with an old girlfriend."

"It wasn't like that."

"How was it then?" She walked over to the oven and gave a vicious twist to the dial until it reached three hundred and fifty degrees. She turned and leaned against it. "And if you dare give me that old 'it didn't have anything to do with us, babe,' I swear I'll slap you silly."

"It had everything to do with us. You never gave me a chance to talk to you, to explain…"

"Come on, the last thing I needed was explanations and excuses."

He shook his head. "Reasons but no excuses."

"Oh, really?"

"When you flew off to the Dominican Republic and came back divorced a week later, I couldn't believe it."

"One of the perks of being a legal secretary in a big firm. They take care of their own. I warned you the day I married you that the one unforgivable sin in my book was infidelity. I watched my mother trying to live with her devil's bargain with my father year after year. You knew damn well what it would do to me. But you're different from Daddy. He always tried to hide his latest. You wanted me to find out. You sure as hell set it up that way."

"Ah, are we going to be dining soon?" Arnold said from the doorway. "If not, I don't believe Dub is going to be awake." He made drinking motions and raised his eyebrows at them. "So sorry if I'm interrupting anything. Amazing how raised voices carry in this house."

David scowled at Arnold, but Kate grabbed him and shoved him toward the counter. "Put those rolls in and watch them. They burn quickly." She turned to David. "Is there a bathroom on this floor? Suddenly I am feeling extremely dirty."

CHAPTER FOUR

"I'M WORRIED about Dub," David said to Kate as they carried the last of the dishes holding the dregs of peach cobbler into the kitchen. "He seems distracted, and his color's not good. This thing has hit him harder than he lets on."

"I hardly know the man, but he's not what I'd call distracted. He ate a good dinner, and kept us in stitches. In fact, he's giving Arnold a real education in the genus good ole boy."

"Dub's acting as though if he ignores all this, it'll go away on its own." David shook his head. "By the way, he has an honors degree in political science from Brown. A good ole boy he is not."

"I recognize that, but Arnold grew up on Long Island. He's only recently been transplanted to Atlanta. Mississippi is as foreign to him as Bosnia and not nearly so civilized." She rinsed the last of the dishes and slid them into the dishwasher. "But I agree that Dub keeps veering away from talking about the murder. He's treating this little dinner party as though it were a purely social occasion."

"He always jokes and clowns around to avoid hearing things he doesn't want to hear and dealing with situations that don't suit him. Deep down, he's scared."

"He's right to be scared. I haven't had time to do more than hit the high spots in the arrest report, but they definitely have enough to indict."

"And convict?"

"That's something else again." She wiped the counter clean and rinsed the sponge under the tap. David sidestepped her to pick up the coffee carafe and pour himself a second cup of decaf. Suddenly, she leaned on her hands and closed her eyes. How often had they cleaned up after their own meager parties in New York? No dishwasher, of course, but the rhythms weren't that different. It was as though their bodies still remembered the logistics of living together, even though their hearts—well, her heart at any rate—rejected the idea.

"You okay?" David asked solicitously.

"Just tired." God, how tired! This day seemed to have started last week. "And we still need to discuss what happens next with Jason."

"Stay here tonight."

"David…"

"Listen to me before you say no. It makes sense. You can work on strategy over breakfast when everyone's fresh."

She shook her head. "Not a good idea."

"I told you I won't be here, if that's what's bothering you."

"What's bothering me is being unable to get away from my clients to confer with my colleague in anything remotely resembling privacy."

"I'll give you the key to my office. You and Arnold can have all the privacy you want out there. The rooms upstairs are much nicer than that motel. You'll have your own bathroom, and I can guarantee plenty of real hot water."

"The Paradise Motel has hot water."

"Occasionally." He raised his eyebrows and lowered his voice seductively. "King-size bed. Your bathroom has a whirlpool tub."

Sinking into a hot whirlpool, feeling her tense muscles relax, big fluffy towels and a huge bed to sprawl on. She groaned and closed her eyes.

"It would make Dub happy. He gets lonely out here."

"Jason's here," Kate answered. "Why, by the way?"

"Why what?"

"Why is Jason here rather than at home with you?"

David turned and thrust his hands into the pockets of his chinos. For a moment he stared out at the mist rising off the pool. "He's going through a phase. He doesn't like me very much at the moment."

"And why is that?"

"Nothing to do with this. He feels more comfortable here with his grandfather. They've always been close."

"And you haven't?"

"Is that your business?" He turned to stare at her.

"It is if it impacts my case."

"How could it impact your case?"

She sighed. "The kid is mad as hell at you. It's possible he took out that anger on the first person to cross him. And that would be Waneath."

"Don't be ridiculous. I've always had a great relationship with my son. This is simply teenage rebellion—going away to school for the first time."

"The district attorney is going to put all three of you under a microscope. If there's anything I should know, you'd better tell me. As you may remember," she said dryly, "I don't react well to nasty surprises."

"I promise you, my relationship with Jason has nothing to do with this case."

She stared at him for a moment without speaking, then she said. "I'll have to accept that for the moment."

"So you'll stay here?"

"Oh, what the heck, why not. It's only for one night.

Arnold can cancel the motel reservations. We're leaving for Atlanta tomorrow anyway.''

"Uh-huh. I'll go tell the others. I'll help Arnold get the bags out of your car." He strode out and left the door to the dining room swinging.

She reached for the carafe of coffee and touched the glass instead of the plastic. "Damn!" She recoiled and looked down at her fingertips. She blinked back tears, not so much in pain, although her fingers stung, but in frustration and exhaustion.

She'd had about enough of all these people. She was worn out with being pleasant and acting domestic. Most of all, she was tired of forcing herself to look away from David's familiar, and unfortunately, still too-handsome face. From his eyes, which always seemed to be searching hers out every time she looked his way. Mostly she was tired of trying to ignore the heat he generated in her from across a broad dining table.

She should feel nothing after all these years except contempt. Instead, she felt like an iron filing being inexorably dragged toward a very destructive magnet.

DAVID STOOD in the dark under the portico of the guest house and watched Kate's sleek silhouette move back and forth behind the sheer draperies that covered her bedroom window. One part of him felt like an overage Romeo pining beneath Juliet's balcony. The other part felt like a peeping Tom. But he couldn't tear his eyes away. Sleep was an impossibility.

He wondered whether she still slept naked.

He could tell even in her clothes that her body had grown richer with the years. He had married a lovely girl. In the years they'd been apart, she had evolved into a truly beautiful woman.

His body ached with sheer physical need. It had been much too long since he'd made love to any woman, and an eternity since he'd held Kate in his arms. No one had ever measured up to her. But then he hadn't loved any other woman. Never would. He had long since admitted that to himself.

He wondered what she'd do if he shinnied up to her window.

Break a lamp over his head, probably.

How many years had he dreamed of seeing her again, of being able to apologize? Explain? But explanations would hurt her all over again. He wanted to hold her, not hurt her.

He'd come close to writing her a note after he'd read that her husband died, then decided it was not the time to notify her that they were both free. He'd fantasized about moving to Atlanta and trying to win her all over again.

But their lives had grown too far apart. Until now, he'd been tied to this land as though he were a serf in czarist Russia. He'd sworn to stay until Jason was safely on his way in school. Now the plans he'd made, the people he'd contacted would all have to be put on hold until he got Jason clear of this murder charge. By that time the money he'd saved would probably be spent on Jason's defense.

What if Jason were guilty? What if he'd lost his temper, hit Waneath and suddenly realized she wasn't breathing? Was he capable of simply walking away and leaving her beside the road for someone else to find?

Just as he had when he'd messed up as a child. Of course, Melba and Dub had always tried to protect him, never really taught him to take responsibility. David had done what he could to oppose them, but Dub and his daughter had been a powerful team and David recognized that Jason found their way easier. That was human nature.

But eventually, you had to take responsibility.

As David had. Twenty years' worth. Twenty years of living with the fact that he'd betrayed the only woman he'd ever loved.

David prayed Jason wasn't guilty. He clung to that hope even as the evidence mounted against his child. The boy had inherited his mother's temper, but basically, he was a good kid, talented and loving. He worshiped his grandfather, and until Melba's death he and David had been as close as any father and son could be.

David understood his need to rebel, but if Kate was right and Jason had taken out his anger at his father on Waneath, how guilty did that make David for her death?

His gaze swung over to Dub's window. Dub had prowled for over an hour before his light went out. When David called Dub "the old man" he used the term the way seamen did for their skippers or infantrymen their generals. Nothing to do with age; everything to do with respect and real affection.

In the few years since Melba's death, he and Dub no longer agreed about much of anything. Certainly not about the way to run Long Pond or raise Jason. Dub had always been irascible, but lately he'd been downright grumpy. In fact, it seemed to David that Dub had aged more in the past three years than he had in the last seventeen.

Maybe he was imagining things. Dub couldn't be worried about business. Even with Dub's hidebound decisions not to try any of David's experimental ideas, both cotton and soybeans had sold high this year.

He'd tried to get Dub in to his doctor for a checkup, but so far as Dub was concerned, a visit to a doctor was tantamount to a death sentence.

Not surprising he should feel that way, first losing his wife so young, and then Melba before she hit forty. He and

Jason were the old man's only remaining family, except for some shirttail cousins whom neither of them had ever met.

No matter how he and Dub fought, David would always love the old man. He was family, after all. And David knew that his father-in-law truly valued him no matter how often they disagreed. Dub probably felt like the old bull about to be displaced by the young bull.

They'd tried hard to keep things pleasant between them at least on the surface. To make it easier on both of them, David had moved into his own house two years ago. But lately their private fights had escalated. David had decided that the time for him to leave Mississippi had come.

Now leaving was no longer an option. At least until Jason was cleared and Dub was back to his old self.

David was trapped all over again.

THE NEXT MORNING, Kate found David already in the kitchen. She smelled fresh coffee and the aroma of hot bread. A pitcher of orange juice sat in the center of the table. As she walked into the room, he filled a glass and handed it to her.

"Sleep well?" he asked.

She lied. "Like a log. The minute my head hit the pillow."

"You look great. Although I miss your long hair."

Kate blushed. "Lawyers don't wear hair down to their rumps," she said.

"In New York you kept it rolled up in a braid. Lawyers can do that, can't they?"

"Not if they're over thirty, they can't. Is that real coffee? I don't do decaf before noon."

He handed her a cup. "You still like it black?"

"Actually, I prefer double mocha latte with chocolate ice cream, but my thighs demand I drink it black."

"I never managed to convince you your thighs were gorgeous."

"Well, they're okay, thanks to hours in the gym and a personal trainer who earned his degree in a torture chamber."

"Impressive."

Arnold wandered in, stared at them morosely and extended his hand without saying a word. Kate poured a cup of coffee and handed it to him. He sniffed, sipped and sighed. "Good."

"He keeps to monosyllables until the third cup," Kate said and sat down.

"Dub and Jason are still asleep," David said. "Or they were when I checked. I don't want a repeat of the denial game Dub pulled last night, so talk to me. Where do we go from here?"

"Officially we can't demand discovery or a list of witnesses from the D.A. until after the indictment," Kate said. She took a hefty swig of orange juice and set the glass down beside her plate. "The sheriff seems willing to cooperate, but the D.A. sees blood and a spot on Court Television. He wants to convict Jason so bad he can taste it."

"Even if he's not guilty?"

"It's going to take incontrovertible proof of innocence to convince him to let go of his juicy prime-time lollipop."

Arnold sat at Kate's right and began smearing homemade fig preserves on a reheated roll from last night's dinner. "One chance," he croaked.

David turned to him. "Which is?"

"Find the guy." He went over, poured himself another cup of coffee and stood swaying over the counter.

David looked at Kate.

"Find the real killer," she translated. "Give your D.A. another raccoon to tree or whatever they say down here."

"How do we do that?"

"Investigate." Arnold said. He sat down and began munching another roll.

"We have an investigator who works for the firm," Kate said. "He's not cheap, but he's good. If Jason didn't kill Waneath, then whoever picked her up on the road is the most likely suspect."

"Yes."

"We've already asked for a private autopsy on your behalf."

"You what?" Jason said from the doorway.

Kate turned to him. "Good morning. Another autopsy from a top forensic pathologist in Memphis. Arnold started the paperwork yesterday afternoon. The body should be delivered to Memphis this morning."

"You can't do that!" Jason said. He wore ragged sweats and an Athena High Panthers sweatshirt that sagged at the neck.

"It's the obvious next step. The coroner in Athena isn't even an M.D., just a funeral director. He barely touched the body. We want to have accurate data on time of death, cause of death, whether or not she was raped…"

"She wasn't raped. Dad, you've got to stop her."

"She knows what she's doing."

"We've also asked for a full toxicology screening to see whether there were any drugs in her system."

"We were drinking beer, okay? I told you that. Listen, you work for me. And I say no."

"And I say yes," Dub spoke from behind Jason's shoulder. "She may work for you, young man, but I'm gonna help pay the bill on this."

"But Granddaddy…"

"Don't you granddaddy me. We've got to nip this foolishness in the bud. I won't have you going to trial over something you didn't do."

"I won't go to trial, and if I do I'll be acquitted. I mean, this is America, right? I mean it's *The Big Clock*. The good guy always gets off at the last minute."

"This is real life, not a movie," David said.

"What the hell do you know? You always get off," Jason snarled. A moment later they heard his bare feet slap the marble stairs as he ran upstairs.

"Ooooo-kay, that's it," Kate said, putting down her napkin and pushing her chair back. "Dub, have some breakfast. I'll be right back."

She reached Jason's bedroom door only seconds after he slammed it. She knocked and called out, "Jason, let me in."

"Go away."

"The heck I will." She opened the door. The room was at least as big as the guest room in which she'd slept, and every wall was papered with movie posters. The horizontal surfaces were drowning in clothes, shoes, papers, books, pages of what appeared to be scripts in shiny black covers. There was a big computer with an oversize screen on the desk in the corner, a scanner, some other equipment Kate couldn't identify and a big handheld video camera on a tripod in the corner. It was the room of a creative male slob with a great many interests, none of which included order. It was also the room of a male who was used to having someone else pick up after him.

"Good grief," Kate said. "Is that an original *Revenge of the Jedi* poster over your bed?"

"Yeah. Cool, huh?"

"Expensive. They're very rare."

"My dad gave it to me for Christmas last year." He turned away and Kate saw his fists clench at his sides.

"Enough small talk. Sit down."

"I didn't ask you up here."

"Don't be a jerk." Kate pulled out the chair from behind his computer desk, stacked half a dozen scripts onto the floor on top of at least a dozen others and sat. After a moment in which she was afraid he'd simply walk out, Jason sat on the edge of the bed with his knees apart and his hands hanging between his knees. He refused to meet her eyes.

"You are obviously planning to use your twenty-five years in Parchman as the basis of a documentary," Kate said.

"Hey!"

She opened her hands. "What else can I think? If you really believe that innocent people don't go to jail in this country, you have been watching too damn many movies. I recommend you watch *The Shawshank Redemption* and *Cool Hand Luke*. Then tell me prison life is what you want."

"Listen, you're my lawyer, you've got to do what I tell you, right?"

"Within reason."

"Then go down to that D.A. and see what kind of a deal you can make me."

Kate's heart fell. "So you did kill her."

Jason swarmed off the bed and bolted toward the window. Kate came up out of her chair. For a moment she was afraid he planned to jump.

"I'm responsible for her death."

"You hit her with your tire iron?" Kate tried to keep her voice level.

He turned to look at her. "What tire iron? No. Man, I'd never hit a woman, and I don't even have a tire iron." He seemed genuinely puzzled.

"Why not? They come with the car."

"Yeah, well, last August I was trying to break my out-board-motor mounts loose on the ski boat and I kind of dropped the tire iron in the lake." He shrugged. "I guess I forgot to get another one."

Kate took a deep breath. "That's one of the things the police have against you—your missing tire iron. If you didn't hit her, then responsible or not, you are not *guilty* of her death."

"But I left her on the road in the middle of the night. Man, it was real warm for Thanksgiving weekend, you know, but it was still cold. And I just drove off and left her." His voice broke, and Kate suddenly saw not a truculent young man, but a very frightened nineteen-year-old boy, eaten up with guilt and pain.

"Tell me something, Jason. You've been at school for less than three months and California is a long way to fly for Thanksgiving. Why did you come home?"

He flushed. "It's just the three of us, you know? I thought my granddaddy would be lonesome."

Not his father, but his grandfather. Kate continued gently, "How about you?"

"Yeah, okay, I missed everybody, all right? It's not like we can't afford it or anything." He turned back to the window. "Man, I wish now I'd gone to Carmel like they wanted me to."

"Who wanted?"

"Some friends, that's all."

"So you came home when?"

"I told you this yesterday."

"Tell me again."

He heaved a cavernous sigh and sat on the bed. "My dad picked me up in Memphis about eight Wednesday night. Thursday we had Thanksgiving dinner around two, and then I lazed around here watching football for a while.''

''Who called who?''

''Waneath called me. Said some of the old crowd were getting together Saturday night and would I pick her up. I mean, she sounded like it was no big deal, you know?''

Kate nodded. ''But it was.''

''The party was out at the Blue Jack. We had a couple of beers, and I was having a good time seeing everybody, but Waneath kept trying to drag me out. Finally we had a fight about it.''

''But still you went.''

''Yeah. I mean she was my date, right?''

''And you thought you'd have sex.''

''Okay, so I thought we'd have sex. What's wrong with that? It's not like it was the first time.''

''Can you show me where you were?''

For the first time Jason hesitated. ''Why'd you want to go over there?''

''I want to see the place you say you left her.''

''I did leave her there. I mean, we had sex, and then she hit me with...'' He took a deep breath. ''Okay, this is the truth.''

It was Kate's turn to heave a sigh. ''Well, finally.''

''She wanted us to get married.''

''I beg your pardon?''

''She told me we could get married at Christmas, and then she could go back to California with me.''

Kate narrowed her eyes. ''To do what? Go to school?''

He shrugged. ''To be the next Pamela Lee to hear her tell it.''

''And you weren't interested.''

''I'm a freshman in college, for God's sake. I don't want to get married!''

"Then she told you she was pregnant."

"No! She never told me she was pregnant. I didn't know she was pregnant until the sheriff told me."

"It wasn't yours?"

"No way."

Kate leaned back in the desk chair and stared at him wordlessly. He squirmed. She was certain he was still holding something back, but she didn't think that something was an attack with a tire iron. She could see him making Waneath get out of the car, but more likely she got out of her own free will, expecting him to sweet-talk her back in so that they could make up.

What she'd wanted meant responsibility and growing up and the end of his career and life plans. He wouldn't have thought beyond putting the pedal to the metal. He was an irresponsible nineteen-year-old nitwit. But not a killer.

She said conversationally, "So you plan to expiate your guilt by going to jail for twenty-five years?"

"Yeah. No! I don't know." He dropped his head into his hands. "I knew I shouldn't have left her there, but, man, she made me so mad."

"You did go back," Kate said gently.

"Oh, sure, I went back. But by then she was gone." The face he turned toward Kate was tear-stained. "I tried to find her. I drove around and I yelled…"

"And then what?"

He shrugged. "I was pretty wasted. I mean, we'd been drinking beer and getting it on and fighting and stuff. I figured somebody'd picked her up. I came home and went to bed. I was still asleep when Sheriff Tait showed up around noon."

"Okay. What are you leaving out?"

"Nothing!" It was a wail. "Look, I saw what Waneath's mother did to you. I knew she'd be mad at me for leaving

Waneath that way, but she really thinks I did it, you know? No matter what happens I can't ever come back to Athena.'' He fell back onto the bed. ''Not that I want to.''

''What do you want to do?''

He sat up and waved a hand at the posters on the wall. ''Make movies. I'm going to make it too.'' He glanced at the door and curled his lip. ''Not like my dad.''

Kate felt her heart leap in her chest. Was that it? Jason thought his dad was a quitter because he gave up an acting career to marry Melba and be a farmer. ''Your dad did what he thought was right.''

''Sure. Like he ever gave a damn.''

''He gives a damn about you.''

''Right.''

Kate stood up. ''Okay, here's the deal. You're going to have to work out your guilt over leaving Waneath on that road, and I have no idea how you're going to do it. What you are *not* going to do, however, is plead guilty to salve your conscience. I guarantee you that two days after you got to Parchman you'd realize what a bad bargain you made. Maybe you can make documentaries that save humanity from famine or something. That's up to you. But if you're telling me the truth about not hitting Waneath, then you didn't kill her. Now, come get some breakfast and act like a rational human being for a change.''

''I'm not hungry.''

''Of course you are. You're nineteen.'' Kate stopped with her hand on the door. ''Oh, and later on this morning you're going to give me the name of every friend the two of you had in high school, everybody who was at that party, everything you can remember from the minute you got off that airplane in Memphis. You're going to make a list of every old beau of Waneath's and anyone and everyone else in this town that she might have run into on that road.''

"But..."

"And another thing. Whether it's me or somebody else, your attorney has one job—to get you acquitted. If you get in the way, I'll run over you."

She left the room before he could say anything. At the head of the stairs she leaned on the balcony railing and looked down at the empty foyer, trying to catch her breath. Maybe she was being too trusting, but she believed he didn't kill Waneath.

Was her sixth sense about Jason because he was David's son? She sure didn't owe David a damn thing. He'd tricked her into coming, he'd tricked her into spending the night thinking about him. Maybe Jason was tricking her as well, but she didn't think so.

She felt the old swell of enthusiasm whenever she got her teeth into a case she believed in. She started down the stairs. By the time she reached the last step, she'd decided.

For better or worse, she was going to get Jason Canfield out of this mess.

CHAPTER FIVE

"WHERE'S ARNOLD?" Kate asked when she walked back into the kitchen.

"He and Dub are in the library," David answered. "He's calling Atlanta to see when that investigator of yours can get here."

"Oh." She leaned against the doorjamb and folded her arms across her chest. "Are you absolutely certain you want to go on with this? With me as defense counsel, that is."

"You'll do it?"

"Answer my question. This is Jason's life we're dealing with. You want the best, not someone who hasn't had a criminal case in over six months."

"Before I give you an answer, you give me one. Why did you stop practicing criminal law?"

She closed her eyes, and the familiar sensation of fear and loathing began to surface. "I owe you that."

"And tell me what the differences are between the civil stuff you're doing now and what you were doing before."

"Sensible questions." She smiled at him ruefully and walked around the table to sit opposite him. "Questions you probably should have asked before you brought me down here."

He picked her cup and his off the table, and went to the half-full carafe of coffee on the counter. She could feel him behind her, hear the soft sound of his breathing. Why had she never been as physically aware of another human being? He laid his hand on her shoulder. His long fingers kneaded her muscles with a tenderness that she'd never known from anyone else.

"I needed you," he said softly. He continued in a normal voice. "But I also knew you were a hell of a lawyer."

She took a deep breath. "So sit down and let's talk. Lawyer talk." She took a hefty swig of her coffee that came close to burning the roof of her mouth. He sat opposite and watched her.

"You wanted to know the difference between civil and criminal law," she said. "The rules of evidence are different, for one thing. Civil verdicts are based on preponderance of evidence; criminal cases are based on reasonable doubt. In civil cases the defendant usually testifies. More and more defendants are not testifying in criminal cases because it leaves them open to cross-examination."

"Have the rules changed in the last year?"

"No."

"Then you still know what you're doing. Where's the problem?"

She walked over to stare out the breakfast-room window at the November sun sparkling on the waters of the swimming pool. "The fault, dear Brutus, is not in our stars, but in ourselves."

"And that means?"

"When Alec was alive I had a mentor and a colleague as well as a husband. Whenever I went off half-cocked on some crusade, he was there to haul me back. Just before he died I was in the middle of a big arson case. My client was a rent-a-cop in an apartment complex. He discovered a fire, turned in the alarm and got everybody out. He was a hero until they arrested him."

"Sounds like an innocent man to me."

"In arson cases the person who turns in the alarm, especially if it's a guard who winds up being hailed as a hero, is invariably the prime suspect. Fits the profile. You know what happened in Atlanta during the Olympics. I was certain this was the same miscarriage of justice. So was the jury. He was acquitted."

"You did your job."

"And I was damn proud of it, until two months later when he was caught red-handed setting a fire in the basement of a nursing home." She turned back to David. "Two people died before they could get them out. I as good as killed those people, because I believed in him, believed in my judgment."

"That's ridiculous." He set his cup down and came to her. He put his hands on her arms and held her at arm's length. "You didn't know."

"I should have known."

Without warning he pulled her to him, wrapped his arms around her and whispered, "You keep forgetting you're only human, Katie. You don't know everything."

He lifted her chin. She knew there were tears in her eyes. She also knew that standing like this against his body felt right, as if he was the shelter she'd sought for so long and had not found. But as he lowered his mouth toward hers, she pulled away and snapped, "Don't."

"It's what we both want."

"No, we don't. Or if we do, we shouldn't." She pushed past him. "The past is dead and buried. You are my client's father, and that's all you'll be or I'll walk away from this now."

"Does that mean you're staying?"

"In the Paradise Motel and only until we get the preliminaries over with. I intend to be in Atlanta for Christmas."

"With whom?"

She flushed. There was nobody, not even Alec's children, both of whom lived hundreds of miles away, or her mother, who had no intention of leaving her buddies in Florida. "That's none of your business. And remember, that's all that is between us. Business."

"I can't promise that."

"Then I'll make that pledge for both of us. I'm going to find Arnold." With that, she left the breakfast room, and walked briskly down the hall in search of her partner. She found Arnold and Dub in the living room.

Dub sat in a big leather wing chair by the fireplace with his everyday boots on the heavy slab of marble that served as a coffee table. His eyes were closed and he seemed to be asleep.

Over the mantelpiece, carefully lit by special lights, was the misty portrait of a woman stretched languidly on a white wicker chaise longue in a flower garden. In the curve of her arm stood a girl of about four or five, barefoot and tousled. It was a beautiful picture, all soft pastels, with the rosy resonance of an early Renoir.

Kate nearly backed out of the room. She had seen pictures of Melba Mays with David, on stage and off, the year before she graduated, before Kate had arrived at school to take David away from her.

This woman looked very much like those pictures, but the clothes were more old-fashioned. And David and Melba didn't have a daughter, did they? She realized he could have a dozen kids by Melba without her being any the wiser.

Behind her, David said quietly, "That's Melba with her mother. Melba was about three at the time."

On closer inspection, Kate felt a frisson of disquiet as she looked at the direct, intense gaze with which both subjects stared out at the world. Although the picture might be ethereal, the two subjects were anything but. Kate had an idea she'd discovered from which side of the family Melba got her unshakable determination to get what she wanted at any price.

Arnold sat on the edge of Dub's broad partner's desk with his back to the room, and the phone seemed to grow out of his left ear. "Well, find me somebody," he said, and slammed the phone into its cradle. He noticed Kate in the doorway and gave her an exasperated shrug. "Mahoney broke an ankle jumping off some cheating husband's second-floor fire escape," he said.

"Drat," Kate said. She said to David, "The firm's P.I." Then to Arnold, "Are they going to locate a substitute?"

"Not immediately. Are we turning this over to Haskind and Vortiger?" He glanced at David. "Remember Kate told you about the murder twins?"

"As of this moment," Kate said, "you're moving us to the Paradise Motel. We're back in the criminal-defense business."

"Yes!" Arnold said and pumped his arm straight up and down. "About time you stopped having the vapors."

"Thank you very much."

Dub stirred and opened one eye. "Shoot. More foolishness. Good money after bad."

"What happens now?" David asked.

"We start interviewing the kids at that party after we get the list from Jason."

"I know most of them," David said.

She sighed. "Arnold can set us up at the motel, and baby-sit the paperwork with the sheriff and the D.A. All we need is a couple of other suspects. And somebody who knows Jason hasn't owned a tire iron since summer."

"I know that much," Dub said.

"Great witness you'd make, old man," David said affectionately.

"David's right," Kate added. "Let me go get my stuff ready, and we'll head out."

"See you sometime this evening at the motel," Arnold said, turning back to the telephone. "Great to have you back, boss-lady."

She made a face at him.

"I KNOW YOU'D RATHER do this without me," David said as he turned his car in the direction of town. "But this is one time when you need me as your stalking-horse. I know the people on that list Jason gave you. I can at least introduce you—pave the way." He glanced over at her. She stared out the window as though the endless acres of plowed fields were the finest scenery in the world.

"I wrote you a dozen letters when your husband died," he said abruptly.

She turned to stare at him. "I never got them."

He grinned ruefully. "That's because I tore them all up. Save you the trouble, I guess."

"What did they say?"

"That I was sorry for your loss." They'd said a great deal more than that. The pile of letters he'd written to her over the years, far from being in bits and pieces, lay in the bottom drawer of his desk in his office under lock and key. He kept telling himself he ought to destroy them. Some of them, especially the early ones when he was very young and very horny, were pretty raw.

He'd started writing them first when she refused to see him, refused even to let him know where she was staying. He'd hoped to get friends to pass them along to her, but before he could, Melba had dropped her bombshell.

He supposed there'd been other alternatives to marrying Melba and moving to Mississippi. Live in New York, try to get Kate back, struggle after a second-rate career, or take up working as a full-time waiter. Let Melba have the baby alone. Send support checks when he could. Neither abortion nor adoption had ever been an option. Not for him.

If he'd been able to talk to Kate, maybe he would have explored those other options, but once the divorce was final, he felt he had only one responsibility—to be a decent husband and a good father. The prospect of his baby was the only thing that kept him sane. That, and Dub, who'd set about turning him into a farmer the first afternoon they'd met. David had always loved growing things, working beside his father among the roses. But that was entirely different from farming as a business. At least it had given him a way to submerge his misery.

What did it matter where he lived or with whom? It wasn't as though Melba had not been a good friend in times past. Even a good lover, before he discovered real love with Kate.

Even after he realized Melba had set out to break up his marriage, he couldn't hate her, because he understood her. She'd always had her own way. If he was the golden boy, she was definitely the golden girl. The only difference between them was that she was willing to do just about anything to make her desires come true. And nobody, least of all David's wife, was going to stand in her way.

Give her credit. She'd settled down to try to make him happy once she got him.

That was the thing. They'd both tried too hard. Trying had probably killed her. They'd both spent their time compensating for wrongs they'd committed. She, because she'd destroyed his marriage, and he, because he could never truly love her.

He realized Kate was speaking to him and drew his attention back to her. "What did you say?"

"I asked where we're headed first."

"I've got to go by the gin to make sure the last of the cotton is baled and ready for shipment before we get started on Jason. You mind?"

"Not at all. I've never seen a cotton gin in action."

"You probably won't today either. Just a bunch of trucks being loaded. After that, our next stop is Jimmy Viccolla. He's the best mechanic in these parts and Jason's best friend."

"You think he saw Jason drop his tire iron in the lake last summer?"

"Possibly. And he would know whether Jason replaced it." David shook his head. "Kids. If he had managed to break that motor mount loose, he'd have dropped the motor into the lake as well."

"He has his own ski boat?"

"Actually, it's Dub's big bass boat, but in the summertime Jason uses it most weekends, or did. He's a safe driver. I never had to worry about him on the water."

"How about on land?"

David nodded. "Here we are." He turned into the gravel parking area in front of a high metal building with open sides. Several men were sitting around smoking, while a big truck with its tailgate wide open sat backed up to the loading dock. There were several enormous bales of hay on the truck, but room for plenty more.

"Hell," David snapped. "Wait here." He climbed out of the car and sauntered toward the men, not betraying his anger by so much as a clenched fist or tightened shoulder muscles.

The moment they saw him approach they dropped their cigarettes and ground them out underfoot. They knew the restrictions against smoking around the cotton. He'd ream them out later. At the moment his primary concern was that cotton. "Morning, gentlemen," he said casually. "Little early for a break, isn't it?"

"We're waiting for you," one of the men said. He hesitated a moment, then stuck his hand out. "Sorry about your trouble, Mr. David. Jason's a good boy. He never did this."

The other men made affirmative noises. David felt his throat close with emotion as he took the man's hand. "Thanks, Wylie, that means a lot."

Wordlessly, each man stepped up and shook his hand.

David took a deep breath. "Now, come on, y'all," he said. "What say somebody mans that forklift? Need to get this truck loaded and out of here in the next hour."

"Huh?"

"I'll be back in an hour. That truck better be loaded and on its way to New Orleans by then or Dub'll give us all Hail Columbia." He sauntered away and called over his shoulder, "And after that, I got a list of chores long as my arm, so nobody disappear."

They'd do the job. He never stood over them, and they appreciated that. He was certain they'd been talking about how Jason's trouble might affect them, but he felt grateful for their support, all the same.

"Men are worse gossips than women ever thought of being," David said as he climbed into the truck. Through the windshield he saw the first bales shifted onto the forklift.

"Impressive," Kate said. "I don't remember your exerting that sort of authority."

"Over who? The busboy at the pizza joint down on Thirty-third? I was about as low on everybody's totem pole in New York as there was to be."

"What does a farmer do in November?"

"You mean when he's not trying to find defense witnesses in a murder?" David made a right onto the road and accelerated. "Get in the last cotton if he hasn't already. Fix everything that's broken during the year. Repaint. Mend. Do endless paperwork on the blasted computer. Read the *Wall Street Journal* and track the stock market. Line up crop loans for next year, and research fertilizer and seeds and crop rotation. Go to seminars with other farmers—"

"Stop! Enough." Kate laughed. "I figured you, Dub and Jason probably spent the winter in a duck blind somewhere shooting at innocent mallards."

"That, too. And getting a deer or two for the freezer."

"You never used to hunt."

"Still don't. Makes me highly suspect among the local male population. Sitting up to your armpits in ice water at four o'clock in the morning in a duck blind is not my idea of fun."

"Does Jason enjoy hunting?"

David nodded. "His grandfather taught him. I handled the less glamorous stuff like Little League and soccer."

"Little League? You?"

"Why not? You forget you are talking to the Hilton High School starting pitcher. Jason's not beefy enough to play football, but he's a hell of a center fielder and a darned good soccer player."

"You're proud of him, aren't you?"

"Of course I am. That's why I can't believe he did this. Can you see that?"

"What if he is guilty?"

"Here's Jimmy's garage. That's Jimmy over there." David pointed to the lower half of a person in coveralls protruding from under the hood of a perfectly restored early Thunderbird in fire-engine red.

"Hey, Jimmy," David called as he stepped out of the car. He sauntered over with his hands in his pockets, the picture of the relaxed male getting ready to kibitz over cars.

But Kate, who walked behind him, could see the tension in his back and shoulders, the cords that stood out in the back of his neck. *He can still act,* she thought. *I can't allow myself to forget what a good actor he is even for a second.*

The young man raised up, and automatically reached for a grimy rag at his waist to wipe his hands. "Hey, Mr. Canfield." The young man's eyes darted warily past David to settle on Kate.

"Kate Mulholland, this is Jimmy Viccolla. He went to school with Jason. He's also the best shade-tree mechanic in the state of Mississippi." David grinned engagingly.

Kate watched the young man relax as an answering grin spread over his face. "Shoot, I'm not that good."

"Keeps my old farm pickup running," David said. "Thing is, Jimmy, Mrs. Mulholland here is Jason's lawyer…"

Kate saw the young man stiffen and take a single step backward so that his thighs were pressed against the grillwork of the Thunderbird. She stepped forward, pasting what she hoped was an equally infectious smile on her face. "We know you want to help Jason out of this mess," she said.

He glanced at her suspiciously. "How can I do that? I don't know nothing about what happened."

"Were you at the party?" David asked.

Jimmy's eyes slid away from Kate's face. His was an unprepossessing face with large teeth in a small mouth and close-set eyes. He wiped his hands convulsively on the cloth that hung from his belt.

"For a little while. Left early. Had to go to church with my momma on Sunday."

Kate nodded. "Did you hear Waneath and Jason's fight?"

He shook his head violently. "No, ma'am. Left early, like I told you." Suddenly he turned to David. "Jason wouldn't a' hurt Waneath like that, though Lord knows somebody was bound to.''

Kate stiffened. ''Why would anybody hurt her?'' she practically whispered.

Jimmy's shoulders hunched away as though she'd struck out at him. ''I shouldn't a' said nothing.''

''Please,'' Kate said. ''I need to know as much as I can if I'm going to help Jason.''

''Listen, ma'am,'' Jimmy said urgently. ''Mr. Talley, Waneath's daddy, has the biggest—heck, the only—car dealership in Athena. If he finds out I was talking to you, I'll never get a lick of business out of him again, and I do all his regular maintenance and service and stuff.''

''Surely he wants to find out the truth.''

''He thinks he *knows* the truth. He thinks Waneath was some kind of pure little angel. Well, let me tell you, she was anything but an angel. I wouldn't hardly blame Jason none if he hauled off and smacked her one.''

''He didn't,'' David said. ''He'd never hit a woman.''

''All I'm saying is that if he did, he probably got provoked or something. Didn't mean to hurt her, got scared and bugged out.''

''Is that what people are saying?'' David asked, and Kate heard the menace in his tone.

She stepped in. ''Actually, I really wanted to ask you about something else. Did you do much skiing with Jason last summer on the lake?''

Jimmy looked confused. ''Nearly every weekend, why?''

''Do you remember one time in August when the outboard went out?''

''Sure do. Turned out we'd wrapped one of the towlines around the propeller,'' Jimmy shook his head and raised his eyebrows. ''I mean that was a flat-out mess. Couldn't get the motor off, and finally Jason had to take his scuba gear and go down underwater and fix it there.''

Kate sighed. ''Were you with him when he was trying to get the motor off?''

''I tried to help.''

''What was he using to break the motor mount loose?''

''Shoot, the darned fool was trying to use a tire iron.'' Jimmy laughed. ''Darned if he didn't drop it overboard right into three feet of Mississippi mud at the bottom of the lake.'' He shook his head. ''Never did find it.''

Kate took a deep breath. ''Would you be willing to testify to that in court?''

He rubbed his jaw. ''Like I said, about Mr. Talley...''

''I understand, but if the case goes to trial, we need you to tell the truth.''

''Oh, shoot, Jason's my friend. And I never did lie real good.'' He grinned and shrugged.

''Thank you, Mr. Viccolla.'' She extended her hand, and after another swipe with his towel, Jimmy took it gingerly.

''Now, about the party,'' David began, but Kate laid a hand on his arm and shook her head.

He looked confused, but followed her to his car anyway. As they drove away, he turned to Kate and asked, ''Why didn't you ask him some more about the party?''

''We got one piece of corroborating evidence that Jason did not have a tire iron—at least he didn't in August. It's a teeny piece, because he probably could have snitched one from one of your other cars, but unless the prosecution can produce evidence that he bought or borrowed one, that's a small point in his favor. That's enough for one witness, certainly one who obviously believes that Jason was justified in 'smacking Waneath' and is scared to death of her father.''

"Yeah. Okay." David obviously didn't agree, but didn't intend to contest the issue further at this point.

Kate made up her mind immediately. "Look, I've got to rent another car. This won't work. Nobody's going to open up to me with you tagging along."

"Nobody's going to open up to a stranger either. I want to know what people are saying."

"There is a certain cachet attached to talking to a lady lawyer. With you standing guard behind me, everybody's going to want to spare your feelings."

"What's wrong with that?"

She closed her eyes. "Pull over a minute and shut off the engine," she said.

He complied and swiveled in his seat to look at her.

"Are you worried he's guilty?" she asked.

"Hell, no!"

She raised her eyebrows and glared at him until he moved restively, then she nodded. "But you're not as positive he's innocent as you've been trying to convince me, are you? You want to get him off because he's your son, but you also believe in justice. You always did, at least when I knew you."

He leaned back against the seat and closed his eyes. "I still can't lie to you, can I?"

"You practically made a career out of lying to me, and I never tumbled to it, not once." She turned to look out over the muddy fields. "Maybe I'm smarter than I used to be, or a damn sight more cynical."

"I tried never to lie to you." He reached across to touch her shoulder. She flinched.

When she turned to him, she knew her eyes were brimming with unshed tears. She sniffed and willed them not to spill over. "Just left out a few things, right? Listen, David. I don't represent clients I don't believe in. I did when I first got started, but not anymore. That's one of the perks of being a senior partner in a law firm. And it's why I'm sticking to civil law these days. Because the cops are right most of the time. They arrest people because they're guilty and deserve whatever punishment they get. Jason knows more than he's telling, but I don't think he killed Waneath. I don't give a damn what you believe. What matters is what a jury believes. So you can knock off the act, Daddy dear, and drive me somewhere I can rent a car.''

CHAPTER SIX

"NOBODY IN ATHENA rents cars," David told Kate as he pulled back onto the road. "I think Big Bill Talley has a couple of loaners for people to use while they're getting theirs worked on at his dealership, but he sure as hell won't let you have one."

"Hardly."

"So," David continued, "you take this car. I told you Jimmy keeps my farm truck running like a top. It's an antique, but it gets me where I need to go."

"I'd rather have a car not quite so recognizable as this," Kate said. "But it's better than nothing."

"I would still prefer to drive you around, even if I stay in the background. I don't want you running into Waneath's mother again. There could be others just as angry. You have no idea about life in a small town, Kate. Feelings run deep."

"I beg your pardon?" Kate said. "You're the city boy, in case you've forgotten, Mr. Greensboro-High-Point-North-Carolina. The biggest thing in my town was the college, and it only had fifteen hundred students."

"College towns are different. Not quite so insular."

"Equally inbred however, and with secrets within secrets within secrets. Secrets so pervasive that everybody assumes everybody else knows them. That's the kind of thing I have to find out if I'm going to get Jason out of this."

"You really believe Jason's innocent?"

She shook her head. "I believe he's not guilty of murder. That's not quite the same thing. I don't think he ever expected to be arrested." She shrugged. "Of course, part of that is his grandfather. Dub is convinced this is all some big joke that'll go away if he simply ignores it."

"That's the way Dub always treats real problems. He never believed Melba was as sick as she was, even though his wife died young from the same heart problem. He thinks he can bull his way through life charming everybody in sight and getting his own way. Most of the time it works."

"With you, too?"

"Until lately we've never had a cross word, but I guess that was because we pretty much agreed on the way the farm was supposed to run."

"No longer?"

David shook his head. "I've got some ideas on ways to increase efficiency and cut cost—new herbicides that are environmentally friendly, no-till planting. Even some new hybrids. Dub's a businessman, but he's dug in his heels. Says he doesn't believe in messing with success. If it ain't broke, don't fix it."

"And your philosophy?"

"If it ain't broke now, it'll be broke five years from now, and by then it's too late. The way developing countries are coming on…" He stopped. "Sorry. At the moment, I can't think any further than getting Jason out of this mess." He turned across more endless fields. In the distance a group of pines stood on the only rise within miles. David turned down a gravel road and dropped his speed. "So what do you think happened that night?" he asked.

"I think Waneath got out of the car, or maybe Jason shoved her out—he's certainly feeling guilty about something. She started walking, and somebody—probably someone from that party—came along and picked her up. She was still half-drunk and mad as a wet hen, remember. Maybe whoever picked her up wanted to have sex, and she didn't.''

"So this unknown stops the car, walks around to his trunk, gets out his tire iron, pulls her out of the car, hits her with it, leaves her body beside the road and drives off?'' David shook his head. "And what was she doing all this time?'' He dragged his hand along his jaw. "I knew Waneath, Kate. She had a very high opinion of herself. In the mood she must have been in, she'd have been a handful. I can't see her sitting quietly waiting for some man to kill her, can you?''

"Okay, so maybe he said he thought he had a flat tire, or told her he had a blanket in the trunk that they could spread out. Maybe he drove a truck and carried his tire iron in the back seat. Maybe it wasn't a tire iron—that was only that funeral director-cum-coroner's best guess. We'll know more when we get the results of the autopsy in Memphis. Those guys have a national reputation. If there's anything to discover, they'll find it.''

"Meantime, we're looking at a possible indictment just after Christmas. Some Christmas.'' He slowed for an intersection and waited while a big cotton picker trundled through.

Kate watched it, fascinated by the bits of cotton that blew in its wake like snow flurries. "Everything in our lives always seems to happen around Christmas, doesn't it?'' Kate said.

He took his hand off the wheel and dropped it on Kate's thigh. "I'll never forget how beautiful you looked with the holly wound through your hair that Christmas Eve we got married. Like a Druid priestess.''

Kate removed his hand and said dryly, "Actually, it's the following year I remember so well. 'Now, Kate, for your first Christmas as a married woman, and for your first anniversary present, here you go—a cheating, lying husband.'"

"It wasn't like that." He pulled around a pickup and ignored the wild barking of the pair of Australian sheepdogs that occupied its bed.

"Oh, really? You actually didn't cheat?" Kate said as soon as she thought her voice could be heard above the yapping.

"I didn't lie to you."

"You didn't run home and confess you'd committed adultery either."

"When you asked flat out if I'd been unfaithful, I admitted it." He swiveled his head to look at her. "You never considered forgiving me, did you? Not for a minute."

"I warned you before we were married that adultery was an unforgivable sin in my book. I might even have been able to deal with it if you'd picked some little actress you met at an audition—a one-night stand with a stranger." She stared out the window. Along the sides of the road bits of cotton were caught in the weeds. "But you had to pick the one woman in the world I knew I could never replace."

"You didn't replace anyone. You were my wife. I didn't ask Melba to marry me, I asked you."

"And discovered what a bad bargain you'd made. So you went back to plan A. Did you intend to tell me eventually, or were you simply going to continue the liaison whenever she could get away to New York?"

"I never expected to see her again. It was damn near a one-night stand."

"And the worst Christmas of my life." She turned to him. "Before that year, I always loved Christmas. Even my father stuck around on Christmas. We acted like a real, normal family. The campus was always decorated, and we had an enormous tree—you remember, when you came down to marry me. There were carols in the chapel, and parties with wassail and carolers in costume in the faculty quadrangle. It was the happiest time of the year. Until that Christmas in New York. Since then I've never trusted it. If you can't trust Christmas, what can you trust?''

David drove through a stand of pine trees and pulled into a gravel turnaround in front of a small house that looked as though it belonged on a cliff in Big Sur—all peaked roofs and glass. Beside the front door sat an aged red pickup seemingly held together by the patches of rust and mud that covered it. David climbed out. ''Come on in. I'll get you my spare set of keys.''

''This is your house?'' Kate said as she followed him up the front steps. ''It doesn't have quite that old plantation look that I would have expected from Melba.''

''That's because I didn't build it until a couple of years ago. We lived with Dub until Melba died. Jason refused to move when I did. I decided not to force him out of the only home he'd ever known. I knew he'd be leaving for college soon anyway. He'd had enough upset. He took his mother's death hard.''

''But you went ahead and moved without him?''

''Yeah. I needed some distance from Long Pond. I bought this land a long time ago. It's only twenty acres, and it's not great crop land. I used to come out here sometimes and just sit in the trees. Made me feel almost as though I was home in North Carolina.''

''It's nice. Not so flat.''

''The house is plenty big enough for me, and Jason too if he ever decides to move in.''

He opened the broad front door and ushered Kate in. The house consisted of one large room with stairs on one end leading to what must be at least two bedrooms, if there was space for Jason. The kitchen was open along one wall. Furniture was sparse, modern and upholstered in leather that looked as though it had been salvaged from old saddles and gentlemen's clubs in the Edwardian era. The floor was dark red quarry tile. A stone chimney ran up the wall by the stairs leading to the loft. The whole place looked as though it could simply be hosed down. There was no evidence of a female presence—no pictures on the walls, and only an untidy stack of magazines on the scarred coffee table.

David opened a rolltop desk in the corner to reveal a computer. He dug into one of the cubbyholes beside the mouse and came up with a set of keys dangling from a John Deere–tractor key ring. He handed them to Kate, and as she took them, he closed his fingers over hers. "Don't go."

She swallowed, but left her hand in his. "I've got things to do, people to see."

"Kate, do you have any idea what it's like to see you again? To have you here?"

"David…"

"Listen to me. It was all I could do yesterday not to sweep you up in my arms and drag you off to my cave."

"And leave Jason sitting in jail?"

"That's the only reason I didn't." He grinned ruefully, "That, and the fact that you would have fought me like a tiger." He turned her hand over and bent his head to brush her palm with his lips.

She felt the waves of heat welling up from her center, heat so strong that for a moment she felt as though she'd pass out. She couldn't deny that his touch, his voice, the sight and sound of him opened her to emotions she had denied for far too long. She should turn around and run, but as his lips found their way to the pulse in her wrist, as his other arm encircled her waist and drew her to him, she resisted only for a moment before she let herself be drawn against his chest.

Her body remembered him, fitted against him so familiarly that twenty years were wiped out in an instant. She closed her eyes and felt his lips sweep her temples, her eyelids, and finally touch her lips. She opened to his kiss as she always had, feeling tendrils of flame lick her, torment her with a need for him she'd denied for too long.

Suddenly she stiffened. "No! I can't do this. Not again. Not ever again!" She tried to pull away, but he held her. She felt his breath on her cheek. She couldn't breathe without scenting him. "Please, let me go." She twisted out of his grasp and started for the door.

He called after her, "Kate, stop, please."

"My memory's not that convenient. You obviously don't remember our last encounter."

"I remember," he said, and followed her. The urgency of his voice stopped her with one hand on the doorknob. "But what I remember most is your soft eyes when I'd look down into your face while we made love, the taste of your tongue, and the hills and valleys of the roof of your mouth." He moved behind her and ran his hands down her shoulders and arms.

Against her will she closed her eyes and leaned back against him.

He whispered, his voice close to her ear so that she could feel his breath. "I remember the way your lovely long hair fell across my chest like a damask curtain when you made love to me. I remember the way your breasts fit my hands. I remember the way you opened to me and the arch of your back when you came... I remember the wild times and the tender times and the crazy experiments where we wound up on the floor laughing our heads off. All of it, Katie. Sometimes nearly a whole day goes by when I don't remember and I think, I'm over her. And then it all floods back and I know I'll never be free of you. There's not an inch, a molecule, an atom of you that I don't remember and want.''

She clenched her fists and crossed her arms over her breasts. ''Then why wasn't I enough?''

''You were more than enough.''

She slipped out of his grasp. As much as she wanted to run, maybe it was time to have this out between them. She strode to the fireplace and braced her hand against the rough-hewn mantel. ''If I'd been enough, if you'd loved me, you wouldn't have needed anyone else.''

He followed her, and she raised her other hand to stop him five feet away. He sighed deeply. ''I could never convince you that I loved you. God knows I tried. When you found out about Melba, you weren't surprised. You were mad as hell and never wanted to see me again. You walked away without a backward glance, never gave me a chance to explain or to apologize. But you weren't surprised, because you'd always expected it. I thought then it was because of your father and what he put your mother through, but it wasn't that, was it?''

She looked at him squarely now and tried to keep her voice steady—the voice she used on judges and juries. It was important to stay in command. Now that confrontation was unavoidable, she wanted everything clear between them. Then maybe she could do her job without thinking about David, being aware of him. ''Maybe I wasn't surprised,'' she said carefully. ''I knew someday you'd see what a mess I was, how unworthy I was of you. That's why I tried so hard to make myself indispensable, to do everything I could to help your career, to be the perfect helpmate.''

"You *were* perfect, Kate. That's the real reason I went to bed with Melba."

"What on earth are you talking about? You're blaming Melba on me? Because I did too much?" She heard her voice rise and fought to keep her anger under control. "My God, David, I thought I'd heard every argument in the world from husbands in court. 'If only she hadn't folded the towels wrong, Your Honor, I wouldn't have broken her jaw. If only she hadn't gotten the wrong brand of beer, Your Honor, I wouldn't have knocked her down the stairs.'" She laughed. "This is the first time I've ever heard of a man sleeping around because his wife was too perfect."

"I didn't sleep around, Kate."

"Once is all it takes. So, please, do tell me how my being too perfect caused you to go to bed with another woman. I'm fascinated."

"I've never told anyone this. I couldn't tell you. All those plans we had when we got married, I was going to set the acting world on fire..."

"And you would have. You had everything."

"You know what it's like never to fail, Kate?"

She blew out her breath. "Hardly, I spent most of my life failing everything from kick ball to 'plays well with others' to differential calculus."

"Lucky you."

"Yeah, right."

"No, I mean it. You learned early. You failed, you picked yourself up, you dusted yourself off, and you either tried again or went on to something else. You learned it wasn't the end of the world. I never failed at anything before we went to New York."

"Don't I know it."

"Listen to me, I'm trying to tell you something here."

She stared at his anguished face a moment, then she said quietly, "All right, I'm sorry."

He went to the back windows and stared out at the pines. She could barely hear his voice when he started, but the more he spoke, the more he seemed to find the strength to go on.

"My mother taught me I was the golden boy. She put me right on top of that pedestal, and I liked it up there. What I wanted I got, whether it was starting quarterback or starting pitcher, the lead in every play from the sixth grade on, honor roll, Beta Club, national merit scholarship, valedictorian of my class..." His voice trailed off.

She took a step toward him. "David, please don't stop."

"People liked me." He shrugged. "They didn't seem to resent me. I hope they didn't, anyway."

"No," she whispered. "Nobody resented you. You never acted as though any of it was your due. You worked hard, you cared about people, and everybody knew you were going someplace. That's why I never understood when you picked me."

"Oh, Kate. I picked you because you believed in me so much," he said. He moved to the counter and sat on one of the tall bar stools with one foot crooked over a rung.

"I never believed in me. Not once. All my life I thought, one of these days somebody's going to catch on and then where will I be? I didn't have a clue who I was or what I wanted, so I tried to want what people said I ought to want. What you said, what my mother said."

"You were a wonderful actor."

He shook his head. "In college I could read all my glowing reviews and convince myself maybe I was as good as they said I was. Within three months after we moved to New York I knew damn well I was mediocre and always would be."

"That's not true. It's just hard to break in."

He leaned back on his elbows and grinned, but there wasn't any humor in his face, just a sardonic lifting of his upper lip. "The first time I auditioned for the Actor's Studio, the director thanked me, and told me I'd done a workmanlike job." He curled his lip.

"Bastard."

David shrugged. "I knew he was right. All those classes we sweated bullets paying for showed me that. I could do a great first read—really impressive, you know. But I never got any better. I never forgot there was an audience out there watching me, judging me. I saw some others—a few of them are household names today— who submerged themselves in the characters they played. I couldn't do that."

She sank onto the couch and leaned toward him. "You were learning your craft as a professional." How could she have loved him so much and not known he was prey to this kind of insecurity? It was as though she were seeing him for the first time. No, as though he was allowing her to see a part of himself he'd always kept hidden from her. It frightened her, and yet at the same time she resented him for not trusting her.

"I had a very small talent. I wasn't good enough. And I found out something else. I didn't want it."

She sat up, bewildered. "But it's all we ever talked about, what we planned for, what we worked for."

"No, Katie, what you worked for. To pay for my tuition, my clothes, my fancy portfolio of pictures, my classes, that crummy apartment with hot-and-cold-running rats and roaches, when I wanted to give you a mansion in Connecticut."

"Everybody starts out that way."

"You don't understand. For the first time, people caught on. I was a fake and a phony. I failed. I didn't know how to handle it. All of a sudden, I didn't know who or what I was. I just knew I wasn't the man you thought I was. And every time I lost another role and came home to you, you told me that I'd get the next part. I knew I was betraying you, lying to you. You made a lousy bargain when you married me.''

''You were never a lousy bargain.''

''Yes, I was.''

''Why didn't you tell me? Why didn't you trust me?''

''I couldn't. You invested everything in my dream…''

''I thought it was our dream together.''

''It wasn't my dream any longer. I didn't have any more dreams. I was so damn miserable that I didn't even want to come home to you for fear you'd read it in my eyes. I was the husband, the breadwinner, the big Broadway star-to-be, and I was a fake and a failure. I wanted to go somewhere, anywhere, where we didn't have to scrub the soot out of the bathroom every morning, and where my wife didn't have to work sixty hours a week to keep me in lessons that wouldn't ever make a difference. And I was afraid if I told you, I'd break your heart. Worse, that you'd leave me.''

''Never.'' As she said the words, she wondered if they were true. She wouldn't have left him, certainly, but she'd have had to adjust to living with a man who was suddenly someone completely different from the person she thought she'd married.

He'd grown in a different direction. Could she have caught up with him? Could she have changed gears from being the wife of a budding New York star to being the wife of a man who didn't know who or what he wanted to be? To being the wife of an accountant? Or even a farmer?

''When I was at my lowest, that's when Melba showed up,'' he said. ''I know now that she came to New York specifically to seduce me, though God knows why she wanted me. She hated you, you know that? She wasn't used to being dumped. Maybe in the beginning she just wanted to have sex with me to prove she could get back at you. I don't think it had anything to do with me.''

Now came the resentment, bubbling up inside her. He couldn't trust his own wife, but he could sleep with an old girlfriend? ''But you went along with her.''

''Oh, yeah. I could have taken her out for a drink, or even dinner, Instead I got drunk and wound up taking her upstairs at the Plaza.''

''You were drunk?''

He shook his head. ''I can't use that as an excuse.'' He ran his hand over his hair. ''I was like a kid who sticks his hand near the stove. I wanted to see how close I could get without getting burned.'' He turned away from her to stare out the window as though he could get some answers from the broad fields where he had spent so much of his life. ''With Melba I could pretend to be the man I used to think I was for a little while longer. Maintaining a fantasy is a damn heady thing. And I swore to myself you'd never find out.''

''But I did.''

''Yeah. I wasn't even a good enough actor for that.''

''You could have convinced an audience, but not me. I saw it in the way you avoided my eyes, touched me, laughed too loud and too often. My father was a great role model, remember. You might as well have written, 'I was unfaithful' across the bathroom mirror in her lipstick.''

He looked back at her curiously. ''But you were already looking for the signs. I did everything I could do to keep you from finding out. I never knew how you did.''

''Oh, come on. Midge Rider couldn't wait to call me to

tell me she'd seen you and Melba all over each other in the Plaza bar.''

"Midge never saw us. And we were never *in* the Plaza bar. Or any bar.''

Kate looked confused. "But that's what she said…''

"Midge was Melba's friend. I guess that's what Melba told her to say.'' David sighed. "Dub got drunk one night and told me it was a setup from the start. But he never told me about Midge. Maybe he didn't know.''

"And I fell right into the trap.''

"We both fell. But when you disappeared that way, when I found your note, and then when I got the divorce papers… I tried every way I knew to find you—to talk to you.''

She stood, reached for the car keys which she had dropped on the table beside the sofa and started for the door. "And what would you have said if you had? Given me all these reasons why you cheated on me, on us?''

He intercepted her and laid a hand on her arm. "I don't know what I would have said. Maybe I'd have tried to blame you, or justify myself, or even blame Melba or the liquor. I hope I would have said what I'm saying now. I'm sorry. I was stupid. Please forgive me.''

She caught her breath and shook off his arm. "I have to process all this, David.'' She stepped around him and opened the door.

"Don't disappear on me again, Kate.''

"Not possible so long as I'm your son's lawyer.''

"Kate…''

She hesitated in the doorway with her back to him. "Maybe I should share the blame. You should have been able to talk to me, but you're right. I had you up on that pedestal too. You could be anything except human and scared and fallible.'' She shook her head and ran her hand through her hair. "I was so wrapped up in my own fantasy—the little wifey-poo, standing in the wings applauding her wonderful husband as he receives his first Tony Award. Reflected glory and all that nonsense.''

''Not a bad dream.''

''No, but it wasn't your dream, it was mine. Because I was too scared to have any of my own, just for me. You had to slay the dragons and drag home the mastodons. You had to be strong and sure for both of us.''

''Isn't that what I was supposed to do?''

''Maybe in 50,000 BC.'' She shut the door again and leaned against it with her hands behind her back. ''And all these years I thought you were suffering because you'd given up your dream of a life in the theater for Melba, when actually, she gave you the one thing I couldn't—she let you escape.''

''Not escape. More of a prison than you can imagine. But a compensation of a kind. Jason and the land, that is.'' He took a single step toward her. ''Can you forgive me?''

She didn't so much make a decision as realize it had already been made somewhere deep within her psyche. It was time to let go. ''We were twenty-two years old. We didn't have a clue about who we were. We were playing at fantasy and great sex and all the rags-to-riches movies we'd ever seen. Could be it's high time to ditch the old baggage.''

''Not the love. And maybe not the great sex.''

''Don't push your luck.'' She managed a wan smile. ''But at the very least we have to stop superimposing the faces of the people we were onto the people we've become.''

''Can you do that?''

''I don't know. I do know that you're a very different man from the boy I married. You're gentler, but stronger too. And there's an edge of sadness in you that wasn't there before. You've been tempered. When you were twenty-two I think you'd have talked a lot about that mastodon, and brought it home and presented it to me with trumpets blaring. Now, I think I'd just look in the freezer one day, and there'd be all those mastodon steaks you never bothered to mention.''

''Is that a compliment?'' He moved toward her as though he planned to take her in his arms once more.

She reached for the doorknob behind her and opened it. Too soon to touch. She needed to be alone, away from his eyes, the scent of his body, the sight of him, the feel of his fingers and his lips. ''A compliment? I think it is. You've gotten on with the business of living in a way I haven't managed. I'm a little jealous.''

''Me? Look at you. You're at the top of a tough profession. You're strong and smart and you don't put up with garbage from anybody or need anybody. I'm just a dirt farmer.''

''Inside I'm still the scared kid who flunked 'plays well with others.'''

''You had a good marriage—''

''Alec was my best friend, my occasional lover and my colleague, but the fireworks never went off in my heart when he walked into a room. I'd almost forgotten what it felt like to be in love.''

''I want to make you remember.''

''Maybe you already have.'' She turned and ran down the steps to the car. As she drove away, she heard him calling after her.

She had been so sure she was free of him, and now she felt ensnared as completely as she had the first time she saw him. Was there really only one woman for one man in the entire universe? If he truly was the other half of her soul, then it was a darned inconvenient pairing.

He swore he never wanted to lie to her, but his whole life with her had been a sort of lie. Melba was simply the last, and maybe not even the worst. All those months in New York he'd kept up a facade, although he must have been desperately unhappy. Was he right about his talent?

Didn't matter. What mattered was that he believed he had failed, had lost his way, and had been afraid to share his failure with her, as though she was only allowed to share his triumphs, and couldn't be trusted to share his defeats as well. What kind of a marriage was that?

And he'd been right, damn him. She hadn't seen it then, but Melba was a defeat for both of them.

Had she let him go too easily? Was principle really more important than love? She'd been so blasted self-righteous at the time, so wounded, so angry, that she hadn't even allowed him to open up to her then. Who had she been punishing? David, for betraying her? Her father? Herself? Other marriages survived adultery to become stronger than they were before.

God knows she had been wounded deeply in the one place she was most vulnerable.

No. Moral principle was important—at least the one about fidelity. Sympathy and understanding were all very well, she thought as she felt the old anger well up in her again. In the final analysis, he was the one who had gone to bed with someone else. His choice, not hers.

She'd had a right to protect herself. Cheating husbands didn't reform—her father had protested over and over again that he'd never cheat again. He always had. And her mother had endured.

Well, Kate hadn't endured. Why live through the heartache, the broken trust, and hope that things would change, that his fling with Melba would be his only fling, when two months later David would probably have bedded some chorus gypsy?

One adultery invariably led to another. She'd been right to cut her losses the first time it happened.

She could never have lived with herself if she had let him get away with it as her mother had. She deserved better than that. She had been faithful. He hadn't.

DAVID WATCHED her drive his shiny new Navigator somewhat erratically down the gravel road and wondered whether she had any idea which direction to turn to go into Athena. He'd planned to draw her a map, but there hadn't been time.

What he hadn't planned to do was kiss her that way and unload all his emotional baggage into her lap. Nothing could justify what he'd done with Melba all those years ago, but even murderers were paroled eventually. He'd spent those years knowing that Kate was out there somewhere in the world and he wasn't with her. Knowing was the hardest part of his sentence.

He went back into the house and picked up the telephone to dial long distance.

He heard the cheerful hello on the other end of the telephone with a lifting of his heart. "Hi, Mrs. Hillman," he said.

"David? Did you manage to reach my daughter?"

"Yes. She arrived yesterday. You were right to convince me to call her."

"Oh, I'm so glad, dear. Has it been terribly awkward meeting her again?"

He laughed. "Awkward enough."

"I'm so terribly sorry it has to be under these circumstances. I feel almost as though Jason were part of my own family—my own grandson. He should be. How are you holding up?''

''Better than I would without Kate. She managed to secure bail, so at least he's not sitting in jail. She wasn't happy that I conned her down here, Mrs. H.''

David heard the laughter of a young girl echoing down the line. ''She'd be furious if she knew you and I had stayed in touch.''

''She's always been a pretty tough cookie,'' he said.

''We both know that inside she's very fragile. I suppose when you live with the professor and his ways for most of your life, you develop a skin like one of those alligators I see on the golf course.''

''Your marriage survived,'' David said. ''Mine didn't. How did you manage to hold it together?''

''For one thing, one always assumes children are blind to the problems and affairs of adults.''

''But Kate knew.''

''Oh, yes, she knew. Blamed me. Thinks I was weak not to kick him out.''

''Why didn't you?''

''Kate needed a father as well as a mother. I had no career, no desire to be anything except a faculty wife. If I had divorced Walter, there would have been a nasty scandal that might have ruined his career, probably forced him to resign from the college. Whatever else he may have been, he was a fine teacher.''

''But didn't your patience wear thin?''

''Certainly. I was furious for a very long time. I began to realize after about five years that he was simply congenitally unable to be faithful to any woman. He had to have that wonderful elation you feel when you first fall in love— only he had to have it over and over again. He always said his relationships had nothing to do with us.'' She laughed.

"That's what they all say, of course, but in his case I think he meant it. I did learn to live quite a full life on my own and conceal my pain better. The amazing thing is that we remained friends despite everything. His affairs became— irrelevant. You were never irrelevant to Kate."

"I was sure you'd never forgive me, either."

"My dear, when you hurt my daughter I was ready to dismember you, but you were so contrite, and she was so adamant. How many years did it take you to get back into my good graces? Four? Five? You paid the price for her father's sin."

"I paid the price for my own sin, Mrs. Hillman."

"You've paid enough. So has my daughter, come to that. She and Alec Mulholland were a nice couple, but he treated her more like a daughter than a wife. He wasn't a passionate man. All women need passion, David, whether they admit it or not."

"I still love her, Mrs. H.," David whispered.

"Then, dear, go after her. What have you got to lose?"

CHAPTER SEVEN

FIFTEEN MINUTES LATER, Kate nearly drove past the Paradise Motel before she spotted the small neon sign in front. It didn't look much like paradise. More like one of the early motels from the thirties where Bonnie and Clyde hid from the police.

Still, it was better than staying at Dub's where she might run into David unexpectedly. Each time she met him she felt a nearly physical blow to her senses. One extra quirk of those eyebrows, one good tilt of that smile, and she might just fall into his arms like some sappy Victorian heroine. Well, she wouldn't.

She pulled in and checked in the office, where a fiftyish lady with dyed red hair took her credit card and read her name with avid curiosity.

"Has Mr. Selig checked in? Mr. Arnold Selig?" Kate asked.

"Uh-huh, he's in the room right next to yours." The woman arched an eyebrow. "Don't have no rooms with connecting doors."

"That's all right."

"Y'all here about that Canfield boy killed Waneath Talley?" the woman asked.

Kate picked up her room key. "We're here about the boy who is accused. That's not the same thing at all."

"I don't know how it is in big cities, but in Athena the sheriff don't arrest innocent folks."

Kate smiled. "We'll see." She turned away. "Oh, could I have some extra towels and hangers?"

"Sure. I'll send Myrlene down with some."

Kate pulled David's car down to the end of the row outside room fourteen. Arnold's rental car was not in evidence, so he'd obviously gone out again.

She dragged her two big bags into the room and grimaced. Quite a comedown from her suite in Los Angeles. Although it seemed clean and neat, the room looked as though it had been caught in an early sixties time warp with an orange and blue geometric bedspread and orange shag carpet. The walls were paneled in the cheapest possible veneer and the television set was small and balanced precariously on a combination bureau and desk. Kate wished for a moment she'd taken Dub up on his offer of a room at Long Pond.

No, she and Arnold needed independent space, and this one was certainly not conducive to romance. Much safer than Long Pond or David's house in the woods.

If she and Arnold stayed in Athena very long, they might want to rent someplace more congenial, particularly when and if they hired a private investigator to look into the case.

She threw her largest suitcase onto the bed, opened it and began to hang up her clothes in the open rack opposite the bathroom.

She started at the knock on the door. When she opened it, a young woman wearing jeans and a T-shirt with her blond hair in a ponytail smiled at Kate over a stack of blindingly white, but suspiciously thin towels.

"Hey, Mrs. Mulholland, Momma said you needed some towels and stuff."

"Come in," Kate said, and stood aside. "Just put the towels on the counter in the bathroom. I'll take the hangers. Did you bring extra skirt hangers?"

"Sure did." The girl returned from the bathroom empty-handed. "Well," she said, obviously stalling.

Kate pulled out her purse and took five dollars out of her wallet.

"Oh, no ma'am, you don't have to do that."

"Sure I do, uh, Myrlene, was it?"

The girl blushed. "Yes'm. You need anything else, you just tell me."

Kate sat on the bed. "Myrlene, you look about Jason's age. Did you know him?"

"We graduated together in June."

"Really." Kate gestured to the straight chair beside the window. "You have a minute to talk?"

The girl shrugged. "Sure. I'm just cleaning part-time for Momma. I don't have to be at work at the hardware store until two."

"So you were in Waneath's class too?"

"Uh-huh. We were sorority sisters."

Kate blinked. "Really?"

"Sure. Les Debs. Everybody is mostly in it. We have parties and stuff. I was a cheerleader," Myrlene said proudly.

"Was Waneath?"

"She didn't have time for stuff like that. Too busy with trying to be Miss America." Myrlene sniffed.

"Stuck-up?"

"Well, Momma says I shouldn't speak ill of the dead..."

"You should tell the truth, whatever it is."

The girl hesitated a moment, obviously dying to unburden herself about Waneath. "We weren't real close, you know? I mean, my momma runs a motel and her daddy's rich. I wouldn't have gotten in the sorority if I hadn't made cheerleader."

"Did you get along?"

"She didn't pay much attention to anybody except Jason, and that's just cause his granddaddy owns most of the county and she thought he'd take her off to Hollywood. They were going to get engaged at Christmas."

"Really? Waneath told you that?"

"Sure did. I ran into her at Wal-Mart a couple of weeks ago, and when she saw my ring, she said Jason was going to give her her ring at Christmas." Myrlene held out her left hand. A tiny diamond sparkled on her ring finger.

"Lovely. So, you're engaged?"

"Uh-huh. Me and Jimmy Viccolla are getting married after Easter."

"I've met Jimmy. He seems very nice."

She shrugged as though it didn't matter, but the flush on her cheeks belied the casualness of her words. "My momma says he'll be a good provider."

"I'm sure he will. Did Waneath say when she and Jason were planning to get married?"

Myrlene snickered. "I'll bet Jason didn't know a thing about it, tell the truth. Waneath always figured she could make him do anything she wanted if she pouted and sulked hard enough."

"So she wasn't angry at Jason?"

Myrlene kneaded her left shoulder with her right hand while she considered. "I hate vacuuming," she said by way of explanation. "Waneath was sure mad at Jason that last night. Man, they went at it in the parking lot like Hail Columbia, which is what my momma says when she blesses me out."

"Do you think maybe Jason told her he didn't plan to give her a ring?"

"She'd have been mad about that, all right. But she still had her backup plans."

"I beg your pardon?"

"Waneath had all these plans from the time she got her first bra. She was going to be Miss America, but she only came in third runner-up for Miss Mississippi. She said that was all right because a lot of rich men wanted to date the runner-ups too."

"I take it she liked rich men."

"Did she ever! Her momma's been teaching her since grade school that a woman's job is to marry a rich man. Jason Canfield's going to be real rich when his granddaddy dies. He gets Long Pond. I mean, I used to go to parties out there. Have you seen how big that place is with that pink marble staircase and all?"

Kate nodded. "But if Jason didn't want to marry her...?"

"He was just her first choice. I mean, he wants to be something in the movies, and Waneath thought she could marry him, move out there with him, and become a big star or something while they waited for the old man to die."

"What was her backup plan? Do you know?"

Myrlene frowned and waved her hands. "Sure. Waneath talked about her plans all the time. Like anybody cared." She sniffed again and considered. "Well, she was still in training for Miss Mississippi, although I don't think she was doing many pageants this year. She was going to the junior college and taking sports education, or something like that."

"And she was in pageants to meet rich men?"

"Sure. She used to say beauty queens marry doctors and lawyers. Around here they mostly do, too. Waneath wanted a big house and to be in society. Her daddy's rich trash, and her momma thinks she married beneath her. She wants Waneath to marry rich *and* socially prominent. She wanted, that is. 'Cause her sister is never going to do it."

"Her sister? I didn't know she had a sister."

"Sure. Coral Anne. She's only sixteen, and she inherited her daddy's looks, poor thing. She's smart, but that never cut much ice with Mrs. Talley."

"So Waneath was the favorite child?"

"Listen, next to Waneath, what chance does fat little Coral Anne have?"

"Interesting. Did *anybody* like Waneath?"

"Sure. All the boys. And most of the girls made up to her because of who she was. She was head of the 'in' crowd, you know. Jason always seemed to. I mean, they were close all through school."

"From what you've said, I can't see Waneath sitting at home alone and waiting for him to come home on vacation. Was she seeing anyone else?"

"Don't know. If she was, it was probably somebody from the junior college. She wouldn't give the time of day to anybody she was in school with. Not that way, at least."

"Thanks, Myrlene, you've been very helpful."

Myrlene stood up. "Yeah, and my momma's gonna kill me if I don't get the rest of the rooms clean before work." She walked to the door. Again, she eased her shoulder.

"Thanks for your help," Kate said.

Myrlene stopped with her hand on the door, and said, "I don't think Jason killed Waneath, Mrs. Mulholland. He's a real sweet boy."

"I'll tell Jason you said that. He's feeling pretty abandoned at the moment."

Kate shut the door after Myrlene. So Waneath had expected her ring at Christmas? Not from any undying love for Jason, apparently, but because he would inherit Long Pond, and in the meantime, he could take her to Hollywood to try her hand at starletdom, or whatever passed for starletdom these days.

And then there was always the backup plan. *Somebody*

was going to marry Waneath, somebody rich and socially prominent. At least if Waneath had her way somebody would. In the meantime, how was she keeping her hand in? Even courtesans needed to practice, didn't they?

Kate decided she'd go to the junior college that afternoon, get a list of Waneath's classes and speak to some of her teachers. Maybe they knew if she'd been seeing anyone regularly. For now, she decided, she'd finish unpacking and getting organized.

She unpacked both bags and stowed everything, set up her laptop computer on the small round table beside the window and looked around with satisfaction. Getting organized always made her feel as though she was on her way to progress.

In this case, however, progress seemed pretty illusory. She reached into her briefcase and pulled out the photographs from the crime scene. She had seen plenty of gruesome pictures during the years when she was handling criminal law, and some almost as grim in civil cases. But Waneath's pictures were almost attractive.

Kate curled up on the bed and spread them out around her. Waneath's body had been found lying on the grass ten miles outside of town on top of some kind of levee. The farmer who had discovered her body had been on his way to check on a sow who was having problems farrowing.

Kate read his statement aloud under her breath. ''Thought it was some kind of joke. Almost drove right past. Looked like she was lying down sleeping.''

Kate checked the pictures. Waneath did look as though she were sleeping. Her body lay neatly, dress down over her knees, legs straight, arms by her side. Arranged. Not tossed out of a car, or abandoned by a rapist or dumped by a terrified killer. Almost as though whoever had laid her out had done just that—laid her out as she would lie in her coffin. Decently.

Someone who cared about her.

Jason?

That's what the district attorney would say.

Kate already knew he'd have to drop the rape charge. There was no evidence of trauma indicating rape and there was a history of consensual sex.

She might even get him to go for voluntary manslaughter instead of murder if Jason would plead guilty. Arnold would, no doubt, be investigating that option on his own this morning.

If so, she'd have to put the deal up to Jason. She didn't think he'd go for it, but even an innocent man might prefer a guaranteed short sentence to the risk of standing trial.

Her stomach rumbled and notified her in no uncertain terms that she'd eaten that breakfast roll a long time ago. She moved off the bed, changed to slacks, a heavy sweater and ankle boots that might protect her feet a bit from the mud on the levee where Waneath had been found. She shoved her arms into her black blazer. If she intended to stay in Athena, she'd have to get someone from the Atlanta office to raid her closet and send her some warmer clothes, or maybe she'd stop by the Wal-Mart and pick up a down jacket.

She shoved the pictures back into their envelope, picked it up, closed down her computer and checked to see that she had her room key.

And realized she had no idea where to find lunch. She had no intention of going to another drive-in.

She saw one of the motel doors open two rooms down from hers and walked over. As she expected, Myrlene was inside changing the bed.

"Hi again," Kate said. "Where do you eat lunch around here?"

Myrlene considered. "The best place, I guess, would be the Athena Café on the square downtown. That's where most folks eat when they don't drive into Jackson." She looked at the watch on her wrist. "This early, probably won't be crowded."

Kate got directions and drove away. In her rearview mirror she could see Myrlene standing at the still-open door of the room watching her, and as she drove by the office, she caught a glimpse of hennaed hair behind the window. She sighed. Obviously, she was the biggest attraction in town at the moment.

TEN MINUTES LATER, she found a place to park on the square and opened the door of the Athena Café to the sound of chatter and clinking dishes. Suddenly the room went silent. Every eye swiveled in her direction. She felt like Wild Bill Hickok stalking into the only saloon in a new cow town.

"Well, sugar, fancy meeting you here."

She recognized Dub's voice behind her and heaved a sigh of relief. She spent a good deal of time eating alone in restaurants and had learned to hate it. But he was probably meeting someone. Oh, Lord, probably David. If he was meeting Jason, she'd kill both of them.

"Dub," she said.

"Come on, sugar, join an old man for lunch."

She nodded gratefully. "You're not meeting anyone?"

"Just you." He put a hand in the small of her back and steered her toward a booth near the rear of the café and waited while she slid in.

"'Scuse me a minute," he said, and proceeded to work

the room with the ease and practice of a master politician, shaking hands, slapping backs, exchanging jokes.

He gave his enemies no chance to draw away. Anyone who did not respond to his bonhomie would look crass and mean-spirited.

When he came back and slid in opposite her, she nodded and said, "Impressive. I've seen senators handle scandal with less aplomb."

"What scandal?" He grinned. "This is just a little bump on the road. Now, when my great-aunt Harriet ran off to Saint Louis with a trumpet player and left three babies under the age of six—*that* was a scandal."

She laughed. Then she reached across the table and touched his hand. "This is not a bump, Dub. You have to understand how serious this is."

"Heck, you'll fix it."

"Not without help and a great deal of luck."

They placed their orders and waited while the waitress brought them iced tea. David had been right yesterday. She felt as though every ear in the place was attuned to their conversation. She decided she'd better stick to subjects that had nothing to do with Jason or Waneath. But what?

"Bet you wish you'd stayed at Long Pond, don't you?" he said. "Told you the Paradise isn't much of a place to stay."

"It's fine." She cast around for some other topic. "Tell me about Long Pond. How did it get that name?"

"The Calloo River runs right through it. Not so much runs, you understand, as saunters. More like a pond than a river."

"Ah, I get it."

"Yeah. When my folks came over in the thirties—that's the 1830s—they figured they could use the water to irrigate the land. Worked, too. We been here ever since. Even saved the original house from the Yankees. Then my momma burned it down.'' He laughed. ''She didn't really, of course. But she was glad when it went. She was a caution, my momma. What she wanted, she got. My daughter, Melba, took after her that way. Hardest-headed woman about getting her own way I ever did see.''

Oh, boy. Kate sipped her iced tea and wondered how on earth to change the subject.

''Named her Melba 'cause she was like a little peach right out of Long Pond orchard when she was born.''

''You wife died several years ago, I believe,'' Kate said quickly.

''Yeah. Same thing that killed Melba. Damn shame.''

''You never remarried?''

''Nope. Long as Melba was alive to be my hostess never saw the need. Neva looks after the house and the cooking.'' He arched an eyebrow. '''Course, if the right woman was to come along…''

Kate leaned back in her seat. The man was flirting with her. He was attractive, rich, and probably in his early sixties—not much older than Alec Mulholland. But he was David's father-in-law, for God's sake, and Melba's father. Obviously, he had no idea she'd ever known David in the past.

At that point their lunches arrived—meat loaf with four vegetables and hot-pepper corn bread. Kate realized she was famished.

''Like a woman with a good appetite,'' he said, as he too, dug into his meal. ''My wife never ate more'n a bird. No meat on her bones. Nothing for a man to hang on to in bed.''

Kate choked on a bite of corn bread, and downed a swig of iced tea. He looked at her with concern.

She wiped her teary eyes with the edge of a paper napkin and coughed to clear her lungs of corn-bread particles.

"What's going to happen to Long Pond if Jason decides to stay in California?" Kate asked after another sip of tea and a deep breath.

"Shoot. He'll come home. Long Pond matters more than any Hollywood nonsense. David should never have let him go out there. Should have made the boy go to Mississippi State to study agriculture like I wanted." He broke off a piece of corn bread. "Jason's got a lot of fool ideas in his head. but he's young, he'll come around. Just like his daddy did. Born farmer, that man." He snickered. "Did you know when Melba married him and dragged him down to Long Pond he was gonna be an act-or." He pronounced the word in two distinct syllables.

Kate froze. She had to stop the man, but how?

"Yeah," he said. "New York, Broadway. Now, I like to visit New York as well as the next man, but an actor? Nobody real does that stuff. Shoot, Melba knew better than that. She brought him on down to me, and I made a farmer out of him."

"I thought you said he was a born farmer."

"Hell, yes, but didn't know it till I taught him." He shook his head. "Never did understand why Melba was so hot to marry him in college. 'Course, I never met him before she brought him down here, and then she had to get pregnant to catch him."

"Had to?" It was like picking at a scab. She couldn't stop herself even though she knew darned well she was going to bleed if she kept at it.

"Yeah. He got caught by some girl he met after Melba graduated, and damned if he didn't marry her." Dub laughed. "Melba took care of that all right. Went right on up there and snatched him out from under her nose.'' He laughed. ''Fool woman probably never knew what hit her.''

''I'm sure she was deeply hurt.''

''Oh, shoot, if she'd a' been half a woman she wouldn't a' let Melba have him so easy. Not Melba's fault she didn't know how to hang on to her man. She kicked him out the minute Melba let her find out she'd slept with him.'' He chortled. ''Didn't know then Melba was pregnant, of course, but once she found out and told David, he came straight down and married her like he should. Good man. Even if I don't always agree with him.''

''Were they happy?''

''Well, heck, yeah, they were happy.'' Dub suddenly looked embarrassed. ''Happy as most married people, I guess.''

''Why did they live with you?''

''Why not?'' He looked baffled. ''Plenty of room. Melba didn't want to move. Her home. Never lived anywhere else. Neither did I, come to that. Neither will Jason, if I have my way.''

''But David moved out after Melba died, didn't he?''

''Damn-fool idea, building that shack out there in the trees.''

Ah, here was one source of trouble between the two men.

''Don't know what's got into David,'' Dub said. ''First he builds that house, then he lets Jason go off to Malibu, California, to learn how to make movies, and now he's talking about maybe leaving Long Pond and going to China or someplace crazy like that.''

Kate froze. ''China?''

''Shoot. Teaching the Chinese to take our cotton markets away. Don't know what's got into him.''

She realized with a start that she didn't want David half a world away—not now that she'd found him again. She pushed the thought from her. What did it matter to her if he colonized Venus? But it did. Heaven help her.

DAVID CHECKED the cotton gin and found the truck pulling out in good order and five minutes under his deadline. He laid out the schedule of maintenance and cleanup for the remaining men, made certain there was plenty of hot coffee in the office and notified the port in New Orleans of arrival time for his truck. He double-checked the paperwork, faxed copies to the appropriate factors and sat down with a cup of coffee to think about the morning. He'd wanted to tell Kate about Melba for so long. He'd written her all those never-mailed letters, and picked up the telephone hundreds of times in the years since they'd been apart. But he'd had no right.

Besides, it wasn't safe. He was afraid that if he ever heard her voice, he'd drop everything and drag her away from her husband to some desert island and to hell with his responsibilities.

He finished the coffee and left the cup on the desk. One of his responsibilities needed a good talking-to. He decided to call on his son.

Since Waneath's death, Jason had refused to say more than a couple of sentences to him at any one time.

In the last year of his mother's life, as Melba drifted further and further away from everyone and everything that bound her to this world, Jason had grown angrier and more resentful, as if his mother were choosing to leave him.

After her death, Jason transferred that anger to his father, as though he should have had the power to draw her back simply by the strength of his personality. David had understood his anger, but that didn't make it any easier to endure.

Neva Hardin opened the front door at Long Pond to him

with a smile. "Hey. Dub's not here. You want some lunch?"

David smiled at her and shook his head. "Jason up?"

"Barely. That boy! I swear he'd sleep the clock around. He took a couple of sandwiches back to his room a while ago." She pointed over her head where the bass beat of music vibrated through the floor. "He's up, all right. How he thinks he's going to direct movies when he's going to be deaf before he's thirty I'll never know."

David nodded and took the marble staircase two steps at a time. He had to knock twice and call out once before Jason lowered the music and gave him a sulky "yeah" from the other side of the door.

David didn't wait for an invitation, but opened the door and entered. Jason sprawled flat on his back in the middle of his disastrous bed. He wore the same clothes he'd had on earlier, and had not shaved. His eyes looked red as though he'd been crying. For a moment, David wondered whether his son could have begun taking drugs in California.

He dismissed the thought. His son's drug of choice was beer, which he obtained illegally and seldom. Until his date with Waneath he'd never shown much interest in that, either. He always said he had to keep a clear head to see the world around him through a camera lens.

"What do *you* want?" Jason asked.

David shoved books and papers off the nearest chair, sank into it and stretched his long legs in front of him as though he were totally relaxed and had all the time in the world. "I want to see how you're doing."

"Fine. Can't you tell? I'm stuck in this house, I'm missing school, I'll probably be expelled if I'm not sent to prison, my career is down the tubes, my life will follow shortly."

"Cynicism does not become you."

"I have a right to be cynical. I come home for Thanksgiving, and I wind up going to prison for life."

"No, you don't. I've contacted Pepperdine. You'll receive incompletes for this semester. You can make up the work in the spring."

"From my cell?"

"Come on, Jason, you're not going to jail. That's why Kate is here. To get you off."

"Even if I'm guilty?"

David caught his breath. For a moment he couldn't speak, and when he did, he didn't trust his voice. "Are you?"

Jason sat up. "Hell, no! But I had you going, didn't I? Even my own daddy believes I'm capable of killing somebody."

"We're all capable of killing somebody under the right circumstances. If we're angry enough, or scared enough. That doesn't always make it murder." He knew he had to tread carefully.

Jason jerked himself upright, shoved open his French windows and stalked out on the balcony.

Momentarily David was afraid that he intended to throw himself off to land on the bricks below. He was on his feet in an instant.

But Jason stood with his hands on the wrought-iron railing and stared past the guest house and out over the fields. "God, I hate this place," he whispered.

"You used to love it."

"Yeah, that was before."

"Before what?"

Jason turned his head to stare at his father over his shoulder. "Before my momma died and you moved out on me."

"I wanted you to move with me. Still do."

"Oh, sure. Bachelor of the year sharing a pad with his son."

"I'm not bachelor of the year."

"Right. Why else did you move out? So you could tom-cat around where Dub and I couldn't see what you were doing."

"That's not true."

"You never loved Momma."

David was so taken aback he had no words for a moment. Then he said, "Yes, Jason, I did."

Jason shook his head. His eyes were bright with tears. "She told me you didn't."

"When, Jason? When did she say I didn't love her?" His whole body felt cold.

"She said you had to marry her because of me, and she shouldn't have done it to you. You were in love with some-body else. You gave up your career because of me. You could have been a star, she said, if it hadn't have been for me and Momma. I could have grown up in New York knowing everybody, doing everything, instead I'm stuck here in Mississippi and I'll never get out."

David leaned back against the white brick and closed his eyes. How on earth was he supposed to deal with this? She'd probably been so sick she thought she was clearing the decks, making her peace with her life. Instead she'd dumped a load of grief on the boy he couldn't possibly have the maturity to handle. David took a deep breath. Better the truth, or some version of the truth, than to make up a lie. "Come on inside, son. Maybe it's time we talked."

Reluctantly, like a child about to be sent to the corner, Jason followed his father into the room, shut the doors be-hind him against the November chill and sank onto the bed.

For a moment David looked at his boy, who would in

time grow into his body. He hoped and prayed he could help him grow into his soul.

"I did love your mother as much as I could," he said. "I won't lie to you and tell you she was the great passion of my life."

Jason moved restively and opened his mouth to speak, then shut it again.

"She was a wonderful mother and a good wife, even when her health was failing. Did she tell you that I was married before?"

Jason sat up. "Huh?"

David nodded. "It—didn't work out. When your mother found she was pregnant with you, I was living in New York and newly divorced. There was never any question that she wouldn't have you, that she—I—didn't want you. That we wouldn't raise you together."

"But your career."

"My career sucked." David managed a small laugh at the shock on his son's face. "True. Whatever your mother did or did not do to my life, she did not drag me away from a great career in the theater. I would have been lucky to scrub toilets on Broadway, believe me. I was a lousy actor. I am a damn fine farmer." He waved a hand toward the window. "I love Long Pond and I love you. You're young, and maybe you have the drive and discipline and talent to be a great director."

"Hell, yes, I do."

"Fine. Then do it. Give it your best shot. That's why when you wanted to go to Pepperdine I fought the old man for you. Because you deserve your chance to make it in the crazy business you've chosen. I had mine. It was wrong for me, but I won't spend the rest of my life wishing I'd gone after it. I tried, I failed, I walked away to do something I love and am good at.'' He opened his hands and offered them, palms up. ''Did I fail at being a father as well?''

Jason sniffed and turned his head away. ''I never thought so before.''

''But now?''

''Now I don't know.'' He rolled over and curled into a ball with his face toward the wall. ''Go away, Dad, please.''

''Jason...''

''Please, just let me be.''

David pulled himself to his feet, walked over and squeezed his son's shoulder. From the way it trembled under his fingers, he was certain that Jason was crying. He didn't know what else to do or say. He slipped out of Jason's room and sank onto the top step with his head in his hands.

Would he ever be able to tell his son that Kate was the woman he'd loved, still did?

CHAPTER EIGHT

"I'LL PAY for my own lunch," Kate said.

"No, you won't," Dub said, reaching for her check. His hand brushed hers and lingered.

She removed her fingers. Since the cost of her lunch would eventually have gone on her bill for expenses anyway, she didn't fight, although she felt a pang for David's pocketbook. She'd have to check with her partners to see whether she could make some sort of accommodation on the grounds that David was, in a sense, family, and deserved professional courtesy rates.

She slid out of the booth, and waited while Dub stood as well. As he came to his feet, she saw a look of total confusion cross his face. He caught himself two-handed on the table, and stood blinking at her as though he had no idea who or what she was.

"Are you all right?" she asked.

He took a deep breath and was his old self. "Shoot, yeah. Sometimes when I get up too fast my blood pressure doesn't catch up with me for a second." He grinned and ushered her toward the front with his hand against the small of her back once more.

There wasn't much she could do about that if she didn't plan to be rude, but the moment Dub reached for his wallet, she ducked out of reach. "I'll wait for you outside," she said, and grabbed the front door.

As she stepped onto the sidewalk, Arnold called to her

from his car, which was parked two slots down from David's Navigator.

"Where have you been?" he demanded.

"Lunch. With Dub. Why?"

"Because your cell phone is either not turned on, or you left it in your room again."

She made a face. "It's in my purse, but I think it's probably out of juice. I didn't plug it in last night. Is there an emergency?" She realized that Dub now stood behind her, listening avidly.

So did Arnold. He smiled at Dub, took Kate's arm and moved toward his car. "Come on. We need to talk."

She slid in on the passenger side and waited until he'd settled behind the wheel.

"We have to ask for a change of venue," he said without preamble.

"I agree."

He continued as though she hadn't spoken. "There's no way in hell to impanel a jury in this county that hasn't already made up its mind one way or the other whether Jason Canfield is innocent or guilty."

"And what brought you to this conclusion?"

"I've spent the morning fighting with the coroner, the sheriff, the district attorney and half the city fathers to get Waneath Talley's body moved to Memphis for the autopsy."

"Were you successful?"

"Yes. She's on her way. I am not going to be nominated for Rotary's Man of the Year in Athena, let me tell you." He wiped his forehead. "The coroner wanted to sign the death certificate as homicide, would you believe, and let her family bury her! I ask you! In the middle of the investigation."

"Poor Arnold. I can certainly see their point. I know it's

hard on the family, but it'll be doubly hard on Jason if we can't get firm evidence about her cause of death. I have a witness to his loss of his tire iron, by the way.''

"Good." Arnold leaned his head back on the headrest and closed his eyes. "When I came down from Long Island, I thought one day I'd like to retire and become a small-town lawyer—you know, like Atticus Finch in *To Kill a Mockingbird.* I am fast changing my tune. There is a great deal to be said for big cities. I prefer being anonymous to having small children dog my footsteps and hurl imprecations at me.''

"You're joking, right?"

"Yes, Kate, I am joking." He opened his eyes, but didn't change position. "I see you managed to get rid of your ex, but retain his car. I do hope he's not lying in a ditch somewhere.''

"Might be simpler if he were."

Arnold raised an interrogative eyebrow. "Oh, really? Are we rekindling the flames of passion, old thing?"

Kate considered lying. She decided against it and opted for at least a portion of the truth. "He apologized for twenty years ago, did some fast explaining that made more sense than it probably should have. The thing is, Arnold, I still respond to him the same way I did the first time I saw him.''

"And how was that? You are the least impressionable female I've ever met. I certainly don't impress you."

She laughed and touched his arm. "Sure you do. Just not that way.''

"My luck, always the buddy, never the lover."

"Lovers come and go, buddies go on forever. Besides, I'm older than you.''

"Not much."

"At any rate, I don't think anybody is allowed more than

one love-at-first-sight per lifetime. Maybe per several life-times. The first time I laid eyes on David Canfield, I felt as though I had known him for aeons.''

Arnold dropped his head into his hands and groaned. ''Oh, no, not one of those 'old souls together' things. I can't stand it. Next you'll be telling me you asked him about his sign.''

''No. I didn't even speak to him. The first time I saw him was at the first read-through for *Death of a Salesman* my junior year. He was playing Biff. I was doing props. I got to the theater early for the first read-through and came into the door at the back of the house.'' She leaned back and closed her eyes. The scene opened before her as clearly as though she were watching one of Jason's movies.

''The theater was dark, the stage was bare and dark except for one naked worklight hanging down center stage on an extension cord. He was sitting cross-legged on a packing case dead center. His head was bent over his script, and the light turned his hair pure bronze. He couldn't see me in the dark, but for some reason he raised his head and looked right at me out of those incredible eyes. I knew in that moment that I wanted to marry him. I didn't even know his name.''

''Judging from what you said yesterday, this was not a good thing.''

''We had nearly three glorious years as lovers and spouses, which is more than most people have, I suspect.''

''Before he screwed it up.''

''I'm beginning to think I was as much at fault in the screwup as he was.''

''Oh, come on! Kate! The guy was an unfaithful louse! You said so yourself.''

''He's changed.''

Arnold groaned again.

Kate laughed. "I am not going to hop into bed with him. But I've made a bargain with myself. I'm going to try to see him as the man he is today, and try not to think of what he was like when we were married. That way, maybe we can at least be friends."

He sat up and turned a serious face to her. "Kiddo, you are out of your mind if you think that guy intends to settle for friendship."

THE LATE NOVEMBER afternoon was already shadowing toward evening, while the sky darkened with scudding clouds as Kate headed for the junior college. She'd stopped off to shop for warmer clothes, and now had to drive around for several minutes before she managed to slide into a visitors' parking space as someone else drove away. The temperature had dropped twenty degrees in the last thirty minutes. For the first time, she remembered that they were drawing a bead on Christmas.

She shivered in her thin wool blazer, and walked quickly into what she assumed must be the building that housed administrative offices, since it was closest to the visitors' parking area.

After one false start she located the office of the dean of admissions. Behind the counter that ran the length of the office stood a bored girl with elaborately braided hair and turquoise fingernails that would have been excessive on a Mandarin. She glanced up from the latest issue of *People* magazine, popped her gum and regarded Kate with basilisk eyes.

Kate smiled politely and introduced herself. "I need a list of the classes Waneath Talley has taken here and the names of the professors who taught them."

The girl shook her head. The beads in the ends of her braids clacked. "That's private."

"Actually, it's not," Kate said. "Her grades would be, of course, and her transcripts and things, but the classes she took—that is a matter of public record." She pointed to the blinking computer terminal at a desk behind the counter. "I'm sure you can call them up and print them out for me in five minutes."

"Uh-uh. Not without the dean telling me I can."

"Ah. Well, then may I see the dean, please."

For the first time, a small smile played over the girl's lips. "Uh-uh. She's in a staff meeting."

"And where might that meeting be?"

The girl raised her eyes. "Upstairs with the president."

"Thanks." Kate turned away, then turned back. "You know, I can get a judge to issue a subpoena for those records, and I can certainly depose you if I have to. And your dean. I'm sure she'll be delighted to drive downtown to the sheriff's office to spend four or five hours giving me a deposition. Pity, when you could have saved us all so much time and trouble." She walked away.

"Hey," the girl called. "You really gonna make my dean give a deposition?"

Kate shrugged. "If I have to."

The gum popped. "Oh, shoot. What was her name again?"

Five minutes later Kate had a list of Waneath's classes, the room numbers where they were held and the names of the professors teaching them this semester. She stopped at the information desk for a campus map, then realized that people were streaming out of offices all around her. She checked her watch. Four twenty-five. Drat. Obviously nobody believed in working late. She checked Waneath's schedule. One of her classes met at six in the evening and another at nine. Unfortunately, they met Tuesdays and Thursdays, not Wednesday.

Since she was here, she decided to take a chance on finding at least one of Waneath's professors still in his office. Three of the offices were in the same building on the third floor. She hurried across the darkening quadrangle toward the largest of three ugly buildings, entered, and was struck by the universal campus odor of cigarettes, paper and sweaty bodies.

She found the first two offices dark. As she rounded the corner toward the third, she walked straight into David. He caught her arms, while she caught her breath. She shook him off and backed two steps away outside the torrid zone that seemed to surround his body when she was near him.

"Kate?" he said. "What are you doing here?"

She felt her heart turn over at the flash of sheer delight in his eyes at seeing her. She took a deep breath. *Keep it professional, kiddo.*

"Checking out Waneath's classes and trying to speak to her professors. What are *you* doing here?"

He fell into step beside her. "I'm an adjunct. I teach two courses in agribusiness."

"I didn't know." She turned to him. "Did Waneath take any of your classes?"

"She wouldn't have been caught dead designing flow-charts on pig farming."

"Did you see her?"

He hesitated. "I ran into her from time to time."

"Do you know whether she started dating somebody after Jason left for college?"

He shook his head. "Never saw her with anyone. I think she was just marking time so that her daddy wouldn't make her get a job, or worse yet, give her one at the dealership."

"Why didn't she go away to school?"

"I doubt that she saw much point in college, except to

be able to answer that she was a student during the question-and-answer sessions at her pageants."

"Here's Professor Gregson's office," Kate said, checking the number above the door. She felt David's breath on the nape of her neck and shivered. "Damn," she said and sidestepped. "Dark as pitch. Don't these people actually work for a living?"

"Come on, Kate. You grew up on a campus. You know how college professors moan if they have to teach three classes a semester and hold office hours once a week."

"I assumed junior colleges would be different."

"Nope. They still tell everybody they're going to the library to do research when they're on their way home for the first martini of the day."

"Yeah. My daddy did a lot of so-called research," Kate said acerbically. David had done his research as well. Have to keep that in the forefront of her mind when he was this close in a darkened hallway. "I wonder if any of these guys was researching Waneath."

"Mark off Gregson. J.T. stands for Janice Theresa. I don't think Waneath swung that way even to cadge herself an easy A."

"Here's the list. Any of these people possibles?"

"I think Mike Ballard is gay. Thomasson is married, but he's the pipe-and-tweeds type that attracts women like flies. I have no idea whether he takes advantage of the offers. Vasquez I've seen, but not to speak to. He's unmarried and what Waneath would probably consider a hunk." He handed the list back. "Sorry I can't be more help."

She folded the paper and slipped it into the side pocket of her purse. "You've been a great help." He followed her down the hall to the central staircase. Kate wondered suddenly whether his arrival had been entirely fortuitous. "Where's your office?' she asked.

He pointed vaguely down the hall in the opposite direction from which Kate had come. "Down there around the corner. I don't have an office as such. I have a desk, a file cabinet and access to the department secretary if I'm desperate."

"And you are here because…?"

They reached the stairs. He put a hand on her arm and turned her to face him. "I wasn't following you, if that's what you think. I haven't been near my office since this thing happened, and I've got a class tomorrow at ten. I had to check to be sure the secretary had dropped off my handout."

She avoided his eyes—those crazy blue eyes. "Plausible."

"Almost everyone's office is either on the third or fourth floor of this building. We're not spread out over a fancy campus."

"Coincidence bothers me." She started down the stairs and he followed. Over her shoulder she asked, "So you don't know anyone Waneath was dating?"

"As Jason's father, I'd be the last person she'd tell."

"We badly need another suspect. So far there's no evidence anyone but Jason was angry at Waneath. If we can prove that Waneath was having a hot and heavy affair with someone else, someone who might have been infuriated when Jason came home and snatched his girl out from under him—probably literally, from what I have heard about Waneath—then we may be able to shift the focus of the investigation onto someone other than Jason."

"I wish I could be more help," he said as she hurried down the stairs. "Wait up, you don't have to run away from me. These stairs can be treacherous."

"I'm the cat who walks by herself, or hadn't you noticed?"

He said under his breath, "I've noticed, all right."

"We've barely started," she continued as though she hadn't heard him. "A good P.I. could find out more in twenty-four hours than I'm likely to discover in a month. Which is why we need to bring somebody in so that I can go back to Atlanta and prepare Jason's defense."

He caught up with her. "You think they'll take him to trial?"

"Frankly, unless the sheriff has more than we know so far I don't think it should get to trial, but I think because of the people involved it will. Unless we can give the district attorney a better scenario."

"What about DNA testing to discover who fathered Waneath's baby?"

"We can probably eliminate Jason, but unless we have a suspect, we can't actually tell whose baby it was. Besides, DNA testing takes three months on average."

"Three months? What about all these television shows where they come up with DNA evidence overnight?"

"Doesn't happen in real life, David. I'm sorry, but it simply doesn't. Jason will be lucky to come to trial before *next* Thanksgiving."

"My God, he'll go nuts. And I'll be broke long before then."

"Don't worry about the money. We'll work something out. You could be considered entitled to a discount as family."

"I wish I were still your family."

She caught the softness in his voice and strode off ahead of him, deciding not to respond to what he'd just said. "The system does not work the way it does on television," she repeated. "Unless we can plea-bargain him down and plead him guilty…"

He caught up with her and put his hand under her arm. "I thought you said you didn't think he was guilty."

She drew away from him, but didn't break the contact. "Nobody can outguess a jury. Three years for voluntary manslaughter is infinitely better than life in prison without possibility of parole. We have to consider all the options."

"Prison would destroy him."

"It tends to destroy everyone." She sat down on a long wooden bench beside the staircase, leaned back and stretched her legs in front of her. "Is he serious about making movies?"

David sat beside her, his shoulder just brushing hers. She suddenly felt as though she could lean against him and stay that way forever. The rough texture of his jacket felt wonderful against her shoulder, and the scent of male in the cloth made her nose tingle.

She hadn't needed his sandalwood soap to identify him at the jail. She still recognized the scent of *him*. Almost a year after their divorce, she'd found an old sweatshirt of his in the back of her closet, and had buried her face in it, hoping to find the smallest trace of him in the cloth. When she couldn't find it, she'd burst into tears—the first serious tears she'd cried since the night she found out about his infidelity.

"Jason's very serious about movies," he said, and stretched his arm along the back of the seat behind her, for all the world like an adolescent boy on his first movie date. She willed herself to slide away, but her body refused to move. She compensated by straightening her spine so that her shoulder didn't touch the back of the seat.

"I bought him his first video camera when he was barely old enough to hold the thing," David continued. "He's seen practically every movie ever made, some of them a dozen times. He started a video club in school when he was in the seventh grade, and for years nobody in the family was safe—he videotaped everything from Neva fixing breakfast in the morning to me stepping out of the shower.''

Kate closed her eyes for a moment against the sight of David's beautiful, young body as he stepped naked out of their hideous shower in New York. Her pulse quickened and she fought to keep her tone even. ''Did he film Waneath?''

''All the time. She loved the camera.''

''Does he have any of those films?''

''I'm sure he does. You should see his closet—his room is incredibly disorganized, but that closet looks like the vault at Turner Classic Movies. He's meticulous about cataloging everything.''

''I need to see some of those films. I want to meet Waneath.''

''I'll stop by Long Pond and get a couple of the latest ones. How about I fix us some dinner tonight and we can watch together?''

Her mind screamed warning at her. Dangerous to have a cozy little tête-à-tête over home movies, even if they were of a murder victim taken by the prime suspect. ''I'm meeting Arnold for dinner at that café downtown where I had lunch. Why don't *we* come by about eight?''

''You think we need a chaperon?''

''Definitely.'' She turned to him. ''I don't know how I feel about you after all these years. Until I do, I, for one, plan to keep our meetings strictly business. I hope you can handle that.''

''Oh, I can handle it all right,'' he said with a grin. ''But I warn you I intend to push the envelope as far as it will go and then some. And I will also do everything in my power to dump your duenna Arnold the first chance I get.''

''You're welcome to try.''

"He doesn't like me, does he?"

"The point is, he likes *me*. He turns bulldog at the first sign that anybody is causing me grief. I'd do the same thing for him." She looked around and realized that the building, in just fifteen minutes, had the abandoned feel of an empty cavern. She shivered.

"Come on." He stood, and reached a hand down to pull her up. "Let's get out of here."

She came up and into his arms in one smooth movement. He wrapped his arms around her. "See?" he whispered as she stepped back. "No envelope is going to be big enough to keep me away from you."

CHAPTER NINE

KATE PARKED in front of her room and beside Arnold's car in the Paradise parking lot, walked over and knocked on his door. After a moment he opened it and stepped back. She walked in, dropped her handbag on his bed and sank onto the end of it. "Hi, honey, I'm home," she said.

He stood in the open doorway with his hands on his narrow hips. "And where have *you* been?" he asked. "Is that some hussy's lipstick I see on your collar?"

She flopped back on his bed and closed her eyes. "Don't start with me. I've been out at the junior college trying to interview Waneath's professors. Talk about your exercise in futility." She kicked off her shoes, heard the door close and squinted at Arnold as he dropped into the straight chair beside the desk. "And what have you been up to?"

"Doing your dirty work as usual," he said, picking up a manila folder from the desk and dropping it squarely in the center of her midriff. "Arrest reports. Coroner's notes."

She groaned and sat up, clutching the folder. "And?"

"They arrested Jason Canfield because he was the last person seen with the girl and because the two of them had a public argument. And because the district attorney scented votes. So far as I can tell, that's it. They went over his car with everything from black light up and down. No blood…"

"I thought she didn't bleed. The blow didn't break the skin, did it?"

Arnold shook his head. "No evidence that he bundled her into his trunk—which, you must admit, is the optimum way to carry a dead body ten miles into the country. No hair or fiber. A couple of her hairs in both the front and back seats, which is understandable if they had sex back there. No signs of a struggle where she was dumped, and no signs where Jason swears the two of them parked."

"Footprints?"

Arnold shook his head. "No. If they were parked on the side of the road, and if Waneath got out and started walking down the road, there wouldn't be any. They did, however, find her panty hose on the floor of his back seat."

"Lovely. But if they had sex, understandable. Tire iron?"

"Check the inventory of his trunk," Arnold said with a grin.

Kate flipped through the pages until she came to the inventory sheet. She ran her eye down the list of items that had been recovered, frowning. "I can't believe anyone could stuff this much junk into the trunk of a Trans Am."

"Turn the page. That's the inventory from the car itself."

Kate shook her head. "Six empty mesquite barbecue potato-chip bags, a dozen empty cola cans…no beer cans, thank God. Candy wrappers, empty French-fry envelopes. He must spend half his time driving through fast-food windows and the other half eating the stuff he buys. Six dollars and forty-three cents in change?"

"And the glove compartment."

Again she flipped. "Whew! This boy has grandiose ideas."

"Hey, I was eighteen myself. It's not grandiose—it's testosterone."

"But one box containing twenty-three unused condoms?"

Arnold shrugged. "There was a sales slip on the floor. Dated the day after Thanksgiving. I checked. A box of that brand of condom contains twenty-four."

"That checks with Jason's story. They had sex only once that night, and in the back seat of the car." She flipped back to the inventory of the trunk. "And no tire iron."

"Ah, it gets better." Arnold picked up a pocket of photographs, slid one out and handed it to Kate.

She glanced at it. "It's the inside of that disgusting trunk. Oh, dear, I'm afraid there would still be room for a body."

"Yeah, he could lay her head on his moldy gym socks."

"What am I looking for?"

He leaned across and pointed toward the back of the trunk. "You can just see the mounts where the tire iron should have been. Anything look strange to you?"

"No. Am I stupid or what?"

"You're female."

"You noticed."

"The mount things—they've got rust on them. The inside of them, Kate. There hasn't been a piece of metal in those clips in quite some time."

"Arnold, I could kiss you!" Kate said. Then her elation faded. "The prosecution will say—" she glanced at the photos again "—with some justification I'm afraid, that Jason simply tossed the tire iron into his trunk and didn't bother with niceties like sliding it into its holder."

"Yeah, but can they prove it?" He grinned.

"No, but we can't disprove it, either." She got to her feet, felt for her shoes and slipped them on. "But it's a damn fine start. I, on the other hand, have been spinning my wheels and making a total jackass of myself. Maybe I should go back to Atlanta and do personal-injury cases."

"Let me do the grunt work. You do the litigation. You

know I can't speak to a jury without throwing up for two days before and a week afterward." He sounded bitter.

"That's why we are the perfect team." She squeezed his shoulder. "One of these days you'll get past the trauma, and then F. Lee Bailey will have to look to his laurels."

"Never happen, but thanks for believing in me."

"*De nada.* Now, I am going to stand under a hot shower—assuming you haven't used all the hot water in this place, put on an actual skirt and then you and I are going prospecting for what passes for haute cuisine in Athena, Mississippi. And then we are going to the movies."

CHRISTMAS HIT THEM the moment they drove onto the square. The old metal lampposts were festooned with wreaths and fake holly garlands, fairy lights glittered among the privet hedges that lined the walkways, and from the center bandstand came the sound of Christmas carols electronically winging from four speakers, one to each corner.

"Was this all here at lunch?" Kate asked.

"Oh, yes," Arnold said. "Too much traffic noise to hear the music, and the lights weren't on, but the decorations were up. You didn't notice?"

"Not really. Actually, it's kind of charming," Kate said. "Looks homemade, like decorations you've kept since childhood."

"You're going soft on me."

"I've always been soft on Christmas. For the past twenty years, Christmas has been hard on *me*. Not the same thing at all."

Arnold parked the car in front of the Athena Café. Although a number of the shops lining the square were open, there seemed to be few patrons on the street, and those who were strode head down against the chill air. Kate shivered, thankful for her new down jacket.

Possibly because the citizens of Athena didn't much cotton to dining out in the middle of the week, the café was largely deserted. Still, Kate and Arnold chose a table in a far corner where no one could overhear their conversation. Christmas carols played softly in the background, and bright green candles had materialized on the oilcloth-covered booth tables.

"You and Alec always went away for Christmas, didn't you?" Arnold asked over the top of his menu.

"We usually stayed long enough to get the office party over with, then it was off to Cabo San Lucas or Lake Louise. He wasn't close to his children."

"They hate you?"

She shook her head. "Actually, they don't seem to care one way or the other. Alec divorced their mother when they were small, and their stepfather raised them. I think the last few years, Alec regretted that he hadn't been closer to them, but it was too late. Their lives simply didn't encompass him, and by extension, me. At his funeral we were all very polite. I haven't seen or heard from them since."

"So what are you planning to do for Christmas this year?"

Kate sat back. "I haven't thought about it. I'll do the open house for the staff and clients, of course, but after that, I truly do not know."

"You could go to Florida to see your mother."

"Maybe I will."

Their food arrived. Kate ate and kept up her end of the conversation, but her mind grappled with the realization that for the first time since law school, she had absolutely no one to spend Christmas with. Unless she descended on her mother, who would, no doubt, have plans of her own, Christmas would simply be a day like any other. She'd probably spend it working.

The florist and caterer would decorate the apartment for the open house, of course, but all that would disappear when they did. She and Alec never put up a tree because they were never there on Christmas Day to enjoy it. She didn't own a single string of lights, a single ornament.

"I'm staying home for Christmas," she said.

"I beg your pardon?" Arnold looked confused.

She recollected vaguely that Arnold had been discussing the terms of Sunny Borland's settlement. No wonder he was confused.

Even if his parents celebrated Christmas, Kate knew he never went home to Long Island. Too many memories, too many ghosts. His dead wife's parents kept trying to fix him up with one of her sisters. "I am going to put up a Christmas tree. Want to come to Christmas dinner?"

He was staring at her as though she'd taken leave of her senses. "Uh, yeah, sure, fine. Can I bring someone?"

"Of course." Now she felt guilty. Arnold would have places to go and people to see. She reached across the table. "If you have plans, don't worry. I'll be fine."

"You sure?"

"Absolutely. Now, have you ever tried millionaire pie?"

Arnold worked his way through his wedge of cream and pecans while Kate looked on in envy and drank her black coffee.

As they walked to the car, she told him where they were going and why.

"Home movies of Waneath? Isn't that pretty macabre?" Arnold asked.

"More like tragic. But I want to get a look at this girl when she wasn't walking a runway. Everybody's been telling me all about her, but I need to see her for myself."

"Is our client going to be there?"

"Jason? Not to the best of my knowledge."

"So I will be the proverbial third wheel? Canfield, you and little old me watching him make goo-goo eyes at you."

"This is business."

"Of *course* it is." He rolled his eyes and opened the car door for her.

DAVID STOOD waiting for them outside his front door. He bent over to kiss her on the cheek, but she sidestepped him smartly. Arnold raised his eyebrows in silent appreciation of the move. Kate could feel the blush spreading up her cheeks and gave thanks that the lighting in the little house was fairly dark.

David followed them into the house and walked over to the VCR. "Jason and I nearly came to blows over this tape," David said. He picked up the remote from the top of the television.

"You only got one?" Arnold asked.

"Yeah. It's one he made late last summer, and it should have enough of Waneath and the other members of their crowd to give you an idea of the dynamics among them. If you need more, I'll go beard the lion in his den again."

"Why didn't he want you to show us his tapes?" Kate asked. "Is there something he doesn't want us to see?"

"I don't think that's it," David said. "He feels it's some sort of violation. I'm really worried about him. He's barely come out of his room since he got back to Long Pond. Neva says several of his friends have called. He won't talk to them, just lets the answering machine pick up."

"And the other calls?" Arnold asked.

David knit his eyebrows. "What other calls?"

"The threatening calls from irate townspeople. The calls from the newspaper and the media. Those calls."

"If he's gotten calls like that, he didn't say."

"Oh, he's gotten them, all right. I'm surprised nobody's camped on your doorstep. Or on ours, come to think of it."

"Athena is a very small town. We have one weekly newspaper that publishes more recipes for peach preserves and birth announcements than anything else."

"Maybe they're waiting for the indictment to be handed down," Kate said. "I promise you that will be news."

David sank onto the sofa beside her. "This is a nightmare." She nearly patted his hand, but one glance from Arnold restrained her.

"It's only beginning," Arnold said cheerfully. "It gets much worse."

"Shut up," Kate said. "Watch the movie."

The tape had obviously been used for several events during the summer. Jason had not made any attempt at editing; he'd simply recorded events. Not much different from other home movies.

Except...

Kate sat forward as Dub and Neva fought a mock duel with barbecue forks on the patio at Long Pond, and then looked at David stretched out beside the pool with a bottle of beer in his hand. He looked completely at peace. Kate felt a pang at the difference between that man and the one who sat beside her, who was now living a nightmare.

Jason had talent. Raw, unformed, untrained, yet palpably there. He seemed able to make his subjects forget the camera, and thus he captured fleeting expressions, movements, body language that were more revealing than they might have liked. He caught the affection between Neva and Dub, and the housekeeper's exasperation. And when he panned back to David, he caught submerged energy that hadn't been evident in the first few seconds. David wasn't at peace—he was merely playing at contentment. Kate felt a pang of guilt. Surely he deserved a little contentment. Didn't everybody?

They had been watching for perhaps five minutes before the scene switched to a boat dock beside a lake. "That's out at Long Lake," David said. "It's where we keep the ski boat docked. Jason and his gang spent most of the summer out there."

Waneath walked down the dock toward them.

"Wow," Arnold whispered.

Even if they had not seen the autopsy pictures, Kate would have recognized Waneath. Off a runway or a movie set, there would hardly be two women like her in any crowd, certainly not a crowd of recent high-school seniors in Athena, Mississippi.

Under a short, nearly transparent shirt, she wore a bikini that barely covered her nipples and pubic triangle. Her shoulder-length honey-blond hair was swept up on one side by some kind of comb, and fell across her other cheek like an old Veronica Lake still. Her eyes were the color of Swiss chocolate, very large, wide-spaced and slightly tilted at the tips. Her mouth was generous with rich full lips. She had a broad forehead, a perfectly oval face and high cheek-bones. Although this was obviously an informal afternoon, she was perfectly made up.

She smiled and waved at the camera. The fingernails that tipped her slender fingers were very long, tapered to soft points and manicured in fire-engine red.

"My word," Kate said. "She was breathtaking."

Beside her, David stirred. "I suppose she was. I've known her since she was three years old. I guess none of us around here saw her the way a stranger would. To me she was just Jason's girlfriend."

They watched in silence as other young people joined Waneath, the ski boat was taken out into the lake, and members of the party skied behind it with differing degrees of success.

Waneath spent the time sunning herself on the back of the boat and posing for Jason. His camera lingered on her lovingly. At least while the camera ran, she never ventured near the water. She did, however, get rid of the transparent shirt, revealing a body that Kate would cheerfully have killed for.

"Nobody's stomach's that flat," she said.

"I figured Waneath was just some southern dumpling with grandiose ideas," Arnold said. "She really might have made it in Hollywood."

The more Kate watched, the more uncomfortable she became. Perhaps she'd been wrong to do this. Much easier to defend Jason if Waneath Talley were simply a body. She had learned much more than she wanted to know, and what she had learned turned every assumption she'd made upside down and backward.

As the tape finished, they sat silent. Then David switched on the lamp beside him.

Finally, Kate said, "Oh, dear."

Arnold sighed. "What a waste."

Kate walked over to the counter that divided the kitchen from the rest of the room. "Do you have any soft drinks?"

David went to the refrigerator.

"Diet, please, and the can is fine."

As he handed it to her, he looked into her eyes. "What is it, Kate? What did you see that we missed?"

She ran the cold can across her forehead. "I had the impression from the people I've talked to that Waneath was simply a gold-digging tramp who manipulated everyone to her advantage and planned to acquire wealth and status no matter what she had to do or who she hurt."

"That's pretty harsh, and only partially accurate," David

said. "She was cursed with a stage momma who force-fed her the wrong priorities since birth. I think she felt obligated to fulfill her mother's expectations. That meant marrying money and social position."

"She must have been terrified when she found out she was pregnant," Kate said thoughtfully. "It would mess up every plan she'd ever made. Her mother would have been appalled, and I'll bet her father would have been furious. She was betraying everybody who'd invested in her."

"She was certainly no saint," David said. "She expected everybody to dance to her tune, especially Jason. She was the ringleader in every bit of devilment they got into even as children. He always took the blame. If anybody tried to discipline her, she'd cry very prettily. If that didn't work, she'd pitch a temper tantrum."

"I'll bet Melba was thrilled with that," Kate said dryly.

"Waneath was Jason's best friend. Melba gave up trying to dislodge her in Jason's affections about the second grade and prayed he'd get over it before she dragged him to the altar."

Arnold leaned back on the sofa. "So, Jason goes off to California, and comes home for Thanksgiving a different person. He doesn't want to get engaged, much less married. She's pregnant and scared to death. He's abandoning her. She tries to use sex to bring him back in line, but it doesn't work any longer. So she throws a tantrum, gets out of his car and storms off into the night, expecting him to follow her."

"So far I agree," Kate said. "But it doesn't get anywhere near deep enough to the root of the problem."

"What's that?" David said. "The real father?"

"Much more elemental." Kate pointed toward the VCR. "She was a truly beautiful woman. I don't mean girl, either."

"Yeah, your son was one lucky dude," Arnold said to David.

"In more ways than one," Kate continued. "Maybe I'm attuned better than the two of you, maybe it's a female thing. I don't know. But I do know what I'm seeing on that tape. I don't know how good an actress she was, but unless the entertainment business has lost the next Meryl Streep, Jason was much more than a meal ticket to her."

CHAPTER TEN

"The point is," Arnold said, "was Jason in love with her?"

"No," David said.

"You say that as though you're sure."

"He was fond of her, and probably loved her as a friend, but he never mooned around her like a boy in love. I don't think he saw her as Mrs. Jason Canfield, whatever she thought." He glanced at Kate. "I'm familiar with that pole-axed, kicked-by-a-mule feeling when you find the only woman you can ever love."

Kate stood and walked to the window before she turned back. Her fists were balled in her pockets. "Waneath had always been there," she said. "He took her for granted. She never made any real demands on him until the night she died."

For a moment David's eyes held hers. Then he shrugged and joined the conversation. "And he refused her," David answered. "There should have been a better way to do it than simply to drive off and leave her stranded. I can't believe he'd do that to her, no matter how bad an argument they had."

"Yet he did. If we believe him, that is," Arnold said.

"I can't get into his head any longer," David said. "But he's never made any secret of wanting to leave Athena and never come back."

"How does his grandfather feel about that?" Arnold asked.

David echoed the words Kate had heard Dub say at lunch, and in almost the same words.

"He thinks it's a phase, that Jason must learn to run the farm. It's his destiny."

He continued, and this time Kate listened carefully. Dub had definitely not confided this little gem to her.

"Jason has a little money of his own in a trust fund his grandmother left, but it's not enough to pay for a school like Pepperdine," David said. "Dub always promised Jason he'd put him through college, even one of the Ivy League schools, but when Jason was accepted to Pepperdine, Dub hit the ceiling. We had one hell of a row about it."

"So who won?"

"I backed Jason. I'm paying his tuition. The money I inherited from Melba will be Jason's sooner or later anyway."

"So that's why you and Dub aren't getting along?" Kate said.

"That, and my teaching at the college, and the way I want to run the farm, and this house, and a few other irons I've got in the fire. There was no way I could consider leaving Long Pond myself until Jason was safely settled in college."

"And now?"

"All my plans are on hold until this thing with Jason is settled."

"Then you're going to leave?"

"It's a possibility. I've always considered the Long Pond stock Melba left me to be in trust for Jason. It's time I began to build something of my own. Time to find some happiness in what's left of my life."

"Long Pond is a corporation?" Arnold asked in surprise.

"Hey, this is big-time agribusiness. Long Pond is a closely held corporation with three stockholders—Dub owns forty-nine percent, I own forty-nine percent, which I inherited from Melba. Jason's grandmother was given two percent as a wedding present. She left it to Jason. Which, of course, makes him the swing vote."

"An awful lot of power for a boy," Kate said.

"I'm his trustee, so until he turns twenty-one that two percent is mine to vote. Dub knows I wouldn't sell to anyone, and I've never used that stock to go against his wishes. It's his family's farm, after all. Jason can't consider selling his share until he's twenty-one, and then by the terms of the corporation he has to offer that stock to me and to Dub first. In the meantime, Dub and I scrape along and try to accommodate each other."

"Does Dub resent your ownership?"

"He resents the fact that he needs me. He's still a vigorous man, but I've been de facto manager of Long Pond for ten years now. He's lost touch with the day-to-day operations. The men look to me for decisions. I think that rankles."

"But you *could* walk away?"

"Theoretically." He looked at Kate hard and said softly, "With the right incentive, I'd move to the far side of the moon to dig ditches."

She ignored him. "And when Dub dies? His shares go to Jason?"

"I'm sure they do, although we've never discussed it."

"So it's terribly important to him that Jason return to farm the land."

"What does that have to do with Waneath's death?"

"Nothing, so far as I can tell. But it helps to get the complete picture. No wonder Dub was furious when you let Jason go off to Pepperdine."

"Jason deserves his chance to fulfill his dreams. If at some future point he decides to come back and run Long Pond, fine, but he's not going to be forced into it by Dub or anyone else."

"And you? Do you intend to become your son's farm manager after Dub dies? Or are you planning to buy your own land?" Arnold asked.

"Listen, Arnold. Even at conservative figures, the smallest amount of acreage on which I could make a decent living would cost about three million bucks. There's no way I could support an operation with the capital investment in equipment and buildings and manpower, and still manage to pay off a mortgage that size. I'd be lucky to pay off my crop loans at the end of the growing season."

"So you're stuck?"

"There are alternatives."

"China?" Kate asked.

"Who said anything about China?" David said.

"Dub mentioned it at lunch. Was he right?"

David walked over and removed the videotape from the VCR before he spoke. Then he said without turning to look at them, "I've had a few preliminary talks with some people, that's all."

"What about Long Pond?"

"Jason would have to hire someone else to run it for him."

"Could he?"

"Of course." He dropped the tape on top of the television set, turned and stuffed his hands in his pockets. "This is all moot anyway. By the time Dub retires or dies, Jason will either be winning at the Cannes Film Festival, making low-budget porn flicks or doing something else with his life. He might even decide he loves farming. I did."

"In the meantime," Arnold said, "you're all three stuck together in some kind of devil's bargain."

"I enjoy what I do. Everybody makes trade-offs."

Arnold pulled himself to his feet. "We've seen what we came for, Kate. I'm worn-out. You ready to go?"

"Stay," David said and turned to her. "If you don't mind riding in the truck, I'd like to drive you back to the motel."

"Definitely not a good idea," Kate answered. "I should stick with Arnold."

Arnold looked from one to the other. "Stay. I'll see you in the morning for breakfast, okay? And I'll listen for your door tonight."

"Mother hen," David said.

Arnold grinned at him. "I'm already making concessions. Don't push it."

Kate stepped in quickly. "Listen, David, I'll make you a bargain. Do you know where they found Waneath's body?"

"Yeah, down on the levee."

"I've been wanting to see the spot, and it might not be a bad idea to see it at night. Drive me down there, then drive me back to the motel. Period."

"You won't be able to see much."

"There's still a moon. Not quite full, but full enough. And the night is clear. I'll see pretty much what Waneath's killer saw, won't I?"

"Right. If that's what you want."

"Arnold," Kate said, "bang on my door for breakfast when you wake up."

"You'll be up before I am. You always are," he said.

Fifteen minutes later Kate sat on the bench seat of David's old truck. She had to admit that for all its decrepitude, it ran as quietly as a limousine. Jimmy Viccolla must be as good as David said he was.

"I met Jimmy Viccolla's fiancée today," Kate said.

"Myrlene? Nice girl."

"Did you know all of Jason's friends?"

"Athena is a small place. One primary school, one middle school, one high school. I not only know Jason's friends, but most of their parents as well."

"Were he and Waneath always together?"

David laughed. "Are you kidding? They broke up on an average of once a month from the ninth grade on."

"So she wasn't Jason's only girlfriend?"

"The only serious girl. The others came and went, but he and Waneath always got back together."

"And Waneath?"

"She dated all the top people at one point or another. Quarterback of the team, president of the class—she was selective."

"Round heeled?"

"I have no idea, but I would have said no. That's why this pregnancy thing has us all thrown for a loop. Waneath always impressed me as being focused. And careful. What the seminar people call goal-oriented."

"Could she have been raped?"

He swiveled in his seat to stare at her. "And not reported it?"

"If she got into a situation she couldn't control, date rape, maybe, would she report it, or even tell her parents?"

"No. No, I don't think she would tell anyone. She'd keep very quiet and hope there were no consequences."

"And when there were? When she discovered she was going to have a baby?"

"She'd do just what she did. Try to get Jason to marry her. She'd be frantic."

"Was Melba frantic when she found out she was pregnant by you?"

David winced at the sudden change of subject. Kate could see his hands tighten on the steering column of the truck. After a moment he replied, "Determined." His voice was tight. He obviously did not want Kate to pursue this.

But if they were going to get along, it was time to let go of all the secrets. "And if you'd refused to marry her?" she continued doggedly.

David took a deep breath. For a moment Kate thought he'd refuse to answer, then he said, "All right, Counselor. She made it clear that she'd go off somewhere, have the baby and put it up for adoption. Maybe today I would have some rights, but back then, it was her choice. I would have had no say in the matter."

Kate caught her breath, then whispered, "So you either married her or lost your child forever?"

"Basically."

"Peachy basis for a marriage—start off with a spot of blackmail."

"She didn't see it that way."

"Did you?"

He hesitated before he answered. His knuckles were white. "Yes. Blackmail. But also my penance. It would have been damn easy to hate her, and maybe if I'd known that she'd come to New York to try to break us up—maybe I would have. But I didn't find out until much later, when I couldn't bear the thought of giving up my son. Hell, Kate, Melba and I were lovers for two years before I met you. I thought we were still friends, that she understood that I loved you."

"No woman understands a man's love for another woman. We resent it. I did."

He glanced at her. His eyes were fathomless blue in the

light reflected from the dashboard. ''I only thought I loved her.''

All this talk of love, and yet he'd never been able to say the words, not in all their time together. ''And after you married her?''

''We both really tried to make the marriage work for Jason's sake. For our own sakes. We expected to spend a lifetime together. We had to figure out a way to spend it as contentedly as possible. We couldn't live together or be decent parents if we hated each other.''

''Did you manage?''

''Not really. Toward the end, when she knew she would probably die before long, she said she was certain that if she just got me back, that she could erase you from my mind and my heart. I never spoke your name, never mentioned our time together, but she knew the way I felt about you. I wound up hurting her as I hurt you. I always seem to hurt the people I care about.''

''A week ago I wouldn't have said this, but both Melba and I share some responsibility for our own pain.''

''Do you truly feel that?''

''I keep coming back to how young we were, and how insecure. You and I both seemed so strong, didn't we? And yet I was worried to death that you didn't give a damn about me, and you were worried to death that if I knew how miserable you were I'd leave you. We didn't have a marriage—we had a charade with great sex.''

''We had a heck of a lot more than great sex.'' He grinned and reached for her hand. ''Not that great sex is a bad thing.''

For several minutes they had driven along a die-straight two-lane road between more endless fields washed with moonlight. They reached a curve and Kate saw the glint of water in the distance. "Long Lake," David said. "The levee starts up ahead."

"Can you find the exact spot?"

"I doubt it, not unless the police tape is still up."

It was. Kate spotted the fluttering end of ribbon tied to a scrub locust tree. David pulled over and cut the engine. Beside them the incline was not steep, but about ten feet high.

"The grass is short," Kate said as she opened her car door.

"That's why there were no footprints. They keep it mowed. Wait," David said. "Warm as it's been, the snakes are still out, but they're too sluggish to get away from you." He reached across her, opened the glove compartment and took out a long, heavy black flashlight. He clicked it on, and shone it out Kate's door toward the slope. Something rustled away.

Kate caught her breath and drew her feet into the truck. "Do I really want to do this?" she asked.

"You said you did." He chuckled. "Come on, I'll protect you."

She waited until he opened the door for her. She glanced down and saw that he wore heavy brown boots.

He followed her glance. "These suckers will stop the fangs of a timber rattler."

She pointed down at her own chic little black ankle boots. "Well, these suckers will not."

He swept the light back and forth over the grass. "Don't worry, anything that was here is long gone at this point, and mighty annoyed that we disturbed it in the middle of the night. Come on, I'll help you. The grass is slippery." He reached for her hand, entwined his long fingers with hers. Even their hands fit like two halves of a puzzle. "Kate," he began.

She shook her head. "Up, up and away. This is business, remember?"

Five minutes later they stood on the top of the levee. Long Lake glinted under a path of moonlight. On the far shore stood a thicket of some kind of scrub trees. The water barely rippled against the reeds and cane at their feet. A night bird called grumpily, but this late in the year, there were no insects to buzz or bullfrogs to thrum.

"We could almost dance on that moonlight," David whispered. He slipped his arm around her waist. For a moment her head rested on his shoulder.

"Such a beautiful place." She shivered and moved away. Business. She had to keep reminding herself she wasn't some teenager out spooning.

"The dam's that way." David pointed to his left. "It's not much of a lake, but it's big enough to ski on."

"And Waneath's body was all the way up here?" Kate asked.

"Top of the levee."

"Then he wanted her found quickly," Kate said.

"How do you get that?"

She kicked a clod and sent it spinning down the slope toward the reeds. "Because if he took the trouble to drag an inert form up that slope, it would have been simpler just to roll her down the other side and into the water."

"You're right," David said.

"That fits with the way the body was laid out—very neatly, as though she were sleeping."

"Someone who knew her well."

"And didn't want her parents to worry any longer than they had to. How much worse would it have been for them to wait and search for a week or so until the body floated up out of the bottom of the lake? And how hideous would it have been at that point?'' Kate shuddered. ''A caring killer.''

David put his arm around her shoulders. ''But a killer nonetheless.''

She leaned against him. ''Not a premeditated murder. My guess is the father of her baby.''

''Have you seen enough?'' he asked.

''More than enough.'' Kate turned and started down the slope.

''Wait a minute,'' David said.

Two steps on the dew-slick grass in her shiny boots and her feet slid out from under her as neatly as though she'd slipped on a banana peel. ''Oh, damn!''

David reached for her, missed and ran down the levee beside and past her. She slid all the way down to sprawl at the foot of the hill on her rear.

David reached for her and pulled her up. ''Are you all right?''

''Nothing injured but my dignity.'' She brushed her wet, muddy bottom. ''And my clothes. Yuck!''

He wrapped his arms around her. She realized she was breathing hard. She could feel the pulse in her chest against his shirt. She tried to pull away.

''No,'' he whispered. ''Stay here. You feel so damn good.'' He bent his head and buried his face in the angle of her neck. ''I need to hold you again.'' He raised his face to look into her eyes, then he bent to kiss her.

This time there was no denying the fire that leaped in her veins when his mouth met hers, his tongue touched hers. Twenty years fell away in an instant, leaving her gasping and hungry for him as she had always been. When his fingers trailed her throat and slipped down to caress her breast, she felt as though her heart would burst. She pressed her body against his. He was erect against her and breathing as hard as she was.

What would happen if they allowed their bodies simply to slip down on the levee? David dropped the flashlight, and suddenly they were surrounded only by moonlight.

His fingers were slipping under her sweater to find the clasp of her bra when suddenly headlights swept around the bend and caught them as fully as though they'd been in a spotlight center stage.

Kate jumped away.

Instead of sliding by, the truck pulled to a stop.

"Oh, good grief," Kate whispered.

Behind her, David began to chuckle. "Hey, Jimmy," he said.

"Hey, Mr. Canfield," Jimmy Viccolla answered. "Y'all got trouble with the truck?"

As Jimmy opened his door, the dome light came on to reveal Myrlene sitting beside him, wide-eyed. "Hey, Mr. Canfield," she said. "Mrs. Mulholland."

"We're fine, thank you, Jimmy," David said.

Kate was aware that he kept his body behind hers to hide the state of his arousal.

"Okay," Jimmy said doubtfully.

"Come *on*," Myrlene hissed. "Jimmy, you are such a fool."

"Huh?"

She reached across and slammed his door, and a moment later waved out the window as they drove away.

David leaned against the fender of his truck, crossed his arms and began to laugh. After a moment's silence, Kate joined him, but when he opened her arms to her, she sidestepped him. "I think you'd better take me home."

"Kate, come home with me. Finish what we started."

"Uh-uh. Arnold expects to find me in my own bed tomorrow morning and that's where I intend to be."

"You're a hard woman."

"And don't you forget it, buster."

KATE ROLLED OVER in bed to check the luminous dial on her alarm clock. Six-thirty in the morning. Still dark outside. The day loomed ahead of her.

She had a good idea that her clinch with David would be common knowledge all over town long before noon. Lovely.

And if they hadn't been interrupted? Would she have allowed David to drive her back to his house to spend the night? Possibly. No, probably. When he touched her she still caught fire. If anything, the flames had grown hotter for having been banked for twenty years. She thought she had outgrown wild passion. Apparently not. She squirmed in bed and realized that her nipples had grown hard.

Well, why not? What was the harm? Their lives had taken such different paths that there was no chance they could ever get back together on any permanent basis, but what was wrong with savoring the re-creation of the passion they had shared? They might even continue to see each other from time to time the way old friends and lovers sometimes did. They were adults. They were both free.

Bull. One night with David and she'd be as much in thrall to him as she'd ever been at twenty. He'd consumed her then, and he was a lot more man now than he'd been in New York.

Nope. She'd have to continue to fight him and her own desires unless she wanted to wind up traipsing after him down a soybean field for the rest of her life. Which, she did not intend to do. No way. Never.

She jumped out of bed, brushed her teeth and threw on

sweatpants, sweatshirt and running shoes. She needed to get her blood moving in her veins if she intended to think clearly.

She let herself out of her room into the semidarkness and strode off through the parking lot. One good thing about a town the size of Athena. She was safe on the streets, and there was little likelihood she'd get lost.

She warmed up by power walking, then swung into an easy lope along the tree-lined streets. November had stripped the leaves so that she had to watch her step where Athena's residents hadn't yet raked their front lawns or swept their sidewalks.

The streets were well lighted with old-fashioned lampposts. Many of the houses were already lit up as children got ready for school and adults for work.

Nice town. About the same size as the town she grew up in. Still rural, although this close to Jackson, chances were it would become a bedroom community before too many more years.

Would Long Pond survive? Kate found herself hoping that Jason would discover he didn't like directing movies. Places like Athena and Long Pond were fast vanishing, and that was a shame.

But she hadn't thought that when she was Jason's age and setting out to become the wife of a star. Young people fled places like Athena all over the country. Making a living could be tough. Most farmers had to take second jobs to make ends meet. Even wealthy planters like Dub were having to work harder and smarter to keep their heads above water.

Would he survive without David?

She didn't begrudge David his need to run his own show. She simply wished he weren't thinking about moving away in order to do it.

The problem was that all three of them seemed to be right, and yet no matter who won, the others would lose. If David left, Dub and Long Pond would suffer, and in the final analysis, so would Jason. If Jason stayed away, Dub and David would suffer. If Jason came home, he would suffer.

And probably make everybody else miserable as well.

Kate gave great thanks that she was not a part of the equation. Or was she?

By the time she rounded the corner back to the Paradise Motel parking lot, the nape of her neck was sweating. She dropped back to a walk to cool off. Halfway across the parking lot, she heard the sound of a car engine behind her. It was coming much too fast. She looked over her shoulder and froze as a red Trans Am careened into the parking lot, jammed on its brakes and skidded to a halt two feet from her thighs.

She was too stunned to move.

The door opened and Jason Canfield jumped out. He didn't bother to turn off his lights and left his door gaping She looked into his furious face and felt fear. Whoever he had been before, the young man in front of her was more than capable of murder.

CHAPTER ELEVEN

"YOU'RE MY DADDY'S EX!" Jason screamed.

"What?"

He waved a newspaper at her. "It says so right here!"

"Give me that." She snatched it from his grasp, looked at the headline on the front page of the little Athena newspaper that David had assured her never printed anything but wedding announcements and recipes: Canfield Hires Ex-Wife to Defend Son in Murder Trial.

"Oh, Lord," she said. Beneath the headline was a picture of her, Jason and David leaving the jail after the bail hearing. Without knowing any better, she'd have picked herself as the murder suspect rather than the lawyer.

"It's true, isn't it?" He took a step toward her.

She backed up a pace. "Come to my room, sit down and let's discuss this before somebody calls the cops and tells them there's a riot going on in the parking lot."

"Just tell me, is it true?"

"Calm down, park your car, turn off your lights and come in." She hoped she sounded strong and certain, because she felt as though she were about to fall through the asphalt straight to perdition. She turned her back on the boy and walked over to unlock her room. With each step, she expected him to smack her. Instead, she heard his car start, move a few feet and then turn off.

She left her door open and pulled up her bedspread

quickly. No sense in allowing the boy to see how restless a night she'd spent.

He slammed the motel-room door so hard that she jumped. When she turned, he was leaning against it. She realized suddenly that he was every bit as tall as his father and both broad and muscular.

"Well?" he said.

She nodded. "Yes. Your father and I were once married."

He crumpled. He felt for the chair beside the window and sank into it with his head between his hands. "Oh, man, I'm screwed."

"What are you talking about? I'm sorry you had to find out this way, but it doesn't alter the facts."

He stared up at her. "My momma broke up your marriage, didn't she? He married her because she was pregnant with me, didn't he? If it wasn't for me, you'd still be married. It's my fault. I caused it all."

"You give yourself entirely too much credit. Besides, how do you know all that?"

"She told me before she died. Man, talk about getting back at somebody." He ran his hands through his long sandy hair in much the same gesture his father used when he was distraught. "And he didn't want to use Dub's lawyer because he wasn't competent. Oh, man, I can't believe this."

"Listen," she said, and sat down opposite him. "Whatever else I am, I am a damn fine lawyer. I'm also about the only person around here who truly believes you didn't kill Waneath, although the way you're acting at the moment, I'm beginning to wonder."

"Yeah, that would make it better, wouldn't it? Get me sent to prison for something I didn't do?"

"I beg your pardon?"

"Talk about payback. Man. I spend the rest of my life in jail and you get my dad back."

Kate threw up her hands. "You can't be serious. Turn that into a movie script, why don't you? This is the real world."

"Can I fire you?"

"Officially, your father is paying me, but you can in theory fire me. Why would you want to?"

"Because you're gonna get me convicted is why."

"Oh, Jason, don't be ridiculous."

"It makes sense. He's a lot better off with me in jail."

"Are you crazy? Your father loves you."

"Yeah, right." He turned his face away from her. Despite his hunched shoulders, she could see that he was breathing hard. Every muscle in his body was taut. She wondered if she should bang on the wall and summon Arnold.

Nonsense. This was just a boy. He'd had a blow, but it wasn't fatal.

And maybe now, when he was vulnerable, he could be persuaded to tell her the truth. She took a deep breath and spoke in what she hoped was a calm and rational tone. "You haven't fired me yet, so everything you tell me is privileged. I can't divulge it even if I want to. Why don't you tell me the truth about what happened between you and Waneath? All that nonsense about girlfriends at Pepperdine never did wash."

A cunning look crossed his face. His eyes narrowed and his upper lip curled. "What the hell, why not, since you're so hot to get back together with my daddy."

She blinked at the non sequitur.

"Yeah. When I told Waneath I didn't plan to marry her or anybody else for a long time, that's when she hit me with the baby."

"So she did tell you about the baby. I was certain she had."

He shrugged. "I knew it wasn't mine."

"Condoms aren't a hundred percent safe."

"They are when they don't break or leak, and mine never did."

"So you argued?"

He laughed mirthlessly. "You could say that. She started screaming at me, then she jumped out of the car and slammed the door. Said she'd walk home before she'd drive another mile with me. I got out and followed her. I wasn't about to leave any girl on the side of the road, even one I was mad at." He glanced up at Kate. "I mean, it being late and all."

Kate nodded, afraid to interrupt him.

"Anyway, she started walking down the road away from me. That's when she said that if I wouldn't marry her, she'd just have to go tell the real father that he'd have to."

He paused, and that cunning look came back into his eyes. Kate braced herself. Something told her this was not going to be good.

"Said he'd had plenty of practice since he had to marry my mother."

She caught her breath. Whatever she'd been expecting, it wasn't this.

"Yeah, dear old Dad." Now that he'd told her, she could see that his eyes were full of tears. He was deeply angry, but he was also deeply wounded.

And something else lurked in his eyes. Fear?

"You believed her?"

"Why would she lie? Daddy doesn't have any money— not real money. Waneath wouldn't give a poor man the time of day unless she was trapped into it."

Whether Waneath's story was true or not, it was obvious to Kate that Jason believed her.

He dropped his eyes. "I kind of lost it then. I jumped back into the car and drove off to find my dad. I don't know what I was planning to do—beat the hell out of him, probably, for stealing my girl when my back was turned."

"Why didn't you?"

His voice dropped to a whisper. "He wasn't home. His car was gone and the house was dark. I banged on the door and yelled for ten minutes. Then I sat down on the step and tried to think straight. That's when I started worrying about Waneath out there alone. I drove back to where I left her, but she was gone." He dropped his head in his hands. His shoulders shook and he began to sob. "I loved her and I left her out there."

"Did your father say where he'd been?"

Jason shook his head, but didn't raise it from his knees. He spoke through his sobs. "He doesn't even realize I know he wasn't home." He looked up. "Where was he? I mean, it was past midnight." His voice elevated to a wail. "Where was he?"

"You can't seriously believe he killed her?"

"No!" Jason yelped. His eyes, his body language, all said yes.

Kate leaned forward and took both his hands. He froze, but he didn't jerk away from her.

"Do you honestly think he'd let you take the blame?"

"No. Yes. I don't know. He got you to save me, didn't he?"

She shook his hands. "Make up your mind. Did he hire me to get you convicted, or because he was guilty and wanted to save you? You can't have it both ways."

He jerked back sulkily. "Yeah, I can. He hired you to

save me, but you want to get me convicted. So I'm screwed, no matter which way I go.''

Kate ran her hands through her hair, stood up and walked over to lean against the desk. ''Jason, you have the imagination to be a great director, but you live in a fantasy world. Why don't you ask him where he was and stop worrying about it?''

''No!'' It was a piercing cry.

''Because you're afraid to hear the answer?''

''Oh, God.'' He turned away from her and crouched low in the chair, curling into some kind of sitting fetal position.

''Even if he did it, I can't send him to jail.''

''You think he just happened by when she was walking home? I don't believe in that sort of coincidence.''

''Maybe he was coming home from someplace, or out hunting for us. If somebody called him from the joint about our fight...''

''Had he ever come looking for you before?'' She heard her voice turn lawyer in an instant. She had no idea whether the tone would help or hinder the situation.

''Yeah. He's dragged me out of parties a few times when he thought there was dope or liquor. He's always kept me on a pretty tight rein.''

''But you and Waneath were sleeping together since ninth grade?''

''Well, not that tight a rein—I mean, parents forget it's just as easy to get into trouble at four in the afternoon as it is at four in the morning.'' He managed a tiny grin.

''Very true. So you think he was worried about you and went cruising to find you, found Waneath instead, had a knock-down-drag-out fight with her and beat her to death? Then drove ten miles and deposited her on the levee?''

''Maybe.''

''Even if I buy that, which I don't, I can't see your father allowing you to take the blame even for a second. He knows how serious this thing is, unlike your grandfather, who thinks it's all a big joke.''

"Maybe he wouldn't let me actually be convicted.''

"He wouldn't have allowed you to spend five minutes in jail, young man, and if you weren't so angry at him, you'd know that was true.'' But was it? He'd ducked out on the truth at least once before. If Waneath's death had been an accident, might he have been afraid to come forward, afraid of the scandal?

No, she couldn't believe it of David.

What she could believe was that he and Waneath had had an affair. She'd been a beautiful woman, much more mature than her years. David was an extraordinarily handsome and charismatic man, as she had reason to know. Maybe it started simply as two people who missed Jason. Things could get out of hand quickly, especially if Waneath pushed it.

The main thing was that David might have lied about his relationship with the girl.

Big surprise.

She stood up.

"Go home, Jason, before somebody recognizes your car and starts a bunch of gossip we don't need.''

"What are you going to do?'' Jason asked.

"I'm going to find your daddy and ask him if he killed Waneath.''

"You can't!'' Jason squawked. He surged to his feet. "Listen, you said you could maybe plea-bargain for me. Could you maybe get me parole if I plead guilty to manslaughter?''

"I doubt the people of Athena would be amenable to parole and no jail time for killing another human being.''

"I can't let you send my daddy to prison.''

"Nobody's sending anybody to prison. But I am going to talk to him and clear this up once and for all. For pity's sake, Jason, he's baffled because of your attitude and you're scared to talk to him. What kind of family do you people run anyway?"

"The kind where everybody keeps his mouth shut and minds his own business," he said angrily. "And as my lawyer, I order you not to talk to my father."

"Good try."

Jason stepped in front of the door. David had said Jason was too small to play football, but at the moment he looked capable of taking on an entire defensive line. "I can't let you do that," he said.

She stood her ground. "Move, Jason."

"No."

"Listen. Arnold is coming over here to pick me up for breakfast any minute now. He's more than capable of handling you, even if I'm not."

His shoulders sagged, and suddenly he looked about twelve, very tired, very frightened and very confused.

She patted his shoulder. "Don't worry. I'm sure your father has a perfectly good alibi for the night of Waneath's death. You have to give him a chance to explain." She moved him gently away from the door so that she could open it. "Go home. Let Neva answer the phone. Take a nap, watch a movie, eat something. I promise I'll call you after I've talked to your dad."

He began to cry again, and this time she put her arms around him. In a moment, he hugged her back. She patted him and wished she'd had more experience in mothering. She had no idea how to handle him.

After what seemed like a long time, but was actually probably no more than a minute, he snuffled and looked at her. "Everybody thinks I'm such a jerk, you know, for leaving her." His face crumpled again. "I loved her, I really did. I miss her so much."

She nodded. "I know," she said quietly. "Go home. Try not to worry. Everything's going to be all right."

She watched him drive off and turn toward Long Pond. Then she began to shake.

Had David lied to her again? Had he done the same thing he'd done in the past—simply not told her the entire truth? Old habits died hard.

In actuality, he was free; Waneath was free. The disparity in their ages was not much greater than the difference between hers and Alec Mullholland's. If she ignored the fact that Waneath was ostensibly his son's girlfriend, then David was well within his rights, if not his right mind, to get involved with the little gold digger.

David had a history of getting women pregnant. Maybe he'd expected Waneath to be on the Pill. His and Kate's generation didn't talk quite so openly about birth control as Jason's did.

But irrational though it was, she felt betrayed all over again, not only as a woman but as a lawyer. She always said she expected clients to lie, but this seemed gratuitous. Unless, God help them all, he actually was responsible for Waneath's death. How could she handle that knowledge? She couldn't cover up a killing, even for David.

She called Arnold's room, and when he answered, she said, "Sorry, I won't be able to have breakfast with you. I've got someplace to go."

He said muzzily, "Wha...?"

"Don't worry about it. Have coffee, eat. Get yourself into your right mind. I'll either see you at the café, or I'll catch you here later."

"Where?"

"I promise to leave my cell phone plugged into the car. Bye." She hung up on Arnold's second "wha?"

She showered and dressed hurriedly, all the while trying to keep her mind from racing ahead. It wasn't easy. David made a kind of grim sense as the father of Waneath's baby. He taught at the college she'd attended. Had he really gone down that list of professors so casually, knowing all the time that he was the man she sought?

He's an actor, she kept repeating under her breath.

DAVID HEARD tires crunch on the gravel in front of his house and walked to the front door with his first cup of coffee in his hand. He looked out the window, recognized his car and felt his heart lift.

He opened his front door before she reached it, picked up the *Athena Weekly Sun* from his front steps and held it folded in his hand while he waited for her to come to him. He knew he was smiling like a lunatic, but he couldn't help his feelings. He hoped she'd spent as lousy a night as he had, and was here because she couldn't wait a moment longer to throw herself into his arms, ready for a long leisurely morning of making love as they used to do on weekends in New York.

He held out his arms to her, but she sidestepped him and stalked past him into the house. Not the actions of a woman come to make love. "Kate?" he asked.

She dropped her handbag beside the fireplace and turned to face him. Even in the dim light from his reading lamp he could see the set of her jaw. She was breathing hard.

"What is it?" he asked, and went to her.

She put her hands up in front of her like a shield. "Stay on your side of the room, okay?"

"What's the matter?" His blood chilled. "Jason. Is anything the matter with Jason?"

"You could say that," she said. "You could say that there's twenty years of secrets and lies and mistrust the matter with him." She raised her hands to her temples as though fending off a headache. "I was crazy to think you'd changed."

His frustration began to make him angry. "What are you talking about?"

"How come you neglected to tell me that Waneath was carrying your baby?"

He gaped at her. Whatever he'd expected, it wasn't this. He shook his head. "She wasn't."

"Are you denying that you had an affair with her after Jason left for Pepperdine in September?"

"Hell, yes, I'm denying it! Are you nuts? Why would I do that?"

"She was a beautiful woman. Lonely. You saw each other at college. Nothing odd about Jason's daddy comforting his girlfriend."

"Kate, I saw her in the cafeteria three or four times. Joined her for dinner once or twice. We talked about Jason and how much we missed him."

"Oh, really. You didn't mention those little dinner parties before."

"I didn't think they were important. I felt sorry for her."

"Sorry enough to take her to bed?"

"No!"

"Well, David, that's what she told Jason right after he refused to marry her. Right before she walked off to find you to tell you that you were about to become a father for the second time."

"Say what?" He felt his heart pounding in his chest. His skin felt hot, as though he were suddenly sick with a fever. He had to sit down. He felt behind him for the wing chair and sank into it. His mouth turned dry in an instant. He swallowed, trying to get enough moisture to speak.

She stalked back and forth in front of the windows with her arms crossed on her chest. He saw suddenly what a formidable litigator she must be.

"Waneath had no reason to lie," Kate continued. "She didn't expect to die that night. She was annoyed at Jason all right, but what she told him could easily be proved or disproved. She was telling the truth."

He shook his head. "I don't pretend to know why she lied, but she did. I promise you, Kate, I never slept with the girl."

"And is there any reason why I should accept your version? Do you have an unblemished reputation for honesty in these matters?"

He surged to his feet. "Yes, I do, dammit!"

"Then why, when your son drove over here that night to talk to you about Waneath's allegations, were you not here? Where exactly did you spend the remainder of that night? Do you have an alibi? Or did you just happen to pick up Waneath on the side of the road where Jason dumped her?"

"Lord God in heaven," David whispered. "He thinks I killed her."

"Damn straight. Killed her, dumped her and brought me in to get him off so you don't have to confess to save him. He asked me to explore a plea bargain for him. He's willing to go to jail to save you."

He shook his head. "That's crazy."

"Oh, you haven't heard the best part." She walked over and took the newspaper from his limp hand, unfolded it and held it in front of him.

He looked at the headline and the accompanying picture. "Holy hell!"

"Wedding announcements and recipes?" she said sweetly.

"How did they find out?"

"Some housewife-turned-reporter ran across my full name somewhere, no doubt. Who cares? Jason knows I'm your ex-wife, and by now so does Dub and the entire state of Mississippi."

"Kate, I'm sorry."

"Oh, there's more." She wadded up the paper in her hand and paced. "After your giant-size son tried to run me down in the motel parking lot this morning, he explained to me in great detail how I'm planning to get him sent away to Parchman for life to revenge myself on Melba for stealing you away from me."

She threw the newspaper at the couch. It slid onto the floor. Kate ignored it and stormed over to stare out the window.

David stared at her. "That's...that's..." The idea that Kate would do something that Machiavellian was beyond ludicrous. When the laughter began to bubble up inside him, he wondered for a moment whether men got hysterics.

Kate whirled, her face set, her shoulders heaving with fury.

He was instantly sober.

"It's not funny."

"I know," he said. And promptly burst out laughing. "Oh, Kate, the idea that you'd get Jason sent off to prison. I'm sorry. I know this is serious. Maybe it's so damn serious that if I don't laugh I'm going to howl. Surely to God you don't believe him?"

"About getting him sent to prison, of course not. As for the rest of it..."

He surged up out of his chair and went to her. He took

her by the shoulders and spun her to face him. "If I had done it, do you think I'd have let Jason be arrested?"

"Where were you that night?"

He let her go and went to the refrigerator. "I need a drink."

"It's eight-thirty in the morning."

"Milk, orange juice, more coffee—something. My mouth feels too dry to speak."

"You need to stall long enough to think of a good alibi is what you need."

He shook his head, reached into the refrigerator, pulled out a carton of milk and took a long swig straight from the container. He continued to drink for a moment, then flipped the plastic top and set the carton back into the refrigerator, shut the door carefully, turned to the counter and leaned on it with both hands. "This has knocked me for a loop."

"Obviously. Where were you?"

"If you're asking whether I have an alibi, the answer is no. Never occurred to me I'd need one. I definitely was not with another woman."

"You weren't home. Car was gone, house was dark."

"I was restless. I knew Jason was out partying, and I was worried about him. I drove down to the joint to see if I could spot his car, but he wasn't there."

"Did you speak to any of his friends? Hear about the fight?"

"No, I kept a very low profile. I knew he'd be mad as hell if he caught me bulldogging him. I didn't get out of the car, I just cruised by. His car wasn't there."

"You didn't pass him on the road?"

He shook his head. "No. It was a beautiful night. Full moon. I just drove for a couple of hours."

"Oh, come on!" Kate said. "You drove around aimlessly in the middle of the night? You can do better than that.''

''The truth? Celibacy sucks. I'm sick to death of cold showers. The nights can get very long, and frankly, the only woman who haunts my dreams was at that moment handling a lawsuit in California.''

''I'm supposed to believe that?''

''Since the crops are in, I don't go to bed bone tired. I couldn't sleep.''

''Did you stop anywhere? For coffee, maybe? A soft drink? Gasoline?''

''I had a full tank of gasoline. I drove all the way to the outskirts of Jackson and back. Didn't get home until one, two o'clock in the morning.''

''Did you drive by the levee where they found Waneath's body?''

He shook his head. ''I took the back roads.''

''Anyone see you?''

''No one I knew or could recognize. No one who recognized me. Do you believe me?''

''I have no idea.'' She turned away.

He felt a terrible surge of loss, as though after all these years the final thread binding them together had snapped. ''You'll never be able to trust me completely, will you?''

She glared back silently.

''But so far as Waneath's baby goes, you'll have proof of that when the DNA test comes in. That'll prove I wasn't the father.''

''Perhaps it will, perhaps it won't.''

''What?''

''You and Jason share a good deal of DNA. Your patterns could be markedly similar.''

''So I could always be under suspicion?''

''Yes.''

"Then all I can tell you is that it's not true. I don't know why she told Jason that, except maybe she was so damn mad at him that she hit out with the most hurtful words she could. Maybe she planned to force his hand that way. I did not sleep with her. I give you my word."

"And we all know what that's worth."

"I'm sorry you feel that way. Sorrier than you'll ever know," David said. He grabbed his jacket off a hook beside the back door. "But now I have to find my son."

"Can you make him believe you?" Kate asked.

He stopped with one sleeve on and one off. "When I haven't convinced you, you mean?"

She shrugged.

He pulled the jacket on the rest of the way. "Either twenty years ago you married a man capable of killing a woman and leaving her by the side of the road, or I've changed so much in those twenty years that I have become that man. Or a third possibility—I'm innocent. You work it out. And when you come up with an answer, let me know. In the meantime, I'm going to my son."

CHAPTER TWELVE

KATE STOOD rooted to the floor of David's living room and watched him slam the front door behind him. A moment later she heard his truck start and the whine of gravel.

She'd gotten what she wanted all right. No chance of getting back together with David now even for an evening's sexual dalliance. By telling him she didn't believe him, she'd as good as called him a killer.

Lovely.

The problem was that she *did* believe him. All that anger that she hadn't realized still existed had come from someplace deep within her. She'd wanted to hurt him. After twenty years his betrayal still rankled. She wanted to see him bleed, and she'd gone about it with the same single-minded determination she used against hostile witnesses.

She sank onto the sofa and automatically began reassembling the Athena newspaper. She glanced at the story again, then tossed the paper aside. Time enough to read it later, when she could think straight.

Assuming that time ever came.

She closed her eyes and dug the heels of her hands into them as though to keep them from falling out of her skull.

She and Waneath weren't that different. Kate had looked on marriage to David as a career in and of itself. Marriage wasn't a career. It was a relationship between two fallible people who brought emotional baggage with them.

The trick was to fit all the disparate bits and pieces into

the relationship. Tough to manage, especially since neither partner had a clue how much stuff was being dragged along. Hang-ups simply leaped out of closets and crawled from under beds at inopportune moments.

Kate had wanted to hurt David in the worst possible way. Waneath had wanted to hurt Jason. Telling him that David was the father of her unborn child was the nastiest thing Waneath could have said. She probably didn't think any further than the moment. She was furious and scared.

David was right. He was fundamentally decent, whatever mistakes he'd made. He wouldn't have killed Waneath. He'd have been more likely to offer her marriage if he really were the father of her child. That's what he'd done the last time.

But wouldn't it be jim-dandy to have legal confirmation to back up Kate's instincts?

She pulled herself to her feet. With luck Arnold would still be at the motel and ready for breakfast. Suddenly she was hungry and as tired as if she hadn't slept a wink.

Halfway to the front door, she jumped when the telephone rang. She stared at it, wondering whether it was David trying to get in touch with her. She hesitated to pick up his telephone. Let the answering machine pick up, then if it were David, she could interrupt.

After five rings, the machine clicked on. David's voice did the standard machine number. The machine beeped.

As the voice began to speak, Kate gaped.

"David, dear, this is Mrs. H. How is Kate?"

Kate dived at the telephone, picked it up and held it to her ear. "Mother?"

She heard the sharp intake of breath at the other end. "Uh. Good morning, dear."

"What are you doing calling David at eight-thirty in the morning? Or any time, for that matter."

"Um." Silence.

"Well?"

"I wanted to tell him how sorry I am about his trouble."

"Mother," Kate growled. "You're lying through your teeth."

"I beg your pardon."

Kate felt her blood pressure top two hundred. "How often do you two have these little chats?"

"My friends are my own business, young lady. He didn't divorce *me*! I managed to forgive him. Took some time, but he was persistent. He never meant to hurt you. He's very different from your father, even if you refuse to believe it."

Kate sank into the wing chair beside the telephone and dropped her head into the hand not holding the receiver. "How nice. I can't believe this. You never considered telling me you knew where David was and what he was doing?"

Now her mother sounded huffy. "You made it quite clear you wanted nothing to do with him. But the way he suffered without you—well, I started feeling sorry for him. I always liked him. You know I wanted you to talk to him—try to work things out between you."

"So you went behind my back and formed this little 'fool Kate club.'"

"We knew what your reaction would be."

"No wonder he knew Alec was dead and where to find me. Is there anything about my life he *doesn't* know?"

"There's plenty *I* don't know."

Kate groaned. "But what you know he knows. Oh, Mother, how could you?"

"Kate, David was very helpful to me after your father died. In fact, he's the one who encouraged me to sell the house and move down here.'' She waited a moment, then rushed on. ''You were so busy.''

Kate felt a wave of guilt. ''You told me you didn't need any help from me. But now answer me this. Are you the reason I'm here?''

This time her mother sounded guilty. ''I did suggest it might be a good idea. But I'm sure he would have come to the same conclusion eventually. He's very proud of what you've done, Kate.''

''And what the hell right has he to be proud of me?''

''Oh, for heaven's sake. He's still crazy about you. Stop acting like such a…''

Kate heard her mother searching for a word.

''Such a…such a…*lox!*''

That did it. Kate burst out laughing. In a moment her mother joined her.

Kate sputtered to silence. Her mother waited. ''All right, Mother,'' she said. ''What's done cannot be undone. But will you please, please, please keep your mouth shut about my business from here on? That is, if you expect me to confide anything at all to you.''

''Very well, Katherine.''

''Mother?'' Kate asked. ''What are you doing for Christmas?''

Instantly her mother sounded happy and girlish. ''I'm going on a cruise! I've never been on a cruise before. We're going to Puerto Rico and the Bahamas. It's going to be glorious.'' She paused, then asked, ''Why? Where are you going this year?''

Kate hoped she sounded as happy as her mother did. ''Haven't decided. Maybe Saint Moritz.''

''Oh, dear, it's your first year without Alec. What was I thinking? It's not too late to cancel the cruise. You and I will go somewhere. Or you could join me.''

Kate shook her head as though her mother could see her. "No, darling. Go, have a blast. And think of me sliding down the side of a mountain on two very thin pieces of Fiberglas."

"Are you sure?"

"Absolutely. I love you."

"And I love you."

As Kate lowered the telephone, she heard her mother's voice.

"So does he."

DAVID SAW that Jason had driven his car home and parked haphazardly with one wheel buried deep in the azalea beds. Neva would have a fit. He climbed out of his truck as the front door opened, and Dub strode out to meet him. He brandished the rolled-up Athena newspaper in front of him like a club.

"Is this true?" Dub snapped.

David brushed by him. "Talk to me later. At the moment I need to find Jason. He in his room?"

"Dammit, you'll talk to me now!" Dub reached for David's shoulder, but missed.

David raced up the staircase two steps at a time, knocked on Jason's door and opened it without waiting for an acknowledgment.

Jason was working at his computer, and when he saw his father, he stood up so quickly the desk chair fell over backward.

"David! Come back here!" Dub's shout came up the stairs. David ignored it, reached behind him and flipped the latch on the door.

"I didn't kill her," he said without preamble.

"Oh, God, I told her not to talk to you." Jason backed up against the wall.

David went to him, but Jason kept the desk between them. David leaned on it so that his face was less than a foot away from his son's. "I didn't sleep with her. She was not pregnant with my child. None of it is true."

Jason caught his breath. "Why should I believe you? Why would she lie?"

"To hurt you. I can't think of any other reason. Good Lord, son, do you actually think I'd seduce a girl I've known since she was three years old?"

Jason's face turned sulky. "Somebody sure as hell did."

"Well, it wasn't me."

"Then where were you?" Jason wailed. "It was way after midnight when I came looking for you."

David turned away and shoved his hands through his hair. "Driving all over Athena County. I went looking for you at that party, and when I didn't find you, I just took off."

"Alone?"

David walked across and sat on the bed with his forearms on his knees. "I've done the same thing for years, Jason. You never knew because you were asleep, or sleeping over at some friend's house." He pointed at the door. "Ask Dub. He knows."

"He thinks you go to other women."

"What other women? In Athena? I don't know a lot of unmarried women over the age of twenty-five who live here."

"After Momma died, every woman this side of Jackson started going after you," Jason said. "That's why you built that house, wasn't it?"

"No. I built the house for us—you and me." He sighed. "Maybe I should have forced you to move in with me, but you were so adamant about not leaving Long Pond. Adults make mistakes, son, and I've made more than my share, but seducing Waneath Talley was not one of them.''

''How about getting your ex-wife to defend me?'' The sneer was obvious, both on Jason's face and in his voice.

''Now, that was not a mistake—it's the best thing I could have done for you.''

''Yeah, right.''

''Jason, she's one of the best lawyers in this part of the country, and she has a national reputation for defending clients she believes in. If you were a jury, what would you think? That even the woman who has the *least* reason in the world to want to help my son has come all the way from Atlanta to Athena, Mississippi, to put her career on the line for him.''

Jason's eyes widened. ''I hadn't thought of it that way.''

David realized he'd hit the right note. That Kate had not come to Athena for that reason was something he didn't need to tell Jason right now.

''She does say she believes me.''

''She *does*. She told me so in no uncertain terms. And believe me, son, that woman fights like a tiger for the things she believes in.'' He grinned ruefully. ''I've got the scars to prove it.''

Jason picked up his chair and sank into it. For a moment he stared at his father without speaking, then he said, ''Was she the great passion of your life?''

David caught his breath. After only a moment's hesitation, he said, ''Yes.''

''You still feel the same way about her?''

''Yes.'' He shrugged. ''I have no idea how she feels about me. She's spent twenty years hating me.''

Jason grinned. ''Heck, she sure jumped in to defend you quick. Told me you didn't kill Waneath, and even if you did, you wouldn't let me take the blame for it for a minute. Man, she was tough.''

David felt his heart lift. "How do you feel about that, son?"

Jason shook his head. "I don't know. Momma's been dead three years, and I guess you've got a right to go on with your life, but..."

"But you still feel disloyal."

"Yeah, I guess that's it. I just wish it was somebody else."

"You'd feel the same way no matter who it was."

"Maybe," Jason said. "You think she'll get me off?"

David hesitated. Again, this was not the time for complete honesty. "Yes," he said simply.

Jason sighed deeply. "Okay."

"You believe me about Waneath?"

"I guess." He frowned. "But if it wasn't you, then who was it?"

"Probably somebody she met at college. We're trying to find out." He stood, walked over to his son and laid a hand on his shoulder. "Don't freak out yet."

Jason grinned up at him. "You'll tell me when to freak, right?"

"I promise. Now, how about you shave off that stubble, take a shower, open the window to clear the fug out of this room and straighten up."

"Oh, Dad."

"And then come on downstairs, have something to eat with your grandfather."

"I've got an editing project I'm working on," Jason said. "Designing credits for a TV movie."

"Fine. But do it after you're clean, fed, and this room is straight. Smells like you've been keeping goats in here."

"Oh, Dad," he said again.

"I mean it. You can't expect Neva to dig out this pig-sty."

"Yeah, okay."

David squeezed Jason's shoulder and walked to the door. Jason followed him. "Dad?"

David turned and found himself wrapped in his son's muscular arms. He felt tears start and hugged the boy back. He couldn't remember the last time Jason had touched him, much less hugged him. David held him for a long moment before Jason released him and turned quickly away.

David let his hand linger on Jason's shoulder a moment, then unlocked the door and shut it gently behind him. He stood for a moment in the hall with his shoulder against the wall, his eyes closed. Twenty-year-old secrets and lies were being revealed before his eyes. Maybe exposure would lead to healing.

He started down the stairs. Before he reached the bottom step, Dub came out of his study, still holding the folded newspaper.

"That woman sat across from me at lunch and let me make a total jackass of myself," Dub said.

"I beg your pardon?"

"That ex-wife of yours!" He turned on his heel and stormed back into his study, evidently expecting David to follow.

David strolled after him.

Dub threw the paper down on his desk. "Sat right there while I went on about Melba snatching you from your poor little dumb wife who didn't have brains enough to hold on to you!"

David leaned against the door frame. "Oh, boy."

"Did not say a single word about who she was. Just talked about how hurt the girl must have been. You made a pure-D fool of me, David."

"You handled that pretty well all by yourself, I'd say."

Dub's face was dangerously red. "What the Sam Hill possessed you? Hiring that woman, bringing her here and pretending she was a stranger?"

"She's good at what she does. I knew that if anyone could get Jason out of this, she could."

"Out of what? Some little scrape should a' been handled long before it got this far?" He slapped the paper. "Instead we got us a humongous scandal gonna make Long Pond the laughingstock of the county."

"Relax, Dub, before you blow a gasket. Sit down."

Suddenly Dub deflated, felt his way around the desk and sank into his chair.

David rushed to him. "Dub?"

"Let me have a glass of water."

David rushed to the bar and brought him one. Dub drank greedily.

"Let me call a doctor."

"No." Dub waved him away. "I'm fine." He leaned back in the chair and closed his eyes. "Can't believe that woman let me go on that way."

So that was the real problem. Dub hating to look like a fool.

Dub opened his eyes. "Get rid of her."

"No."

"I mean it. We'll hire somebody from Jackson. Don't want her or that Selig at Long Pond again."

David stood over him. The old man seemed to be breathing normally, and his color had dropped to his normal farmer's tan. "Dub, this is my choice, not yours. I'm paying her. Jason is my son. This is not negotiable."

He expected an immediate explosion. Instead, Dub simply waved him away with a sigh. "What the hell does it matter anyway. Damage is done."

"I'm sure Kate won't hold your remarks about Melba against you. She knows you were looking at it strictly from your own point of view."

"Should have told me," he grumbled.

"Probably, but I didn't think anyone would connect her with me, and I'm sure she didn't either. She went back to her maiden name 20 years ago. Then she married Mulholland." He touched Dub's shoulder. "Let it go. We've got worse problems than a little wounded vanity."

Dub looked up at him with narrowed eyes. "Yeah. Like Jason moving to Hollywood and you moving to China."

David walked to the bar and opened a soda from the small refrigerator. "I'm not leaving tomorrow. Maybe not at all."

"Should be me."

David wasn't certain he'd heard correctly. "I beg your pardon?"

"You ever wonder why I got my degree in political science?"

"Good basic degree."

Dub shook his head, pulled himself erect and walked over to stare up at the portrait of his wife and daughter that hung over the fireplace. His rage seemed to have been replaced with a mood that was almost wistful.

"I passed the foreign-service exam first try," Dub said. He stuck his hands in his pockets and turned his head to look at David. "You got any idea how tough that is? Most people—even if they have advanced degrees—take two, three times to pass." He poked a finger at his chest. "I damn near maxed the thing."

"I didn't know."

"Yeah. Going into the foreign service. Wanted to see the world, work in embassies, maybe even get to be an ambassador someday." His voice had grown stronger, but suddenly the strength seemed to go out of it. "Then my daddy had his stroke. I came home to Long Pond. Married Melba's momma. Went to farming. Never did get to join the foreign service." He shook his head. "Ought to be me going to China."

"I'm sorry," David said. "I didn't know."

Dub sighed and shrugged. Then he turned a savage face to David. "Jason has to come home to Long Pond. Maybe if you and Melba'd had a bunch of boys, one of 'em could have played Hollywood, but you didn't. You had Jason. You take over from me, he takes over from you. That's the way it's always been and it's the way it's gonna be."

"We're not serfs," David said quietly.

"Hell, yes, we are!" Dub snarled. "We're bound to the land every bit as much as some damn Russian peasant under the czars and don't you ever forget it!"

"No." David said quietly. "I love Long Pond. I'll stay as long as you need me, even if I have to fight you tooth and nail for every innovation I want to make. That's my choice—for now. But Jason's free to make his choices, and if that means Hollywood, then so be it."

"I won't have it!" Dub shouted. "If I have to, I'll get married again and have me another son, and I'll damn well live to be a hundred so I can pass Long Pond on to him and Jason can starve."

"Dub?" It was Neva Hardin's voice. She stood in the doorway, her hands wrapped in her apron, an expression of concern on her face. "You come on to lunch now. It's getting cold."

Dub turned blank eyes to her. Suddenly he seemed like a very old man. "We're coming."

"You will stay?" Neva asked David. Her eyes pleaded.

He glanced from her to Dub and nodded. "So long as we don't talk business. I'll give Jason a holler." As he passed Neva, she touched his hand. At the foot of the stairs he turned back to Dub. "You and I can discuss this later. Jason doesn't need any more problems at the moment. Agreed?"

For a moment he thought Dub would refuse. Then the older man's face caved in and his shoulders sagged. He nodded. A moment later he pasted a social grin on his face and walked off behind Neva to the dining room.

CHAPTER THIRTEEN

"I REALLY NEED to talk to Coral Anne Talley," Kate told Arnold Selig over his fourth cup of coffee at the small coffee shop across the street from the Paradise Motel. When he gave her an uncomprehending stare, she continued, "Waneath's little sister?"

"Good luck." He looked up from the Athena newspaper in his hand. "I see District Attorney James Roy Allenby's fine Italian hand in this news story," he said.

"Really?"

"Our boy James Roy is no country rube. I get the feeling he could give any big-city spin doctor a run for his money as a media manipulator. Have you read this article?"

Kate shook her head. "Only the headline."

"The gist of it is that the May-Canfield clan plans to use its money to buy Jason a slap on the wrist for killing Waneath, and that you and I are a pair of legal shysters who will use any trick in the book to get the kid off. You'll be interested to know that you have just extorted a fortune in California from a poor, harried female doctor for a greedy, money-grubbing woman named Sunny Borland."

Kate nearly choked on her coffee. "Let me see that." She read with increasing annoyance. "This is just short of libelous. It's not quite lies, but it sure comes close. Who is this Annabelle Wiggins anyway?" She pointed to the byline on the story.

Arnold wiggled his eyebrows. "I called my new best

friend, Sheriff Tait, the minute I read the thing. It would seem Miz Wiggins..." He drew out the "mizzzz" so that it had more than its usual complement of z's. "Miz Wiggins is a thirty-five-year-old divorcée who moved here from Jackson after divorcing the esteemed Mr. Wiggins for flagrant disregard of his marital vows, took a job on the paper and began taking casseroles to David Canfield."

Kate's eyebrows went up.

Arnold shrugged. "The man's a very eligible widower. He probably has enough sweet-potato pies in his freezer to last through the next millennium."

"And did Miz Wiggins's suit prosper?" Kate asked, almost afraid to hear the answer. She had to stop thinking of David as an ex-husband. He was precisely what Arnold said he was. No reason he shouldn't date and bed the entire female population of Athena County.

Arnold grinned and shook his head. "Apparently David has developed a reputation for playing hard to get. Miz Wiggins moved onto greener pastures. Guess who?"

Kate grinned. "Mr. James Roy Allenby."

Arnold nodded. "The *newly divorced* Mr. James Roy Allenby. I'm spending the afternoon in Jackson at Whitman, Tarber and McDonough, getting the papers completed to file for change of venue. You better hope we get it."

"Let's hope it doesn't come down to that. When does the grand jury meet?" she asked.

"James Roy has called a special session on the eighteenth of December to consider Jason's indictment. If we waive time, the trial will probably take place in April or May, if we're lucky. If we fight for change of venue, that could set it back six months."

"Jason might as well write off his freshman year. The courts won't let him leave the state." She sat back. "I suppose he could register at the junior college for spring semester. Maybe those credits would transfer to Pepperdine next year.''

''My, my, we are sure of ourselves, aren't we?'' Arnold grinned at her.

''Hey. I'm sure he didn't do it. That's why I need to speak to Coral Anne Talley. Maybe Waneath told her about the guy she was seeing.''

''The problem with that is twofold,'' Arnold said. ''First, if you go near the Talleys they'll probably shoot you. Second, she's sixteen. You can't talk to her officially without a parent present.''

''And third, I can't get a warrant to depose her this early in the process. Well, damn.'' She began gnawing on the cuticle of her index finger, realized what she was doing and quit. She looked down at her hands. The nearly clear polish that covered her nails had begun to chip and flake. ''I wonder if Myrlene knows somebody who could give me a manicure?'' she asked.

''Might take the opportunity to infect you with blood poisoning,'' Arnold said dryly.

''Maybe Myrlene knows where Waneath had her hair done. If she was seeing anybody, the hairdresser would surely know. Might be time for a little wash and blow-dry.''

Arnold gaped at her. ''That egomaniac hairdresser you go to in Atlanta will kill you if you let somebody else mess with your hair,'' he said. ''You said you had to get his permission and approval to have it cut in Hollywood.''

''Ah, but Michel will never know unless *you* call him up and snitch.'' She smiled at him sweetly. ''And you like your job, don't you, Arnold dear?''

''Woman, you are crazy.'' Arnold said, and slid out of the booth. ''Come on, let's go back to the motel. I'm hoping for the report on Waneath's autopsy sometime today.''

As she paid their check, Kate asked over her shoulder,

"Will they release her body to the family now?" She glanced up into the avid eyes of the woman at the cash register and wished she'd kept her mouth shut. At least until she was out of earshot.

Arnold caught the glance, smiled back and kept his mouth shut. As they crossed the street, he said, "The funeral home should be able to pick up the body from the morgue in Memphis today or tomorrow. I asked the sheriff to notify the family."

"I hate to say this, but one of us needs to go to that funeral," Kate said.

"I'll go. I'm extremely forgettable. You, on the other hand, are not."

"Arnold, you stand out in Athena like an elk in Times Square. And I know the way you feel about funerals."

"And you don't? You think Canfield and Mays will attend?"

"They'll want to. So will Jason. She was his friend. He should go, but it may lead to trouble if he does. Damn. I have no idea what to advise."

"Don't borrow trouble. Wait until the thing is scheduled."

"Yeah." She left him at his door. "If I don't see you today, we can meet for dinner. There's got to be someplace to go other than that café. If you're going to be in Jackson, call me and I'll meet you. It's only a forty-minute drive."

He nodded. "I'll leave you a note if the autopsy report actually shows up."

"Fine. I'm off to find Myrlene."

Myrlene's cart stood in front of an open door to a room at the back of the motel. Kate tapped on the door frame and called out. She heard running water shut off, and a moment later, Myrlene stuck her head out of the bathroom.

"Hey, Mrs. Mulholland," she said. She seemed genuinely happy to see Kate, but a moment later she blushed and stammered, "I—I sure am sorry about the other night. Sometimes Jimmy has fewer brains than God gave a goose."

"That's okay." Kate leaned in the door frame and held out her hands. "I just realized my hands are a mess, and I could use a shampoo. Are there any really good beauty shops in Athena?"

"Well, Momma gets hers done at the Crimp and Curl on the square."

Kate thought about Momma's hennaed and overpermed 'do and repressed a shudder. "Where did Waneath get hers done?"

"Oh, she went to Jackson."

Kate's heart fell. "Do you go to the Crimp and Curl too?"

Myrlene sniffed. "No way. Bunch of old hens. I go to Charlotte out by the bypass."

"Think she could fit in a manicure?"

"Sure. Waneath used to have her nails done there sometimes. You want me to call her for you?"

Kate nodded, and fifteen minutes later drove into the strip mall opposite the shopping center. She decided that a manicure by itself was safe enough, and wouldn't put her life in jeopardy with Michel in Atlanta. Every eye turned to her when she walked in the front door. Charlotte had wasted no time notifying everyone in the shop about who she was. Several women surreptitiously slid copies of the Athena newspaper into their handbags and studiously avoided her eyes. Lord, how she hated this! The chances that anyone would open up while she was here were slim.

She slid into the chair opposite the manicurist, an artistically made-up heavyset woman with skin the color of mocha latte. She looked at Kate's hands and shook her head.

"Whoa, honey, you have not been looking after these nails."

"Uh, I've been kind of busy the last few days."

The woman looked up and grinned. "I'm Juanita. Let's see what we can do."

Around her, conversation had begun again, but eyes turned her way from time to time.

"You do most of the girls in town?" Kate asked.

"Uh-huh." Juanita wiped a cotton ball wet with remover over her thumbnail.

Kate lowered her voice. "I understand you gave Waneath Talley a manicure now and then?"

Juanita looked up quickly. Her brown eyes were extremely perceptive. She nodded. "Uh-huh. Did her fill-ins when she didn't have time to get to Jackson. Never had her hair done here though."

"How about her family?"

"Coral Anne, now, Charlotte been cutting her hair since she was a baby." She arched an eyebrow. "Guess Mrs. Talley doesn't feel like wasting a trip to Jackson on that child."

"You wouldn't happen to remember the last time Coral Anne came in, would you?"

"Couple of weeks." Juanita dropped the cotton into the wastebasket beside her and picked up an emery board. "She sure could use a little highlighting and a body wave. Got hair the color of Long Lake after a bad storm—pure mud. Child has nice hands, though. I made her stop biting her nails."

"You said you did Waneath's fill-ins. She had acrylic nails?"

Juanita laughed. "Lord, yes. Could not grow a nail to save her life. Been wearing fakes since she was thirteen."

Kate remembered the scarlet talons waving from Jason's

videotape and Waneath's incredible body. ''Did she ever have plastic surgery that you knew of?''

Juanita threw back her head and laughed. Instantly all activity in the salon stopped and every head turned to her. She looked around, took a deep breath and snickered. After a moment, activity resumed and Juanita whispered, ''Added a little on the top and took a little off the bottom, if you know what I mean.''

''Liposuction?''

Juanita nodded. ''Everybody in town knows she went off to Birmingham two years ago wearing an A-cup and size-eight jeans and came back wearing a C-cup and size-four jeans.''

''Two years ago?'' Kate gaped. ''She was seventeen years old!''

''You know you can't have breast implants and nurse a baby?'' Juanita said.

Kate shook her head.

''Guess she didn't plan on nursing anyway. Probably would have figured out a way to have some other woman carry it if she'd ever gotten pregnant.''

Kate glanced up at Juanita, but she seemed oblivious to what she'd said. So the Athena gossip hadn't yet picked up on Waneath's delicate condition. ''Was Waneath dating anybody special that you know of?'' she asked.

''Lord, honey, she wouldn't tell me. Didn't seem to me like she was much interested in boys except for Jason.''

Twenty minutes later Kate tipped Juanita extravagantly, paid her bill and left feeling every eye in the shop on her as she climbed into her car.

She drove to the junior-college campus and almost automatically checked for David's car in the faculty parking lot. Not there. But then, it was after eleven. His ten o'clock class would be long over by now. She grabbed a cup of coffee in the school cafeteria and sat in a corner wondering whether every attractive male that walked past had known Waneath, then she went in search of Professors Thomasson and Vasquez.

She caught Thomasson outside his noon class. He looked harried, and ropy rather than muscular, but his shock of iron-gray hair and pale blue eyes might well attract co-eds. She noticed that he wore no wedding ring, and that there were tufts of black hair on the backs of his knuckles. He smelled strongly of a nauseatingly sweet aftershave.

She crossed him off instinctively. Waneath was much too canny to fall for this poor imitation of Richard Gere. Five minutes later, his vehement denials of involvement with Waneath ringing in her ears, she went in search of Vasquez.

She heard a deep male voice behind his office door, knocked and entered at his invitation. Vasquez stood and came around the desk with his hand outstretched the moment she told him who she was. He clasped her right hand in both of his and held on while he led her to the wooden chair across the desk from him.

He wore elderly jeans that seemed painted on his lean, muscular legs, and were worn a paler blue over the considerable bulge at his crotch. His black turtleneck sweater stretched over his chest and shoulders. He was only about five foot seven or eight, and had snapping black eyes, more than the normal complement of blinding teeth, and a head of black curls that would have made Shirley Temple envious.

Maybe Waneath had decided to go for a man who was as pretty as she. If he were the father of her baby, the combination of this guy's genes with Waneath's would probably have produced an exquisite child.

Ten minutes later she decided that he'd probably never tried to get Waneath into his bed. He was the kind of man whose ego wouldn't allow him to bed a woman more beautiful than he was.

Discouraged, she drove back to the motel and found a note from David asking her to dinner. At his house.

She was supposed to meet Arnold in Jackson, but he wouldn't mind if she reneged on that promise. They were both used to last-minute changes of plan.

They'd been friends for a long time. When she'd first come to work for Alec, she'd wondered whether Arnold might be gay.

He never seemed to have a serious girlfriend, but at bar functions he always had a different girl on his arm—beautiful, charming and forgettable.

One long night in Chicago he'd confided in her. She'd come down with a twenty-four-hour bug and had begged him to take over cross-examination of a minor witness in a wrongful-death suit the following morning.

He'd gone into her bathroom and thrown up.

Alec had known, of course, but Alec was a genius at keeping confidences.

Before he came south, Arnold had been an up-and-coming litigator, building a career in New York, and building a life with his young bride, Shirley, in an apartment on Long Island. Life was good.

They'd only been married a couple of years when she burst an unsuspected ectopic pregnancy and wound up in the emergency room.

At the time, Arnold was summing up before a tough judge. By the time he arrived at the hospital, Shirley had bled to death on the table.

Nobody blamed him. He endured the sympathetic stares and pats, and went every Friday evening to dinner with his in-laws, who shoved Shirley's younger sister at him, until he couldn't take it anymore. One day he called Alec Mulholland and asked for a job in Atlanta. One where he would never have to stand up and speak in a courtroom again.

Kate knew that in some way he loved her, just as she loved him. When Alec had died so suddenly, Arnold was the first person she called. He had stayed until after the funeral. He had handled probate of Alec's will, set up the details of the transfer of power in the firm. She trusted him implicitly and worked with him every chance she got.

The perfect team.

But they never spoke of his marriage again. Not quite a secret, but still an unacknowledged elephant in the corner of the room.

An unpleasant thought crossed her mind. Alec had concealed the seriousness of his heart trouble from her. David had taken refuge in Melba's arms to avoid dumping his angst in her lap. Her mother had tried to conceal her father's infidelities.

She must give off serious "I don't want to know" vibes. Was she really that weak a reed?

Her stomach growled. Enough introspection. She went to see what she could dredge up from the vending machine in the motel office to serve as lunch.

She ate a couple of packets of peanut-butter crackers and two bags of potato chips. She knew she ought to be out doing something, but for the life of her, at that point she was so tired and so dispirited she couldn't think what. She sank onto her bed and turned on the television in time to catch the noon news. Halfway through, she looked up at a commercial.

"Hey, folks, Big Bill Talley here, telling y'all to come on down to Talley Motors and let ole Big Bill make you a deal on that new car or truck better'n anything south of the Mason-Dixon line!"

Big Bill Talley deserved his name. Hard to tell on television, of course, but he looked about the size of an eighteen-wheeler with an extra-wide load. He had massive amounts of wavy brown hair that Kate would have bet was the result of a toupee, and his fancy blue-and-white cowboy shirt stretched across his barrel chest and around biceps as thick as her thighs.

And cheerful! Militantly, terrifyingly cheerful. Judging from his short-sleeved shirt and the leaves on the trees behind him, the commercial had been filmed months ago, long before Waneath's death. But there was still something scary about that broad grin. Like an alligator waiting in the shallow water of a lagoon for an unsuspecting crane to meander by.

Easy to tell where Waneath got her teeth and her height. But her enormous eyes came from her mother. Big Bill's were small, narrow, piggy, and set a couple of millimeters too close to the bridge of his nose. Despite his happy demeanor, Kate could well understand Jimmy Viccolla's discomfort. This was not a man to cross.

She felt a frisson of fear. Amazing that Talley had not so far attempted to burn down Long Pond with Jason inside. Or come after Kate herself. He looked like a man who would feel his family, particularly the female members of his family, were his possessions. And resent bitterly anyone who deprived him of one of them.

Nonsense. That sort of thing only happened in bad Hollywood B-movies.

Still, the fact that he had not attended Jason's bail hearing, nor put up more than token resistance to the second autopsy of Waneath's body was worrisome. Kate's grandmother had once warned her that copperheads were more dangerous than rattlers, because at least rattlers gave advance notice that they were angry.

She jumped when the telephone rang, and only then realized she'd been dozing. She brightened when she heard Arnold's voice on the line.

"Kate? Autopsy report there yet?"

"Not unless they're holding it in the office. I haven't checked."

"Nuts. Look, can we cancel dinner tonight?"

"Sure. Why?"

"I intend to work straight through on the change-of-venue thing. They've got a great library here, and I'm coming up with some dandy case law. I feel certain that we can convince a judge that Jason can't get a fair trial in Athena County."

"Great."

"And what have you been up to?"

"I saw two of Waneath's professors. I don't think either of them qualifies as daddy of the month, although I must admit Vasquez could out-handsome Antonio Banderas."

"My, my. Hormones acting up, are they?"

"My hormones are my business, thank you."

"See that you keep them to yourself. Speaking of hormones, what's the latest on Canfield?"

"Give it a rest, Arnold. I don't look back, remember. What's done is done. I don't give second chances."

"Well, see that you don't. You have better things to do with your life than spend it canning peaches and walking behind a plow."

Kate laughed. "I suspect the plow David uses is air-conditioned and cost a quarter of a million dollars. Besides, might be kind of fun. I've always wanted to learn to drive a tractor."

"Bite your tongue!" He hesitated. "Seriously, Kate, watch yourself with Canfield."

"Why do you dislike him so much?"

"I like him all right personally. But it's been less than a

year since Alec's death, and whether you realize it or not, you are vulnerable. You're the sort of woman who needs a man around.''

Kate gaped at the phone. ''I beg your pardon?''

''Well, you are.''

''Am not.''

''Are too. Whether you recognize it or not, you're a very social animal and a born nurturer. I've seen you with your clients, remember. Born nurturers tend to go for the sort of man that doesn't want to be nurtured. Mother Nature is a real bitch sometimes.''

''So you don't think he needs nurturing?''

He laughed, and the bitterness was still there. ''Oh, he needs it all right. Just doesn't want it. I, on the other hand...''

Kate waited.

''Forget it. I may be late getting back from Jackson. I'll see you in the morning after I've dragged my eyes open.''

Kate nodded at the phone as though he could see her. ''Arnold? Be careful, please. I've just gotten a glimpse of Big Bill Talley, Waneath's daddy, on the boob tube. He is immense. I hope he's a gentle giant, but don't bet on it. Be really careful.''

''That goes double for you, Kate. I'm in Jackson. You're there. Watch yourself. Stick close to the motel.''

''Will do.''

She sat looking at the phone for at least a minute after she hung up. There was now no reason why she shouldn't meet David for dinner. No reason except her own nerves. And a feeling of raw longing so intense that she found it frightening.

So, she should face her fears. She took a deep breath, called David's number, waited for five rings and then heard his answering machine pick up. Of course, he'd be at Long

Pond or out in the fields or anyplace except in his house waiting to hear from her. She left a message telling him that she was free for dinner and would drive out to his place about seven. Then she called the motel office and found that no envelope had arrived from Memphis. So no autopsy. Bother. DNA might take as long as four months, but blood-typing on the fetus should be a piece of cake.

She let her head fall back against the thin pillows and allowed her mind to drift. She told herself she needed to go over the case start to finish, but David's face kept intruding. Not the face she remembered from their years together, the face that she had told herself she hated. She couldn't seem to dredge that face up in her mind any longer. She saw him instead only the way he was now, with lines at the corners of his eyes and grooves starting at the corners of his mouth. And sadness buried so deep behind those blue eyes that they were like a chill mountain tarn.

How much of that sadness was her doing? She could no longer avoid her part of the responsibility for the breakup of their marriage.

She had never thought about what might have happened if she and David had confronted his infidelity and Melba's pregnancy together. And then had confronted his lack of confidence in his acting ability together as well.

Her mind shied away. She didn't want to think about any of that. Nothing could change the past.

But what did the future hold?

Someone knocked tentatively at her door. She started, opened her eyes and called, "Yes?"

Again that tentative knock. She rolled off the bed and went to the door. "Who's there?" No answer. She put her eye to the view hole and saw the top of a head of brown hair. Female.

She opened the door. The girl who stood outside jumped

back as though she'd been threatened. Her eyes were wide
and terrified behind her glasses. Kate looked at her mottled
skin and the splatter of pimples across her forehead, at the
lank hair and wide-legged jeans that hung from a tubby
figure, and made a guess. "Coral Anne?"

The girl ducked away.

"Come in," Kate said, and stood aside.

Coral Anne scuttled in and motioned for Kate to shut the
door behind her.

Kate smiled what she hoped was a welcoming smile. She
held out her hand. "I don't think we've met officially. I'm
Kate Mulholland."

"I know who you are," Coral Anne said, ignoring Kate's
hand.

"Please, have a seat. Can I get you something to drink?"

"Got any bourbon?"

Kate blinked. "I meant a soft drink."

"Forget it." Coral Anne looked around the room. "This
place sucks."

"You could say that." Kate sat on the bed and pulled
her stocking feet up in front of her. After a moment Coral
Anne perched on the edge of the desk chair.

"My momma finds out I'm here she'll kill me," Coral
Anne said.

Kate nodded. She didn't doubt it for a minute.

"She told me she smacked you across the face?" The
sentence had a question mark at the end of it, so Kate answered it.

"She did. Good and hard."

Coral Anne snickered. "Lord, I would love to have seen
that. My momma goes at it with both hands when she gets
mad."

For "it" Kate read "me." "She go at you?"

"Me'n Waneath both." Then the girl added proudly,

"My daddy never lays a hand on either one of us. He's a big ole pussycat, big as he is. But my momma, now, she has a temper."

Kate waited, then said, "So why did you come?"

"To tell you it's not Jason's baby."

Kate sat up. "You knew about the baby?"

Coral Anne nodded. "I'm the only one she told. We took one of those home-pregnancy things and I had to drive all the way out to the Dumpster by the levee to throw it away so Momma wouldn't find it in the trash."

"You have a car?"

"Sure. Got it for my sixteenth birthday. My daddy sells cars. Me and Waneath didn't even have to share one." She smiled. "Mine's newer." She sighed. "I guess Daddy'll sell Waneath's car. He had one of the guys drive it to his house and put it in his garage. Daddy cried. Said he couldn't bear to look at it."

"I'm sorry. I know how hard that kind of thing can be for a parent."

"Do you? Really?" The eyes Coral Anne turned to Kate were intelligent behind their thick glasses. "If this was some kind of story, Waneath and me'd hate each other. I mean, she was beautiful, and me…" She looked down at her dumpy body. "But we didn't hate each other more'n any pair of sisters. Mostly, we loved each other. My momma and daddy do *not* appreciate me," she said candidly. "But Waneath did." She laughed. "Shoot, she should. I did her damn homework."

"Even though you're three years younger?"

"I am probably some kind of genius," Coral Anne said. "Maybe when I go off to Harvard or Oxford on a scholarship my momma'll think I'm not such a mess." She shrugged. "Momma doesn't much value women unless they're pretty. Says it's a curse for a woman to be smart."

"Your momma's wrong."

"Oh, I know that." She tossed her head of lank brown hair. Juanita at Charlotte's was right. Coral Anne would greatly benefit from highlights and a body wave. And a good diet and some aerobics classes. Whatever Coral Anne said, Kate suspected she'd be willing to swap a few IQ points for a date on Saturday night. If she was lucky, once she made it to Harvard, she'd find somebody who valued her for her brain.

"Jason didn't do it," she said.

"You seem very sure."

"He's the closest thing to a brother I've got, and if he'd married Waneath like she wanted, he would really have been my brother. I'm sick of my momma and daddy bad-mouthing him and his family to everybody in town when I know damn well that baby wasn't his."

Kate held her breath, then she said, "So, whose was it?"

"She wouldn't tell me. Said it was a stupid mistake, she was only trying to get back at Jason. Showing she could get any man she wanted to."

"When did she think she'd gotten pregnant?"

"We just did the test last week. The way Waneath eats—excuse me—ate, her periods were never regular. She used to flat starve herself and throw up for two weeks before a pageant."

"She was bulimic?"

"Not all the time. Won't catch me doing that even if I wind up big as a house like my momma says I'm going to."

Kate was about ready to slap Mrs. Talley right back for her treatment of her younger daughter. Coral Anne, however, seemed remarkably levelheaded.

"Anyway, I tried to get her to say who the father was, but she wouldn't tell me. I think she was embarrassed. She told me she'd been drinking. My guess is one of those jocks at college took advantage of her.''

"She shouldn't have been drinking, period. Obviously that doesn't stop any of you, does it?''

"Get real. There's always somebody willing to supply beer and stuff. Anyway, she said it was after Jason left for Pepperdine. She was scared he was going to dump her.''

"Did she plan to marry him?''

Coral Anne rolled her eyes. "Oh, sure. He was going to give her a ring at Christmas. Right. Maybe in 2050.''

"And if he didn't?''

"She was really scared. Momma would've been real disappointed. 'Course, Momma would just kill her if she found out about the baby.''

"And your daddy?''

"He'd have been miserable, but he'd have stood by Waneath. She kept hoping she'd lose it, you know.''

"Do you have any evidence as to who the baby's father was?''

"No, but I can testify she said it wasn't Jason's.''

"That might not be such a good idea,'' Kate said.

Coral Anne frowned. "Why not?'' Then her eyes widened. "'Cause he might a' killed her when he found out she'd been cheating on him with somebody else?''

Kate nodded.

"He'd never do that. There's not a mean bone in that boy's body,'' she said, and sounded as though she was repeating something she'd heard an adult say.

"Could she have told someone else, told the father perhaps?''

Coral Anne shook her head. "Nope. We were each other's best friends.'' For the first time Kate saw Coral Anne's eyes begin to tear up. "But sending Jason to jail won't bring her back, will it?''

"No, it won't." Kate reached out and touched Coral Anne's shoulder. Coral Anne shook her off and stood.

"Listen, I got to get out of here before somebody recognizes my car. You tell Jason I know he's innocent, whatever anybody else says."

"Why don't you call him and tell him yourself? He's feeling pretty miserable."

"Yeah, I guess I could call him from the car," she said. "I sure can't call him from home."

"Thanks for coming over," Kate said as she ushered Coral Anne to the door of the motel room. "I really appreciate what it took for you to do it." She opened the door a crack, and saw that the parking lot was in deep shadow. The curtains at the office were closed and there was no sign of Myrlene. "Where'd you park?" she asked.

"Around the corner in back," Coral Anne said as she slipped by Kate. "I'll call Jason." She scuttled around the corner of the building, and a moment later a Camaro, already gray in the fading light, careened around the corner and into the street. Coral Anne drove as crazily as Jason. Maybe everybody under the age of twenty-five in Athena drove like lunatics.

Kate went back inside and shut the door, then sank into the chair Coral Anne had just left. *Momma would just kill her if she found out.* She hated to think that Mrs. Talley could have killed her own child and left her by the side of the road, but mothers did kill their children. As a matter of fact, in cases where children were killed, statistically, mothers were most often responsible.

Had Mrs. Talley been tucked up at home in her marital bed, shared with Big Bill, at the time that Waneath was killed? If David had been cruising the roads looking for Jason, might Mrs. Talley, or alternatively Big Bill, have been doing the same thing? Was Big Bill really a pussycat? Or more like a Bengal tiger?

CHAPTER FOURTEEN

KATE FOLLOWED her nap with a long and luxurious soak in the bath. Her shoulders ached from pure tension. What she needed was a good session at the gym with her trainer or a Rolfing session with her masseuse.

A voice in the back of her head told her there were better ways to dispel tension. She slapped the thought down. That kind of trouble she definitely did not need.

Still, she found herself taking extra care with makeup, wearing her best slacks, her silkiest sweater in just the right color of green to pick up the green tints in her eyes. She told herself she would not under any circumstances wind up in bed with David, but she'd be pretty disappointed if he didn't make a pass or two.

"Just let him hanker a little," she told her reflection. She picked up her purse and walked out of her room. This might turn out to be quite an evening.

The parking lot was not well lit at the best of times. At six forty-five on an early December evening, it was downright sepulchral. She moved quickly to her car, and was just getting her key in the lock when she heard the grate of a footstep behind her on the gravel.

"You drop this case, you hear?"

She froze, then she jabbed at the lock and twisted the key. She recognized that voice from the television. Big Bill Talley, all two hundred and fifty cheerful pussycat pounds, was making his move.

Kate pivoted, prepared to kick his kneecap and rake him with her keys if he came at her.

He swayed three feet away, his face mottled and streaked with tears, a pint of sour-mash bourbon clutched in his paw.

"That boy's got to die for what he did to my baby." His voice caught in a sob. "Don't you go getting him off."

"Mr. Talley…"

"He killed my baby!"

Kate opened the car door an inch. She'd had plenty of experience with drunks as clients. They changed from maudlin to enraged in an instant. One minute that bottle could be hanging limply from his hand, the next he might turn it into a weapon and smash it into her face. She prayed Coral Anne's daddy remained a pussy-cat even when he was drinking and miserably unhappy.

Arguments and explanations would have no effect on him. In his present condition he probably wouldn't listen. If he listened he wouldn't agree.

She felt desperately sorry for him, but frightened for herself as well. She needed to put a locked car door between her and him just in case he did turn ugly. "Go home, Mr. Talley," she said gently. "I'm so sorry for your loss."

Platitudes.

He took a step toward her, his face twisted with grief. "My loss?" His voice rose dangerously. "That's what my baby is to you? A loss?"

"A terrible loss. I lost my husband recently. I understand your grief. But convicting the wrong man won't bring her back."

"He's the right man! Don't you use some lawyer trick to get him off, you hear me? He's got to pay."

Kate heard the grief and the rage in his voice. Even a gentle man could go over the edge when his pain became too great to endure. "Please, Mr. Talley, let me call some-body to come get you..."

A light went on in the office, and the door began to open.

Big Bill cried, "Oh, foot!" and staggered into the dark-ness at the end of the building.

"Anything wrong?" Myrlene's mother called from the office door.

Kate leaned back against her car. She could feel her heart hammering against her ribs. She took a deep breath and said in what she hoped was a normal voice, "I'm fine, thanks."

"Who was that doing all that yelling?"

"Just some guy who'd had a little too much to drink and thought I might like some company for dinner. No prob-lem." That sounded pretty lame, but it was the best Kate could do on short notice. She certainly didn't want Myr-lene's mother making an issue of this. Once he sobered up, poor Bill Talley would probably be horrified at what he had done.

KATE PROTESTED, but Myrlene's mother called the sheriff's office anyway to report a near mugging. Kate intended to keep her own counsel. No sense in making a bad situation worse—not in a town where she was the outsider. Big Bill would look like the victim—which he certainly was—and garner all the sympathy. Everybody would shake their heads in sorrow at the terrible pass to which a good man had been brought by a wicked big-city woman.

"No, I can't identify the man," Kate said for the fourth time. She sat in a patched imitation-leather chair in the mo-tel office while a young deputy sat across from her with a look of concern on his face. "Except to say that he was big and not young."

"How you know that, ma'am?"

"His voice was deep."

"You must have seen him."

"It was dark."

"You sure kept your head better than I would," Myrlene's mother said, "I'd a' fainted dead away."

"Like I said, I don't think he meant to hurt me."

She turned to the deputy. "The man was upset that I wouldn't go to dinner with him. Period."

"Maybe he wanted your purse," Myrlene's mother said, as though that were a comfort. "Getting so not even a town like Athena's safe any longer."

"Kate?" David ran into the office, reached down, grabbed her upper arms and hauled her out of the chair and into his arms. "You all right? Sheriff Tait called me and said there'd been some kind of dustup."

For a moment she let herself relish the feel of him, the warmth of his body, then she shook him off. "No. I am mad as hell, and very, very hungry." She turned to the deputy. "We both know this isn't going anywhere, so I'm going to dinner. Okay?"

"But ma'am?"

"Deputy, just tell the sheriff what I say happened, will you? No real harm was done."

"Ma'am, be careful, you hear?"

"She will be," David said grimly. He propelled her out the door and toward his truck.

"Wait a minute, please," Kate said. "I need to lock the Navigator."

"The hell with it. If they steal it, they steal it. Get in the truck."

He spun out of the parking lot.

"Now I know where Jason gets his driving skills," Kate said.

"This isn't funny. I'm sending you home to Atlanta on the first plane out of Jackson."

"No."

"Kate…"

"No."

"You know damn well who did this, don't you?" David snapped. "Why didn't you tell the deputy?"

Kate sat silent.

"Damnation, Kate. It was Big Bill Talley, wasn't it?"

"What makes you think that?"

"Who else would it be? You said the man wasn't young. That means it's not one of the Athena High football squad looking for a hoo-rah."

"He was very drunk."

David turned to her. "You do know. First, Mrs. Talley smacks you, then Big Bill assaults you in the parking lot. The Talleys are the ones who belong in jail, not Jason."

"Maybe so, but I'm not about to put them there. Talk about garnering sympathy for the other side!" Kate heard David's growl. "He probably never did anything like that in his life—most people haven't. He's much more scared than I am right now. He probably sat around in his dealership this afternoon, got roaring drunk, maybe even heard that Coral Anne came to see me this afternoon…"

"What?"

"She did. And the way gossip flows in this town, I don't doubt someone saw her cut out of the parking lot and told him. So he got drunk and came over to intimidate me. Sounded like a good idea at the time."

"I'll kill him."

"No, you won't. First, because if he'd wanted to do any damage he would have, and second, Coral Anne says her daddy doesn't believe in physical violence."

"And you believed her?"

"I do. Momma's the dangerous one in that menage, as I have reason to remember."

"Do you usually have to put up with getting slapped in the face and mugged in parking lots in your job?" he asked.

"Not usually, but I have been threatened more than once."

"And you're all right with that?" He took his eyes off the wheel to glance at her.

"Of course I'm not all right with that! But no place is safe these days, and when I used to do criminal cases, I took precautions."

"Which I deprived you of."

"No. Lord, David! The minute we get to your house I have to call Arnold in Jackson. He needs to know about this. I suspect Big Bill shot his wad this evening, but if not, Arnold could be in danger. I'm going to tell him to stay in Jackson tonight. He can drive back to Athena after sunrise tomorrow."

"Good idea." David turned into the long gravel driveway leading to his house. "I wasn't certain you'd come tonight," he said.

"Why wouldn't I? I have to eat." Her voice sounded more confident than she felt. She had had some doubts about this evening.

"You need to take your own advice."

"Which is?"

"Spend the night with me and go back to the motel after sunrise."

Kate felt her heart rate increase. "Not a good idea."

"It's a great idea." He pulled in front of his house and turned off the ignition, then swiveled with his left arm along the steering wheel and his right hand on her thigh. "Think of me as your friendly neighborhood rottweiler."

Rottweilers did not have deep blue eyes and crinkly

smiles. She opened the car door and slid out quickly. "Maybe this isn't such a good idea."

He was supposed to be the one doing the hankering. She remembered Arnold's snide remark about her rampant hormones and remembered just how long it had been since anyone—much less David Canfield—had made love to her. Her hormone scale had every right to be off the top of the chart at this point. Not a good sign if she expected to keep her head.

She heard his car door slam and felt him behind her. He pressed his palm against her waist. She could have drawn the outline of David's hand on her skin from the heat it generated in her.

"Come on. Let me feed you. I won't press you, Kate, if you won't fight me."

"My adrenaline bottomed out about thirty minutes ago. There's no fight left in me. I'd take it kindly if you didn't push me right now. I might dissolve in tears, and then where would we be?"

"Better off than we are at the moment, at least from my point of view, that is, if you let me comfort you."

"Well, don't. I need some space. And some food."

Remarkably, he took her at her word, and twenty minutes later they sat across a small round table in his dining area, sipped an excellent Chardonnay and dug into shrimp étouffée and an artichoke salad. A fire crackled and popped in the big fireplace. The only other light came from candles on the table. Kate knew she was being set up. She simply wasn't certain how she felt about it. One part of her wanted to let the evening unfold David's way, making love, the other part warned her what a disaster that would be. She took refuge in chat. And knew David wasn't fooled.

"I had forgotten what a great cook you are," Kate said. "Must be why I married you."

"Must be." He grinned. "Since you and my momma can burn water."

"I'll have you know I've improved," Kate said haughtily. "I can heat up takeout in the microwave with the best of 'em."

"Alec didn't expect home-cooked meals?"

"He already had a good caterer. Alec expected a law partner and a hostess."

"And a trophy?" David asked, then shut his eyes. "Sorry, that was a nasty thing to say."

"It's at least partially true," Kate said. "Except that I'm no long-legged beauty queen, and he'd been divorced for years when we started dating. He wanted company and a colleague."

"Don't sell your legs short. What did you want?"

"I've had my share of anger this evening, David. You're not going to infuriate me with psychobabble. No, I did not seek out and marry a father figure—or at least, not principally a father figure. Frankly, I wanted to be the one loved for a change."

"And that means?"

She shrugged and took a sip of wine before she answered. "You know the old French saying—in love there is one who loves and one who lets himself be loved."

He set his glass down carefully. "And you thought I was the one who let himself be loved."

"Well, weren't you? All that adoration came so naturally to you. Lord knows I did my share of adoring."

"What you adored was some abstract idea of me." He picked up his fork and dug it savagely into a shrimp, but did not raise it to his mouth.

"An abstract you carefully constructed for public view— and I was just another member of the public so far as you were concerned. You never gave me a chance to know the real you—at least that's what you're saying now.''

He laid his fork down and expelled a deep breath. ''I learned early that no woman loves a man who fails. My momma taught me that. When Daddy got laid off, she tried very hard to be supportive, but she nearly tore him limb from limb from disappointment before he got another job. I think if he'd stayed out of work much longer, they'd have wound up in the divorce courts.''

''Not every woman reacts that way.''

''Most women do, no matter how hard they try not to.''

''Don't compare me to your mother. She never thought I was good enough for you.''

David laughed. ''At least you two had the same view of my life. You should have heard her when I told her I was leaving New York for Mississippi.''

''But with Melba? Surely she approved of that,'' Kate said dryly.

David reached across the table to take her hand. She tensed, but did not remove it from his grasp. ''She really liked you, Kate.''

Now Kate did remove her hand. ''Your mother? Get real.''

''She did. But your education and your background threatened her. And then when you threw me out…you have to remember that my mother always thought I was perfect.''

''Most mothers do think their sons are perfect.''

''Mine has mellowed a great deal since Daddy retired. She's softened.'' He shrugged. ''But she still can't cook.''

''But I'll bet she's still a cleaning fool, isn't she?''

He laughed, but then he sobered. ''We can't seem to get past who we were and what we did, can we? Will we ever be able to?''

"Not completely." She shoved her chair back from the table and stood. "Suddenly I've lost my appetite. You better drive me back to the motel."

He stood as well. "No way."

"David…"

"Look, you want to sleep in the guest room, then do it. You can lock the door, put a chair under the doorknob. I don't want you in that motel alone tonight, particularly now that Arnold's going to stay in Jackson."

"I'm too tired to argue with you. I feel as though I've been running for twenty years."

He came up behind her and began to massage the back of her neck. "You feel as though you've got iron bars running across your shoulders," he said softly.

SHE HELD HERSELF taut for a moment, then he felt her relax a bit under the pressure of his fingers.

"You remember when I used to do this every night?" he whispered. Her ear was delectably close to his lips. He fought the urge to take the lobe between his teeth. He knew that used to drive her crazy, but it was too soon. He had to go very slowly and carefully if he didn't want her to spring away from him again the way she had before. He knew darned well she was feeling vulnerable after what had nearly happened in the parking lot. A gentleman would not take advantage of that vulnerability.

He was through playing gentleman.

"I looked forward to it all day at work," she said softly. Then made a long drawn-out "um" sound. He smiled. He knew that sound. He was getting to her. Good.

His fingers stroked up the back of her neck. She bent her head with a sigh.

"I looked forward to other things," he whispered.

"Those, too." She chuckled. A low, sexy chuckle. He felt the hair rise on the back of his neck.

"We were good together, Kate."

"Yes."

"We can be again."

Her lowered head swung left and right in denial. "We're different people. Our lives have gone in different directions."

"Our lives may be different, but our bodies aren't." This time he did run his lips gently over her earlobe, then took it in his teeth and worried it softly.

She shivered against him.

"Being this close to you still sets me on fire." He slid his hands around her midriff and brushed his lips against the soft down at the nape of her neck. She gave a soft moan and let her head fall back against his shoulder.

"We can't do this," she whispered.

"We can. We should." His hands slid up her chest to cup her breasts so that his fingertips just grazed her nipples. They felt like pebbles, hard, erect, swollen under her bra.

She caught her breath as he caressed her, rolling the pads of his thumbs back and forth across her nipples. She didn't fight him, didn't protest, didn't move away. She felt so right leaning against him this way. Her head fit perfectly into the curve of his throat, her back arched slightly so that her bottom pressed against his groin.

"Katie, my Katie," he said softly. He stroked down over her belly and her thighs, then moved his hand to the inside of her thighs, caressing her through the soft wool of her slacks as though he could feel the tender flesh under his fingertips.

He prayed for the moment when she'd commit to him once more. He longed simply to let go, to lay her down and make love to her without conscious thought, letting pure sensation drive him. He fought to stay in control because he wanted this night to be perfect for her.

She'd always been perfect for *him*. From that first night when she'd come to him frightened and unsure, then wildly ardent, he'd only known true joy in her arms, buried in her body, touching her, her scent in his nostrils, her skin against his. He groaned softly.

Then without a word or a sound, in one smooth motion she lifted her arms to encircle his head, and twisted in his arms so that she faced him. Her eyes were half-closed, her lips parted. She was breathing as hard as he was. His heart lifted.

He sought her mouth, felt her tongue reach for his, tease, move over his lips and dart into his mouth. His hands slid down her back to cup her bottom against him. She began to move her hips slowly, sensually, then she stopped.

She broke the kiss to stare up at him with dreamy eyes. "This is crazy," she whispered. He smiled down at her.

"It's right," he whispered as his mouth sought hers once more. "We're right." His fingers worked under her sweater and unfastened her bra.

She ran her hand down the front of his chinos. He caught his breath at her touch. He was more than ready, but he knew from experience she had a long way to go to catch up. He would bring her along every step of the way and relish every moment. His fingers inched around the waistband of her slacks. "Where do these damn things open?" he gasped.

She smiled without breaking the kiss. "In back," she said against his mouth, and guided his hand to the button at the top of her waistband.

"You could help."

"My hands are otherwise occupied."

He caught his breath. "Don't let me interrupt you," he said hoarsely.

He felt his belt come out of the buckle, heard the slight pop as button parted from buttonhole.

"Hey," he said, and picked her up. "If we don't find a flat place before these pants wind up around my ankles, we're going to break both our necks."

She squeaked, kicked off her shoes, wrapped her legs around his waist and her arms around his neck. She bit his ear and began to nibble the edges like a hungry bunny. The feeling that shot through him was in inverse proportion to the softness of her touch. He felt as though someone had hooked up his extremities to electrodes and was cranking up the amperage second by second.

He turned with her locked around him and began to walk toward the stairs with his hands supporting her bottom and hers entwined around his neck.

As he reached the hearth rug, she whispered seductively, "This is flat."

"So it is," he said, and set her down. She slid down his body to the floor. He shoved off his sneakers, stripped off his socks and yanked his sweater over his head.

She wriggled out of her sweater and tossed it behind her, then reached for her bra straps.

"My job," he said. He slipped them off her shoulders, then ran his fingers gently under the bra to pull it away from her breasts. Her skin shone rose gold in the firelight, her nipples as rich as ripe peaches. He bent his head to encircle her nipple with his tongue and was rewarded with a long indrawn breath.

She tangled her fingers in his hair.

After a moment he raised his head, and his fingers found the zipper at the back of her slacks. He slid them down her legs and tossed them across the room. She wore black lace bikinis that barely covered the soft brown triangle at the apex of her thighs.

"I'm ahead," she said, groping for the zipper of his jeans. "You better catch up."

"That's the least of our problems," he said, and stripped.

She reached her arms up to him. "Now," she said.

"No, you don't," he answered. "Not yet." He hooked his finger in the center of the waistband of her panties. As he inched them down, his finger slipped into the crease between her thighs.

"Oh," she said, arching her back. As he tossed the panties behind him, her knees came up and her eyes closed. She encircled him and began to stroke him.

He kissed her breasts, her belly, ran his tongue around the edge of her navel. She moaned and opened her legs to his questing tongue.

"Every atom, every molecule, my Katie," he whispered as he bent his head.

KATE FELT TWENTY YEARS of separation slip away. It was as though she'd grown a thick reptilian skin the day he left, and now it was dissolving. The nerve endings of this new skin were raw and exposed to his lips, his fingers, his tongue, his body. She couldn't protect herself from sensation, from the aching in her loins. Her breasts felt as though they'd swollen two sizes in two minutes.

She'd almost forgotten how beautiful his body was, the soft whorls of brown hair on his chest, the line of down that descended across his navel to his abdomen and below. As she caressed him, she gasped at the size of him. How could she have forgotten how big he was in every way, from shoulders to hands to the erection that she knew would fill her to breaking.

And he would break her, she knew. She couldn't control

him or push him or fake him out. Not that she wanted to. He remembered how long it took her to be as ready as he was. He'd always been able to read her body, gauge her responses. She gasped.

Her eyes widened and her mouth opened. She dug her fingers into his shoulders. He'd learned a few things. His pace increased and she let herself go, feel as though every atom of her being was centered beneath his lips. She screamed as the spasms began.

A moment later he thrust into her, and she broke again immediately. She bucked against him wildly as her nails dug into his bottom as if she could force him even deeper into her. She lost conscious thought. She was all feeling and color—a kaleidoscope of sensation that drowned her in reds and purples.

She felt him tighten in her arms, and his body spasm inside her. As he sank against her, she wrapped her legs around his, wishing she could hold him inside her forever, but she knew she couldn't. When he finally rolled away, he pulled her with him so that she lay against his chest.

"Why did we wait so long?" he whispered against the top of her head. "I feel as though I've just woken up after twenty years."

She raised her head and rubbed her cheek against his chin. "Your beard's not long enough, Mr. van Winkle. It's supposed to be white and all the way down to your waist."

"It's my heart that has been unconscious, Katie, my love."

My love. He'd never called her that. Except for the one time he'd been so drunk he couldn't get his own shoes off, he'd never actually said the words *I love you.* She'd longed to hear them, tried every way she knew to evoke those words, but somehow he could never get them past his lips.

Now here she was at last, his love, when it was too late for either of them.

She didn't realize she was crying until the sobs broke through and threatened to choke her with grief.

"Kate?" he said urgently. "Katie? What have I said?"

She shook her head and sniffed to keep her nose from running. "Nothing. It's okay. Really. Call it endorphins."

He sat up and propped his back against the leather sofa behind him. She sat up as well, turned away and ran her fingertips under her eyes to slide the tears away.

"It's not okay," he said. He took her shoulders and twisted her so that she couldn't avoid looking at him. "Tell me." Then in a gentler tone. "Please, love."

That did it. She collapsed against his chest and let the tears flow. She didn't know precisely why she was crying. For lost youth and lost opportunities. For the two kids they had been. For the love that had shattered. For the years apart when they had grown in such different directions. Because it was too late now for love.

When she could speak, she said through the gulps and hiccups of tears, "You never told me you loved me."

"I told you over and over again, every moment of every day."

"No, never. Not in words."

"I showed you..."

"Doesn't count, David. I needed the words." She sat up and hugged her arms across her naked breasts. "You said I wasn't surprised when you were unfaithful. You're right. I knew you didn't love me because you couldn't force out those three words—'I love you.' They wouldn't come out of your mouth."

"And you thought that because I didn't say the words I didn't love you?" He opened his arms. "But I did. I do. I always will."

She shook her head. "You see. Even now, you can't quite bring yourself to say the words." She stared at the fire.

"Kate," he said. She felt his fingers stroke down her spine, and in spite of herself she shivered under his touch. "Before I met you, I don't know how many girls I said those words to. I had no idea what love was. To use the words with you I'd used so...effectively...on other women... There has to be something better, something beyond those words to express what I felt for you."

She wanted to see his eyes. "And Melba? Did you say those words to her?"

"Yes, before I met you, I did."

She nodded and turned away from him again toward the firelight.

"But after I knew you, Kate, since you taught me what love is all about, I've never said those words to any woman." He touched her shoulder. "Look at me."

Reluctantly, she acquiesced.

His eyes looked almost black in the reflected light of the fire. "Kate, I love you. I always have and I always will."

"Even if we never see each other again after this is over?"

"I won't consider that a possibility."

"It is, though."

"Planes fly, cars drive. Georgia's not that far from Mississippi."

"China is."

"I don't have to go."

"Sure you do. The most important thing I learned is that we have to have our own dreams. We can't submerge ourselves in anybody else's."

"There are other dreams. This, for instance."

The fire had begun to die. She shivered.

"You're cold."

"A little."

He stood and reached down a hand. "Then come to bed. I'll keep you warm."

She took his hand. Whatever else happened, she would remember this night for the rest of her life. For a small moment in time, she was complete again. Let tomorrow take care of itself.

CHAPTER FIFTEEN

DAVID WOKE at dawn with his face buried in Kate's hair, her body snuggled spoon fashion against his.

She still slept so quietly that he ran his fingers lightly over her rib cage to make certain she was still breathing. He blew her hair away from his nose before he could begin to sneeze, and smiled sleepily. The first time they had actually spent a night together—not simply a wild, passionate coupling after which one or the other of them had gone home to a solitary bed—he had woken in a state of terror, fearing that she really was dead in his arms.

That instant of panic had struck him with a sense of bereavement so terrible that he felt his own heart stop, until he felt her respiration under his fingertips. In that instant he'd known that she was central to his existence. He'd never lost that feeling, through all the years when his only contact with her was through newspaper clippings and conversations with her mother.

Why had he never been able to tell her how important she was to his very being in a way that she would understand and accept? Was it, as she said, his simple inability to say "I love you"? If so, he was an idiot. No, it was more than that. She'd held on to the crazy idea that he was somehow extraordinary—some kind of superstar who'd deigned to shower his favors upon her.

Whereas the reality was that she was the extraordinary one. From the beginning he had clung to her like a drowning man. And they had both lived in fear of allowing each one to sense the other's vulnerability. No marriage could survive with both parties working so frantically to maintain a fantasy.

He had seen the way his mother had turned on his father the moment he showed weakness, as though losing his job were a betrayal of her. He had watched his father endure that punishment day after harrowing day without complaint. He didn't have his father's strength of character. He'd rather lie than take a chance that Kate would react the same way his mother had.

He still wasn't certain he'd been wrong. Kate said he was, of course, that she would have understood and supported him. That was hindsight. When warriors failed in battle, they were sacrificed. He hadn't had the nerve to offer himself up that way. He could not allow himself failure, and certainly could never allow Kate or anyone else to see that he'd failed.

He still couldn't. Couldn't allow Dub or his son to see what a sham his marriage to Melba had been, couldn't allow anyone to get close to him, clutched his loneliness as though it were the only possession he had left. It had been a stupid way to live.

And even stupider to let his thoughts drift this way now that Kate actually lay in his arms, her naked bottom against his groin, the nape of her neck within an inch of his lips.

When he kissed her she sighed softly, and moved against him. They made gentle love, slow, sensuous, drawing out the pleasure of remembering one another's bodies again, until finally passion began to assert itself and he entered her. She responded wildly, wrapping her legs around his waist, digging her fingernails into his shoulders and finally crying out and arching her back against him. He sank onto her. She bit his shoulder and said something muffled against his neck.

He raised his head. "What?"

She smiled up at him sleepily. "And good morning to you, too."

He rolled off, gathered her into his arms and stretched luxuriously. "Better than coffee."

"Opposite effect." She snuggled and threw her leg across his body. "I want to go back to sleep."

"So you're still an early riser," he said, his right palm brushing the hair from her forehead.

She giggled. "You were sure up first *this* morning."

He chortled. "Wicked woman." He closed his eyes. "I can't believe you're here."

She caught her breath, untangled herself and sat up. "My God, neither can I! Am I crazy?"

He opened his eyes and put his arm around her waist to draw her back down. "If this is insanity, let's make the most of it." He kissed her, and she responded warmly.

Then she drew away. "We really cannot spend the whole day in bed, David. There's work to do." Her eyes widened. "Oh, Lord, Arnold! He'll probably send the sheriff out here to make sure I'm all right." She leaned across him and reached for the telephone on the bedside table. The action brought her naked breast very close to his face, so he raised his head and caught her nipple between his lips. He was rewarded with a gasp, and she dropped the phone.

Five minutes later, the damn thing began to whine. David looked over the edge of the bed to see that the handset had fallen from the cradle. "Damn," he said.

Kate reached down and replaced it. She kissed him lightly and slid across him, then swung her legs over the side of the bed and sat up. She picked up the phone and sat it on her naked lap. She dialed the phone, listened for only a moment, then said, "Arnold, it's me. Calm down. I'm fine." She listened some more, then glanced down at David. "I spent the night at David's."

He saw the flush spread over her breasts and up her face. "That is none of your business."

David heard the sputter from two feet away.

"It's okay, Arnold, really it is. Any sign of our masked avenger? No? Good." She shoved David over with the hand not holding the telephone and curled back against the headboard. David realized that she had shut him out as effectively as though he had left the room. Which seemed the appropriate move. He left her to it, went to the bathroom, brushed his teeth, shaved quickly and stepped into a hot shower.

He was standing with closed eyes, letting the water cascade down his face when he heard the shower door open. He felt her slide in behind him and grabbed her hands as they encircled his waist. "You want to smell like sandalwood too?" He slipped the bar of soap into her palm.

"Talk about your dead giveaways."

"What can I tell you? It's the only soap I have."

She giggled. "Oh, well, in for a penny, in for a pound. I'll scrub your back if you'll scrub mine."

KATE FINISHED drying her hair, checked her makeup—a fairly slapdash job created from the few items she carried with her in her purse—and opened the bathroom door. The aroma of brewing coffee and some sort of hot bread drifted up the open staircase from the kitchen area. David's king-size bed, which they had so recently ravaged, had been neatly made up; her clothes had been collected from downstairs and were neatly folded on the foot of the bed with her shoes sitting side by side on the floor beneath it.

She considered that she should have brought fresh underwear in her purse. But that would have been an admission to herself that she expected what had happened last night to happen.

"Can't have been that easy to find all this stuff," she whispered. From her recollection they had done some mighty clothes-flinging downstairs last night. "Miracle my bra wasn't hanging from the chandelier," she breathed as she shrugged it on and fastened it, then wriggled into her sweater.

As her head surfaced from the neck hole turtle fashion she caught her reflection in the mirror over David's bureau and walked closer to see whether her night of wild abandon showed in her face.

"Beard burn does a super job of exfoliation," she told her image. "Wonder if plastic surgeons have considered it?" She ran her hand down her cheek, which still tingled.

"Still talking to yourself in the morning?"

She turned to see David lounging against the bedroom door with a cup of steaming coffee held in front of him like an offering. Her heart turned over. Killer smile. Killer eyes. She'd known the moment she turned to face him in that jailhouse corridor that she was dead and done for all over again.

"Only when I'm truly exasperated with myself," she said, reaching for the cup. He tried to capture her waist, but she eluded him handily. "No you don't."

He sat on the bed. "Second thoughts?" He looked concerned, all right, but remarkably smug as well. She wanted to smack him. Instead, she kissed him.

"I knew what I was doing." She danced back. "Or I thought I did."

"So where do we go from here?"

That's the question she'd been dreading. She leaned her bottom against the dresser and sipped her coffee while his eyes scalded her soul and heated her body. She kept her voice light. "We don't go anywhere. Not together."

He came off the bed and had her upper arms in his hands before she could take a breath. "Listen, wench, if you think for one moment I'm going to let you walk out of my life again, you can just forget it."

"Down. Sit. I mean it."

He grumbled, but he went back to the bed.

"More than twenty years ago I walked into that theater, saw you sitting there and fell off a cliff. Took me most of that twenty to put the pieces back into some semblance of order. I'm older and, I hope and pray, at least a little smarter. I sure break easier. This time I'm going to find a nice, gentle pathway and take it one step at a time. And if you try to throw me over the edge, I swear I'll have you arrested for stalking."

"That's fair." He wiggled his eyebrows at her. "As long as I can shove a little in the flat places."

"Is that what you call last night? Shoving a little?"

He laughed, sat back and folded his arms behind his head. "No, that was actual Kate-tossing. Did it work?"

"What do you think? It worked to the point where I am ravenous. Do I smell food?"

His eyes widened and he sprang up. "Oh, Lord, I forgot the cinnamon rolls."

A moment later she heard him clatter down the steps two at a time.

DAVID HAD PROGRESSED from tumbling off his own cliff to figuring out the logistics of a life with Kate. As he took the cinnamon rolls—thirty seconds away from being over-done—from the oven and set them on a rack, he realized he hadn't come up with any workable plan. Of course, Kate would be around until she got Jason off—he'd begun to think she would actually get the boy off—then she would go back to Atlanta.

What the hell. Any time was better than the last twenty years of no time at all.

Going to China was out. No way would he go halfway around the world and leave her, and no way would he drag her with him. She had a job to do, a job she did very well for people who needed her. Besides, she loved it.

What on earth could he do to make a living in Atlanta?

As he set plates out on the counter for the rolls, the doorbell rang. He'd been so deep in thought he had not heard a vehicle arriving. "Arnold," he said. "The man must be part German shepherd."

He wiped his hands on the dish towel stuck in the waistband of his jeans as he went to the door and opened it.

"Dad? We've got to see you."

He barely managed to get out of the way of his son who was closely followed by Coral Anne Talley. She looked as though she'd been crying, and she clung to Jason's hand.

Five steps inside the door Jason stopped. "What's that smell? Man, am I hungry!" He started toward the counter, and David saw his eyes widen at the two plates and two glasses of orange juice as Kate started down the stairs.

She saw Jason and Coral Anne and stopped two steps from the top. David heard her "uh-oh" when Jason's eyes swung her way.

"I spent the night here," she said before Jason had a chance to open his mouth any wider than it already was. "David insisted I not stay at the motel after my encounter in the parking lot with Mr.—"

Coral Anne began to wail. "With my Dad. Are you gonna arrest him?"

"Of course not," Kate said, came the rest of the way

downstairs and walked over to the mantelpiece. "He was drunk as a skunk. Does he know you're here?"

The girl shook her head. "I snuck out and drove to Long Pond to speak to Jason. He said we needed to come see Mr. Canfield to find out what to do."

"The first thing to do is have some breakfast," David said. "There's plenty. Jason, pour some more orange juice. Have you taken up coffee drinking at school?"

Jason shook his head. He hadn't taken his eyes off Kate. "Coral Anne, go wait in the car," he said.

She stared from him to Kate for a moment, made an "oh" sound with her lips and bolted.

The moment the front door closed behind her, he turned to his father. "Man, you really did it. I cannot believe this!"

"Now, wait a minute, son."

"You gonna try to tell me you two didn't get it on last night?"

"Watch your mouth."

"Or you'll what? Have me up on contempt charges?"

"I'll wait upstairs," Kate said, and started for the stairs.

"Shoot, I don't know why." Jason's voice had begun to take on an edge of hysteria. "You've stuck your damn nose in everywhere else you weren't wanted."

"Stop it," David said.

"Oh, right. You're gonna tell me she spent the night in the guest room."

"Where Kate spent the night is none of your concern."

"Hell, yes, it's my concern. She's *my* lawyer. Shoot, Dad, did you kill Waneath just to get your old girlfriend back?"

David's stern voice cut him off. "Not girlfriend, sport. Wife. To have and to hold from this day forth until death do us part. That's the way it should have been, and the way it would have been if I hadn't been a damn fool.''

"David," Kate started.

He raised a hand to stop her.

Jason's breath rasped in his chest. "And if I hadn't been born, right?''

"Your conception was the only good thing to come out of this mess, and nobody—not me, not your grandfather, not your mother—ever thought of you as anything but a blessing. You didn't screw up by getting born. Your mother and I did some stupid things and made some bad choices, but we did the best we could at the time. So did Kate. I don't regret one moment of knowing you and loving you and having you for my son. If your mother were still alive, Kate wouldn't be here, but your mother has been dead for three years, son.''

"She's still my mother!"

"Yes, she is, and she wanted us to be happy—all of us, even me. Nobody knows what happens in a marriage, Jason, except the two people involved, and sometimes even they don't have a clue. But your mother and I both grew up a lot those last years. I know you think that Kate's being here is disloyal to her memory…''

"Not think, Dad, *know!*" Jason dropped his head. The room went silent.

After a moment he raised his eyes and looked straight at Kate. "You back in love with my dad?''

Kate caught her breath and looked at David. "I refuse to answer on the grounds that it may tend to incriminate me.'' She knew that her discomfort was making her glib.

Then, when she heard Jason's exasperated snort, she raised her hands. "You deserve a decent answer. I'm sorry. The real answer is that there is no 'back' to it. I've never stopped loving your father. But whether that means we have a future together, I don't know. Last night may simply have brought us to some kind of closure we didn't have twenty years ago. Does that make sense?''

''Yeah. I guess.''

''Do you hate me?''

''Nah.'' He sighed. ''I hate the *idea* of you, but my dad says I'd probably hate any woman who tried to take my mom's place.''

''I would never try that.''

''Good. 'Cause you couldn't. See, I know my mom had major big-time problems, but she was my mom and I loved her a lot. I miss her.''

''I'm sure you do.''

''So, look, I don't want to think about you and my dad…you know.''

''I can certainly understand that.''

''If we can just act like maybe we don't know…?''

''Son,'' David said, ''I'm not going to treat Kate as though she were simply your lawyer.''

''Yeah, I know, but could you maybe be…oh, shoot…*discreet* or something?'' He stared at his father, who frowned back at him. Then he shrugged and grinned. ''Yeah, I know. Not exactly what I've been the last couple of years, right?''

''Not really, no.''

''Well, I think that's an excellent way to handle it,'' Kate said, crossing to him. ''I don't know how successful we'll be in a town the size of Athena, but I'm willing to give it a shot. Deal?'' She stuck out her hand.

He stared at it a moment, then enveloped it in his large one. ''Deal.''

''Now,'' David said, ''get Coral Anne back in here and let's eat those cinnamon rolls while they're still at least warm.''

"Won't your dad have a conniption when he finds you gone?" David asked Coral Anne. She had already eaten two cinnamon rolls to Jason's three. That left five of the dozen David had baked, and from the avid looks on both youngsters' faces, it seemed fairly certain the others would disappear.

As if in answer, Coral Anne reached for her third roll. "It's Saturday. Daddy's already down at the dealership. I watched him drive off." She turned to Kate. "He's really sorry about last night, I know he is. He forgets sometimes how scary he can be, big as he is and all. He really takes stuff a lot harder than my momma." Coral Anne turned away quickly, but not before Kate saw tears in her eyes.

"It's all right, really," she said, touching Coral Anne's arm. "He scared me, but not that badly. I'll get over it. Please don't cry."

"It's not that!" Coral Anne said, and sniffed. She looked over at Jason, who stared at her with that slightly horror-struck look most men got on their faces when a female started to cry. "Every time Momma looks at me, I can see what she's thinking!"

"What is she thinking?" Kate asked quietly.

"Same as him!" Coral Anne pointed the remains of her cinnamon roll at Jason. "Momma and Daddy and every-body in town looks at me and thinks, 'How come she wasn't the one who died? Why'd it have to be Waneath?'"

Kate's heart sank. She opened her mouth to say some-thing, anything, but Jason forestalled her.

"Man, that's crazy!" he said. "Nobody's thinking that!"

Kate could have kissed him.

"They are! They are!" Coral Anne wailed.

Kate gathered the girl into her arms. "You're here, and you're alive, and thank God for it," she said. "You see that you stay that way, you hear me?"

Coral Anne snuffled. "Yes'm." She raised her head. "I wasn't gonna do anything stupid like kill myself."

"I was thinking more about trying to turn yourself into the perfect daughter to make up for Waneath," Kate said, although she had indeed been thinking that Coral Anne might do "something stupid."

"Fat chance. Look at me."

"I am looking at you. You know what I see? I see what Arnold calls 'a mensch.'"

"What's that?"

"A real person. Someone worth knowing."

"Yeah," Jason said.

"I echo that," David said. "Took guts to do what you did this morning—bringing Jason over here, trying to head off trouble for your dad."

"Took guts to come see me yesterday afternoon too," Kate said. "Give your parents time. I have never had a child to lose, but I've been told it's the worst possible pain any parent can endure."

"I've lost a sister!" Coral Anne said. "They don't seem to even notice that."

"Remind them."

"Anyway," Coral Anne said with a deep sigh, "thanks for not doing anything to my daddy. I think he'd probably like to apologize, but he doesn't know how."

"Don't worry about it. Now, if I can catch a ride back to the motel, I really need to find Arnold and get some work done." She looked at David.

Jason said, "We'd take you, but..."

"No. But maybe you should come with us. You don't need to be seen driving around town with Coral Anne. Her car is very recognizable."

"And I've got to get down to the library so I can tell my momma where I've been without lying about it," Coral

Anne said. "She'll believe that. She doesn't have the first notion whether the library opens at seven in the morning or noon on Saturday. She's not much of a reader."

"Okay that's settled. We'll take Jason home if he doesn't mind squeezing into the truck with Kate," David said.

"Yeah, sure, no problem," Jason replied. "You go on, Coral Anne. Thanks for coming. Do you think you can manage to come back? I'm really tired of staying in that house by myself."

The girl gave a good imitation of a pup that has just been patted on the head. "Sure."

Coral Anne waved out her window as she drove away. Jason looked after her wistfully. Kate wondered whether now that the beautiful Waneath was no longer in the picture, Jason might come to appreciate the intelligence of the younger sister. Probably not. Not when he was surrounded with hard bodies in minuscule bikinis at Pepperdine. Hard on Coral Anne when she so obviously adored him—and not like an older brother. Must have been hard for her to see him mooning around with Waneath.

"It's about time somebody had a little etiquette session with Big Bill Talley," David said as he watched Coral Anne's taillights disappear around the curve in the road.

"Don't you dare!" Kate said. "That's all we need. You make him mad, he'll break you in two."

"Hey!" David said. "I've got ten years on Bill Talley."

"And he's got fifty pounds on you," Jason said. "Drop it, Dad." He punched his father's shoulder. "We Canfields are lovers, not fighters." He realized what he'd said and looked at Kate in horror.

She laughed. "Get in the truck. I've got work to do."

"So do I," David said. "Unfortunately. A whole day of chores. Not the way I expected to spend the day." He surreptitiously squeezed Kate's thigh.

Once they were packed in the front seat, David turned the key. Instead of a purr, a metallic whine like an angry banshee issued from under the hood. "Damn!" David said, and tried again with the same result.

"Sounds like your flywheel finally bit the big one," Jason said as he climbed out. "Pop the hood, Dad."

David popped it and joined his son. Kate climbed out and walked over to sit on the bottom step of the porch. She was rewarded with the sight of two nearly identical tight male jeans-covered butts bent under the hood of the truck. She visualized the near one, which belonged to David, as it had looked when he got out of the shower that morning.

She blinked to cut off the libidinous thoughts she was having. He was a man with a nearly grown son and she was old enough to be that son's mother. But she felt the same as she had the first time she and David made love, when they'd wandered onto the college campus at dawn hand in hand, while the world seemed new, washed with shades of pale gold and lavender. When nothing could tarnish the love she felt.

Enough, already! She had a job to do. Last night was an interlude. Couldn't be more than that.

She watched Jason and David squabbling amiably about the best way to get the flywheel to work. Amazing how alike they were. At least Melba had been honest about Jason's parentage.

And she must have had a good deal to do with Jason's good nature as well. Would Kate have done as well if Jason had been her son? She was finding it more and more difficult to despise Melba. The French said that to understand all was to forgive all. At least in her case they seemed to be right.

Besides, it was considerably easier to forgive Melba dead

than it would have been to forgive her if she'd still been holding on to David.

"Try it now," Jason said.

David walked around to the driver's side and slid in. She heard the key turn. The engine caught.

"All right!" Jason said. "Come on, Mrs. Mulholland."

"Why don't you call me Kate?" Kate said as she climbed back in.

"Yeah, okay. Dad, you better let me take the truck over to Jimmy's. That flywheel's got to be replaced. I'll give him a hand. Get me out of the house. Don't let the engine die or we'll be in deep doo-doo."

"You can take the Navigator," Kate said.

"Not necessary," David said. "We'll drop you at the motel. I'll drive back to Long Pond, pick up Dub's Cadillac, and Jason can take my truck over to Jimmy's."

"Won't Dub need his car?" Kate asked.

"Shoot," Jason said. "Granddaddy's got a brand-new truck he'd a whole lot rather drive than the car. He saves that land yacht for company and church."

ARNOLD HAD apparently been staring out the window of his motel room, because when David drove up, he opened the door before Jason opened his to let Kate out. David jumped out and left the engine running.

"It's a conspiracy," he whispered to Kate as he helped her out. "All I want is to slam your door behind us and take you back to bed."

"Our chaperons would be shocked," Kate said.

"Tonight, woman, you are mine."

"Oh, really?"

"Yeah, really."

"Oh, go fix your flywheel."

She stood beside Arnold while father and son drove

away, then she held up her index finger. "Not one word, Arnold Selig."

"Kate…"

"I mean it. I may be crazy, but I feel more alive than I've felt in twenty years."

"Besides, I'm so thrilled your acne's cleared right up," Arnold said sarcastically.

"He's changed, I've changed. We can be totally honest with each other now. We don't have all the pressure on us any longer."

Arnold looked at her as though she'd grown a second head. "You, my sweet, are living in a bigger fantasy world than Jason. Nobody is ever totally honest with anyone, and certainly lovers are incapable of dealing with each other honestly. We are talking lovers, right?"

Kate felt the blush. "Yes, Arnold. And that is *so* none of your business."

"Don't get snippy with me. I spent a productive night coming up with enough case law to change Jason's venue to the third moon of Jupiter."

"Arnold, you're wonderful and I don't appreciate you. So, come on, show me all this case law. We can finish the paperwork and dump it on that judge first thing Monday morning."

As the final pages slid out of Arnold's portable printer, Kate leaned back and rubbed the back of her neck. "You deserve a raise."

"Make me a senior partner in the law firm."

"Sure." She smiled at him. "Seriously, at the spring partners' meeting I intend to give that my best shot."

"They won't agree. I'm not a rainmaker. Who wants a guy who can't stand up in court without vomiting?"

"Who makes the rain anyway? The litigators or the guys like you who seed the clouds? I couldn't survive without you. You deserve the money and the prestige if anyone does.''

''Prestige, schmestige. And I make enough money.'' He held up a hand. ''I never said that. I guess I'm looking for vindication. Something to say that I'm valued and valuable.''

''You are.''

''By you, maybe. And I was certainly valued by Alec. The others, who knows?'' He propped his feet on the bed. ''So, when's he moving to Atlanta?''

''Who?''

''Big D.''

Kate lay back on the bed. ''We have had one night. He's not moving, I'm not moving. Nothing's changed.''

''Right. It's not nice to lie to your lawyer.''

Kate rubbed her eyes with the heels of her hands. ''When you're twenty you have all the choices in the world. We've both made our choices. We have responsibilities. Whatever he says, he loves Long Pond, loves that charming old bastard Dub, loves his son…''

''And loves you.''

''Possibly. And I love what I do.''

''Kate, I hate to say this, but what you do is one hell of a lot more portable than what he does.''

She opened her eyes. ''Huh?''

''You don't think Pink Tarber in Jackson wouldn't take you on as a senior partner in a heartbeat? You spend half your time on the road in any case. If you are serious about this Canfield guy, maybe you should consider the choices *you* have.''

CHAPTER SIXTEEN

So KATE WANTED him to keep his distance from Big Bill Talley? David pulled Dub's Cadillac into the parking lot outside Talley's car dealership. "I don't think so," he said as he turned off the key. Kate might be willing to forgive and forget, but whether he'd intended to or not, Big Bill had scared her. He needed to know his behavior was unacceptable.

And David didn't require anyone's permission to look after the people he loved. And he did love her. Heaven knew what he could do about it. He wanted the world simply to disappear so that he could spend a lifetime relearning her body, her heart, the feel of her breath on his cheek...

He pulled open the door of Big Bill Talley's showroom and walked in. At nearly noon on a blustery December Saturday, there were precious few people around except three salesmen lounging in their office cubicles drinking coffee and reading *Road and Track*. David walked down the hall past them, and was rewarded with the sound of chairs and boots hitting the floor behind him as they recognized him. He knocked on Big Bill's door and opened it without waiting for an answer.

"Bill? Got a minute?" he said from the doorway.

Big Bill Talley sat behind an acre of walnut desk with his head propped in his hands and a giant mug of what was probably coffee beside him. When he raised his head, David's eyes widened. The man looked deathly ill.

Behind him, David heard footsteps, and a deep voice said, "Bill, you okay?"

David had not thrown a punch in years, although he'd acquitted himself well in a few brawls when he was in high school and college. He would definitely get the worst of it if he wound up fighting off three loyal salesmen, middle-aged or no, not to mention Big Bill, who made two of him.

He stepped into the office and closed the door between him and the man at his back. "Need to talk to you, Bill," he said quietly.

"Hey!" a voice said from the other side of the door.

"It's all right," David said. He wasn't certain that Bill recognized him for a moment. "I'm not here to make trouble," he said to Bill. "Call off your watchdogs."

"Yeah, okay," Bill whispered as though he couldn't bear to hear his own voice reverberate in his ears. "Go 'way!" he said to the door.

David heard grumbles and receding footsteps. He knew they'd all be standing in the doorways of their cubicles listening for the sounds of warfare.

Bill seemed to gather strength and pulled himself to his feet. "What the hell are you doing here?"

"Sit down, Bill," David said. "We need to talk."

"We got nothing to say to each other. Get the hell out of my place of business before I throw you out."

David felt the inevitable surge of adrenaline and resisted the childish urge to say "Yeah, you and what army?" He held up his hands. "Hear me out first. Then if you want to throw me out, have at it."

Bill narrowed his eyes and stayed on his feet, but he made no move to come around the desk. "That lawyer woman gonna have me arrested?"

David took a deep breath. "No. She understands you're

under a hell of a lot of pressure. So do I, because I'm under it too.''

''You?''

''Me. Listen, Bill, you and I don't know each other well, but we've known each other a long time. Our children have practically lived in each other's houses all their lives…''

''I wish to God my baby had never met any of you!''

''We all loved her.''

''Love?'' Bill started around the desk. David held up a hand to stop him.

''Love. I swear to you, Jason did not hurt her.''

''You swear? You swear? What the hell do you know about it?''

''The point is, unless we can find enough evidence to show he's innocent, to get the district attorney to drop the charges, he's going to stand trial. And meanwhile, the person who killed Waneath will get off scot free. At the moment Jason's lawyer is trying to find the real culprit…''

''Do some fancy footwork to get Jason off is what you mean.''

''No. Kate doesn't work that way. Can we sit down here? I promise I won't take but a minute more.'' Bill swayed uncertainly, then collapsed into his chair as though his legs wouldn't hold him any longer. David took a deep breath and sat in the client's chair across from him. He leaned forward with his forearms on his thighs, clasped his hands under his chin and held Bill's eyes. ''Jason is the one who wants to be down here, but I wouldn't let him come. He feels guilty as hell for letting Waneath walk away from him Saturday night. That's all he did, and he's going to have to live with it for the rest of his life. Let the jury decide whether he's guilty of anything else. Punishing him for something he didn't do is not going to bring Waneath back, and it's tearing this town apart—tearing your family apart and mine as well.''

''What the hell do you mean, tearing my family apart?'' Bill started to rise once more.

''You have another daughter,'' David said quietly, knowing that he was venturing into forbidden territory. ''She thinks you and her mother wish she was the one who died.''

''What?'' Talley said. He sounded stunned.

''You lost a child, and she lost a sister. She needs you badly, and she's scared to death that between your parking-lot forays and Mrs. Talley's slapping Kate across the face...''

''She did what?'' Talley surged to his feet.

David stood as well. He didn't intend to get socked sitting in his chair. Bill was near breaking. ''At the jail after Jason's bail hearing she slapped Kate across the face. I assumed you knew.''

''Oh, Lord!''

David took two steps back. ''I came to tell you how sorry I am, we are, for your loss, and to tell you that my son is not responsible. You may not believe me now, but one day you will. When that day comes, I hope we can share your grief. And to ask you not to let your anger spill over onto Jason's lawyers. They're just doing their jobs.''

Bill's chest heaved. David didn't know whether with anger or unshed tears. He decided not to wait around to find out. From the doorway he said over his shoulder, ''In the meantime, the daughter you have left is a very fine person who needs you badly. Thanks for seeing me, Bill.''

He walked back down the hall past the men who lounged in their cubicles in mock relaxation. With every step, David felt certain he'd hear Big Bill's roar giving a command to attack, but nothing happened. He climbed into Dub's car, cranked the engine and backed out of the parking space while a dozen pairs of eyes followed him. He didn't begin breathing properly until he hit the highway. Had he made things worse? Had Kate been right?

Right or wrong, he had to try. Chances were she'd never find out what he'd done. Here he was already keeping secrets from her. Damn.

AFTER LUNCH, Kate left Arnold to catch up on the sleep he had missed the night before. The Christmas carols playing in the square reminded her that she had not yet bought a single present for anyone—not that she had many people to buy for. The office took care of the client presents, and for years the partners had eschewed giving one another meaningless gifts. She still sent her college roommate a book for each of her three children, and there was her mother…

Now there was David. And Jason. And Dub. And Arnold. As good friends as she and Arnold had been previously, these last few days in Athena had brought them closer.

The best present she could give the crew from Long Pond was to get the charges against Jason dropped before Christmas. Monday morning she planned to go at that little chore full bore. Allenby had very little evidence connecting Jason to the crime. With luck, the autopsy report from Memphis would arrive today with some hard facts that would help Jason's case. With luck…and a good deal of prayer on her part.

Wandering down the sidewalks of Athena past the small antique shops, the hardware store advertising ax handles and red wagons, smelling the fresh southern pine and holly, even feeling the soft December breeze ruffling her hair, tossed her back into childhood Christmases when there were packages galore.

She did not want to wake up on Christmas morning alone

in Barbados or Aspen. She wanted to wake up in David's big bed and know that there were scads of packages downstairs under a fresh Christmas tree—none of this artificial stuff—heavy with decorations and lights and reaching to the peak of his great-room ceiling.

She stared in shop windows. What on earth could she buy any of these people? She didn't know them, their tastes, their sizes, even what or whether they read. And suddenly it became very important to spend some money on Christmas now, today, this afternoon, before she lost her nerve or her spirit. She longed to buy David something beautiful and frivolous and expensive.

She hopped into the Navigator and drove out of town toward Long Pond. Neva Hardin would know what to get.

She walked up to the front door of Long Pond shortly after two in the afternoon. According to David, Dub had begun to take naps in the afternoon. With luck she wouldn't see him. He wouldn't even have to know she'd come to the house.

No such luck. The door was opened, not by Neva, but by Dub himself. He did not look overjoyed to see her.

"What do *you* want? Jason's not here."

"I know that. Actually, I came to see Neva."

"Neva? What the hell for?"

For a moment, she thought he would bar her way, then he stepped aside. "Hell, come on in. Neva's in the kitchen."

"Thanks. Before I go hunt her up, I wanted to apologize to you."

"You lied to me," Dub said. "Made me look like a damn fool."

"I didn't lie. I simply didn't volunteer the whole truth."

"Huh. That's lawyer guff." He blocked her way to the

kitchen by simply not moving out of the hall. She could either slip past him or stand and talk.

Okay, that's what he wanted. "Frankly, I didn't stop you because I couldn't figure out how to do it without making things worse. And I never thought Brenda Starr on the local paper would find out who I used to be and publish the facts for the world to see."

"She sure found out easy. You sure you didn't tell her? You or that Arnold?"

"I never made a secret of my name or my first marriage even though I went back to my maiden name after the divorce. If she checked me out in anything that had all my names, she'd have seen Canfield listed as one of them. It's not that usual a name. Enough to set off any decent reporter's radar, I suppose. I've never found they needed more than a hint to go haring off over what they hope is scandal."

"Yeah. Scandal."

"Not that this was a scandal. Admit it, Dub, you're mad at me because I didn't tell you who I was before you mouthed off, not because it matters in any substantive way."

"Well, shoot, never did matter before, when David's ex didn't have a face or a name." He dropped his head.

"Isn't that what generals say? Never put a face on your enemy. It's very hard to massacre someone real. Some faceless nitwitted girl in New York who tossed David out on his ear was a figure of fun—just somebody Melba pulled a good trick on."

"Same's true for you," Dub said. He walked into his study. Intrigued, Kate followed him to find him staring up at the portrait over the fireplace. "You didn't know Melba face-to-face."

"No, I didn't, and yes, it is hard to hate someone you

put a face on. I could hate Melba like poison before. Now that I've met you and Jason, now that I know what she went through, I'm casting around for someone to hang all my anger on. Unfortunately, the only person handy any longer is myself.''

"Yeah. My daddy used to say folks spend their lives doing dumb things and trying to make out like they're smart.''

"Your daddy was absolutely right.''

"About that. Not about much else.'' He sounded desperately tired, and Kate noticed a twitch at the corner of his right eye. Beneath his farmer's tan his skin had taken on a yellow sheen.

He sank into his big chair without waiting for her to sit, and stared at the fire without speaking. Kate walked over and sat on the leather love seat across from him.

"Funny,'' he said, still with his eyes on the fire, "I spent my whole life trying to keep Long Pond and my family out of the way of scandal. Don't know why. We been scandal-prone long as I can remember, from my uncle Willy who got caught up in Peacock Alley wearing a dress, to Momma's burning the house down 'cause she was drunker'n Cooter Brown, to Melba's coming home from New York knocked up by a married man. And now this—this mess—with Waneath.''

"I grew up with secrets, too,'' Kate said softly.

"You are gonna get the boy off, aren't you?'' Dub said, raising his eyes to hers.

Kate was surprised to see that they were red-rimmed, as though he'd been crying. "I hope so.''

"Lord, so do I.''

"So, am I forgiven for keeping my status from you?''

"I'd forgive the devil himself if he could get Jason out of this mess.''

"I'm doing my best, and so is Arnold. Don't underestimate him. He's the real mover and shaker. I just stand up in court and run my mouth. He's the ventriloquist. I'm just the dummy."

"Shoot, I don't believe that for a second." For the first time, Dub's mouth twitched in a smile. "When you leaving?"

"Can't wait, huh? Give me a couple more working days before you kick me out. The autopsy report's due any minute from Memphis. With any luck it'll have enough evidence to clear Jason."

Dub sat up, his eyes narrowed. "How you figure that?"

"No idea, but what passed for an autopsy here didn't do much except take blood and urine samples and say that Waneath appeared to be pregnant and to have met her death by blunt trauma, probably with a tire iron. Let's hope a full autopsy by a qualified pathologist will add some facts to that. Facts that help rather than hurt—things like analysis of the rust on the tire iron. Blood-typing of the fetus. Worst case—we won't learn anything helpful. Best case—we'll have some indications leading to another suspect."

"Can't have that boy standing trial for something he didn't do, even if it does keep him at Long Pond instead of California."

"Keep your fingers crossed. Now, I really did come to see Neva." She stood, but Dub did not stand with her. For a southern gentleman of his generation, that denoted sheer exhaustion or complete oblivion. She left him staring at the fire with his hands on his knees.

CHAPTER SEVENTEEN

KATE PULLED UP at the motel and picked up the flat package from the back seat. Even after her visit with Neva, she'd only been able to come up with a single present, and that one was for Arnold. In one of Athena's small antique shops she'd found a framed Daumier print of a French nineteenth-century lawyer. Arnold would love it.

But she'd found nothing for David. She wondered for a moment how he'd react if she were to wrap herself up and tie a bow around her waist.

The problems between them hadn't been expunged by one night of passion, no matter how glorious. She was afraid he was right when he said she could never fully trust him again. And that would destroy any chance they had for happiness together.

He didn't deserve that.

"Mrs. Mulholland?"

Kate turned to see Myrlene trotting down the walkway waving a thick manila envelope. "Momma said this came in the mail for you. I thought you might want it right away."

Kate took it. The autopsy report. "Thanks, Myrlene. I definitely do."

"You look like you could use an extra hand," Myrlene said. "Here, let me take that." She took Arnold's print while Kate dug in her purse for the room key.

"Thanks. Just put it on the bed."

"Okay." Myrlene lingered, obviously looking for a little gossip.

Kate, who longed to slit open that envelope, tried to keep the impatience out of her voice. "You know that Jason's out working with Jimmy?"

"Yeah. He called me at lunch. Going to take most of the day to replace that flywheel. Mr. Canfield ought to buy a new truck. That one's got almost two hundred thousand miles on it."

"No doubt you're right." Kate smiled, but did not sit down. She fought the urge to shove Myrlene out the door and slam it behind her.

"Well," Myrlene said. "Guess I'll get back to work. Saw you with Mr. Canfield this morning. He sure is a hunk." She turned with her hand on the doorknob. "Funny, the most eligible hunks in town are three generations of the same family." She shrugged, smiled and left.

Kate grabbed the phone and dialed Arnold's room. "Wake up, sleeping beauty. Autopsy report's here."

"Right. Don't open it until I get my pants on."

DAVID STOPPED by the cotton gin, saw that there was no one there—not surprising. The cotton had all been baled and shipped. No reason to work night and day this late in the year. Maintenance could start on Monday morning. He had a list on his computer of parts to be ordered for the farm equipment. He drove around the barren fields aimlessly, unable to focus on anything except Kate.

Finally, he pulled into a small grocery and bought himself a cold drink and a ham sandwich. Then he drove down by the lake to eat a solitary lunch. He did love winter in the South. Plenty of people hated it. Barren trees, too much mud, weather that flip-flopped from warm and sunny to black glare ice and sleet in an hour. He didn't want to leave all this for life in a city. But he also didn't want to lose Kate again.

He sighed, gathered up the remnants of his meal and dropped everything into a trash barrel. Then he climbed back into Dub's car. As he leaned over to slide behind the wheel, a flash of red caught his eye. Dub was downright finicky about his cars. David reached down in front of the passenger seat and picked up the small red oval object.

For a moment he had no idea what it was. Then he felt a rush of adrenaline as his subconscious mind identified it. He'd seen that color enough times, seen talons like that every time Waneath came over to visit Jason. It was an acrylic fingernail. Waneath's color.

He closed his eyes and felt that sandwich threaten to come back up.

Waneath had lost a fingernail the night she died. The sheriff had scoured the spot where Jason parked, scoured the crime scene, but had not found it. He predicated that she had lost it fighting with her attacker.

Now here it was, lying on the floor of Dub's car. That could mean only one thing. Waneath had been in this car the night she died.

But why? When? Why had Dub not mentioned it? Jason never drove the Cadillac. Besides, he'd been driving his own car that night.

Thoughts tumbled through his brain as he started the car and backed out into the road.

It was time for Dub to answer a few questions.

"GIVE IT HERE!" Arnold said, and reached for the still-unopened envelope.

"Well, don't stand there, open it!" Kate said as she plumped down on her bed. Arnold pulled the sheaf of papers and photographs from the envelope and ran his eye down them quickly.

"She was barely two months pregnant," Arnold said. "That lets Jason off the hook. Oh, God, look at what the first autopsy missed."

"What?"

"The pregnancy. It was ectopic." He dropped the papers on the bed and walked out of the room.

Kate found him standing across the parking lot staring up at the bare December trees.

He turned to look at her as though he didn't see her. "Sorry, Kate."

"Arnold, I'm so sorry."

"Yeah. Sometimes I don't think about Shirley for weeks, and I think I'm getting better, and then something like this…"

"Can you face it? Do you want to go back to Atlanta?"

"Don't be ridiculous." He put his arm around her.

The gesture startled her. He was not a touchy person. She wrapped her arms around him and hugged him hard. She felt his body stiffen into resistance, then he relaxed and gripped her back.

After a moment he broke the hug and stepped back. "Won't that raise a few Athena eyebrows!" He glanced at the motel-office window. The curtain fluttered, and he curled his lip at it. "It will be all over town in a nanosecond that Jason's lawyers are canoodling on the lawn."

She linked her arm through his. "Passion in the pines?"

"Let's get back to work." They started back to the room, its door still open.

"So, what else did the death doctors in Memphis find out about our corpse?" Arnold picked up the report again.

Kate noted that his hands shook slightly. He was considerably more upset than he let on, but she took her cue from him. He wanted glib, then glib it would be.

"I'll be damned!" he said. He shoved Kate over and sat beside her. "Look at this. There was pink dust in her hair."

Kate grabbed the report from his hand and ran her eye down it. Then she glanced up at Arnold. "We've been seeing this all wrong."

"We're not the only ones. You know what this could mean, don't you?"

"I'm afraid I do."

"We have an obligation to our client. We have to clear him any way we can. We'll have to turn this over to the D.A."

"Not until we're certain of what we're talking about." She stood and pulled open the bureau drawer. She pulled out the crime-scene photos and tossed them on the bed. "Now these pictures begin to make a little sense. Look at them."

Arnold picked up the photos and fanned through them. "What am I looking for?"

"Her knees. And her feet and legs."

"So? She apparently walked away without her panty hose."

"They were in Jason's car, but we already know that. That's not what I mean." Kate leaned over the bed. "I never really paid attention before. See the bruises on her knees? They were made before she died or the blood wouldn't have pooled there the way it did. And the spots of mud and dirt on her legs? And the scratches? They're just visible, but the autopsy makes a note that she has several small scratches from briars or something on her ankles and calves."

"Yeah?"

"So look at her shoes, Arnold. They're perfectly clean. Polished, nearly new leather pumps."

"I'm not with you."

Kate took a deep breath. "Her legs are dirty, the soles of her feet are filthy. Her knees are bruised. The crime-scene reports mud *inside* the shoes, Arnold, but the shoes themselves are clean on the outside. Wherever she walked, she walked barefoot."

"The last of November?"

"It was warm, remember—well into the sixties even that late at night. Otherwise I doubt she and Jason would have been too comfortable making love in the back seat of his car."

"He never said she was barefoot when she walked away from him."

"No, he didn't. We'll have to ask him, but I don't think she was. Even mad as he was, I doubt he'd have let her go tramping off down the road in her bare feet. Come on, Arnold, we need to take a ride out to where Jason left Waneath and then out to Long Pond. I have a very, very bad feeling about this."

DAVID STOOD OVER Dub, who had not moved since Kate left. He held out his hand. On his palm lay the small red fingernail.

"What the hell's that?" Dub asked.

"One of Waneath's fake nails," David said. "Guess where I found it?"

Dub blinked, then shrugged. "No idea."

"I found it on the floor of your car."

"So?"

"She lost it the night she died. That means she was in your car, Dub. Why?"

"What?" Dub sprang from the chair, his fists clenched at his sides. "What the hell are you talking about, boy?"

"Don't lie to me, Dub," David said, his anger fighting with his weariness and despair. "Did you kill her?"

Dub's face turned a fiery red. "You're crazy! Why would I kill her? I didn't even see her that night."

David shook his head. "Then somebody drove your car, and I don't think that's possible." He looked into Dub's eyes. The older man dropped his. He was breathing hard. "She came to you, didn't she, to ask you to drive her home? Why on earth would you kill her, Dub?"

"Stop saying that!" Dub was almost howling. "I didn't kill her. It wasn't like that!"

David leaned his backside against Dub's desk. "Then you know who did, and it wasn't Jason. How in hell could you put him through this? I thought we all loved each other."

"Oh, right, you love me, Jason loves me." Dub threw up his hands and strode over to the fireplace to stare up at the portrait. "You've been a damn prisoner for twenty years just waiting for your chance to break out of jail." He turned malevolent eyes toward David. "Now you've got your chance—you and that ex-wife of yours. God, Melba hated that woman!"

"Melba hated Kate because she knew Kate was the only woman I ever loved, ever could love." David heard his own voice rising. "Hated Kate because she felt guilty over what she'd done to her, to me, to us. Kate did nothing to her, nothing except fall into the trap she set. So did I." He ran his hand over his head. "Hell, so did Melba. It was a bigger trap for her than for me. You want to feel sorry for somebody, feel sorry for your daughter—the woman you taught that it didn't matter who you trampled all over as long as you got what you wanted."

"I've never done that. I've treated you like the son I never had."

"Yes, and I've paid you back a hundred, a thousandfold, and glad to do it. Because I respected you, respected what you'd made of Long Pond and of yourself. Because however mistaken you were, you loved Melba, and I thought you loved Jason."

"I do!" It was a wail.

"That's your idea of love? To let him go to jail for something you did?"

"He'd never have gone to jail. I wouldn't have let that happen."

"But you'd let him sweat bullets, sit in that jail, go up before a judge in handcuffs and chains, put him through hell?"

"Yes!" Dub shouted. "Yes. Oh, I didn't like it, but then I thought, hell, the boy's had it too easy all these years—it's all been handed to him on a silver platter. Doesn't appreciate it, never did. Doesn't appreciate Long Pond. Wants to go off and make fool movies. Maybe a couple of nights in jail, maybe a little worry'll knock that nonsense right out of his head. Know who his real family is, where his loyalties lie. He can't go back to that California school now, can he? He'll go to Mississippi State and take agriculture and come home to Long Pond. Do what he should have done all along." The face he turned to David was stricken. "I had to give up my dreams for Long Pond. Why the hell shouldn't he?"

"You really believe that?"

"Yes." Dub said, and suddenly he thrust his great silver head straight up and pulled himself erect. He stood in front of that portrait of his wife and daughter like a prince or a duke. "This is his destiny, the same way it's yours. I promised my daddy, and I won't break my promise."

"So you killed Waneath to keep Jason in Athena?" David shook his head. Could Dub be this crazy?

"I tell you, I didn't kill the woman!"

"Well, somebody sure as hell did."

"No, they didn't." Suddenly Dub collapsed and sank into the wing chair on the side of the fireplace. He dropped his head into his hands. "It was an accident."

"An accident? You expect me to believe that?"

"I'm telling the truth." Dub looked up. His face had aged ten years in five minutes. His skin looked mottled, a vein throbbed wildly at his temple. He looked away, and when he spoke, David could barely hear the words. Dub stared into the flames as though he could see back in time. "I was upstairs getting ready for bed when I heard the bell. Ringing off the wall." He shook his head. "I grabbed my robe. That time of night—I knew Jason was out. I was afraid something had happened to him."

"It was Waneath?" David asked.

Dub nodded. "She was already in the front hall before I got to the head of the stairs. She knows—knew—where the spare key was." He sighed and leaned back with his eyes closed. "I have never seen a woman that mad in my life. She was barefoot—no stockings. Her feet were all muddy. She was carrying her shoes—one in each hand." He looked up at David, and his eyes pleaded with him for understanding. "She started screaming at me. At first I didn't know what was the matter—thought maybe she was drunk and Jason was out there someplace hurt."

"But she was angry at him."

"Not just him. All of us—Jason, you and me."

"What did she have to be mad at you about?"

"She was carrying my child."

"I beg your pardon?"

Dub nodded. "I'm not proud of it. I sure as hell didn't plan it."

"Dub, she was nineteen years old. You're what, sixty-three?"

Dub sat up straight. "I'm not dead yet, dammit. Those movie stars have babies a lot later than any damn sixty-three!"

"You're not a movie star."

"No, but I'm a rich man!" Dub snarled. "Rich, and prominent, and powerful."

"I don't understand any of this. Maybe you'd better explain it."

"After Jason went to school, Waneath started dropping by sometimes in the evenings on her way home from school. Said she missed the boy the way I did. Gave us something to talk about. We were both lonely, both feeling the boy'd betrayed us by going off and leaving us that way. She kept saying she was gonna marry him in June, but I knew he wasn't about to marry her, and I think she knew it too. We'd watch television together. Sometimes I'd pick up a movie. She'd make me a few drinks. Keep me company, you know, the way Melba used to."

"Neva never found out?"

"Always after Neva'd gone home to her own husband and grandchildren."

"Watching the occasional movie and having a couple of drinks do not add up to a baby, Dub."

"Yeah, they do. Or they did. I told you I'm not proud of it. Damn stupid. One night she was over here, we was watching some historical movie about some English king with four rotten sons. She said that's what I ought to do— get myself a new, young wife, have me a passel of kids and disinherit the lot of you. I'm not too old to father sons."

David nodded. "No, you're not too old to marry again or to father sons."

"Damn right." He looked away. "Looking back on it, I think she'd been making those drinks of mine stronger than usual. Had a couple herself—rum punches. Taste like fruit juice, but they don't call 'em punches for nothing.

"Waneath said it would serve Jason right if she was the one to give me those sons. It started out being funny. Then things got out of hand. I didn't intend for it to go that far. To this day I don't know whether she planned it or not. Everybody always said she was a gold digger. Maybe I was a better bet than waiting for Jason to get out of college." He took a deep breath, and continued.

"I was also a hell of a lot likelier to die sooner. Afterward, she cut out of here like a scalded cat. I called her the next day, said I didn't think it was a good idea her coming over here at night like that anymore."

"How'd she take it?" David asked.

"Acted snippy, but I think she was relieved. It was really Jason she wanted. I think she just got carried away thinking about being mistress of Long Pond and how pleased her momma would be."

"I can just bet," David said. He glanced up at the portrait above the fireplace. Didn't Dub see the correlation between what Waneath had tried to do to him and what Melba had accomplished with David? He looked at Dub, who sat slumped in his chair. No, he hadn't made the connection, and David wasn't about to point it out to him.

"Can I have a drink? I'm spitting cotton," Dub said.

David went to the bar in the loggia and came back with a soda over ice. He noticed that Dub's hand shook when he took the glass. "Tell me about that night."

"I didn't have the first notion she'd actually gotten pregnant, David, you've got to believe me!"

"What would you have done if you'd known?"

"Probably offered to marry her. She never gave me the chance. Not until that night."

"So you killed her?"

"No. I keep telling you it was an accident. She didn't want to listen to me. Just started running up those stairs with her shoes in her hands like hammers. She was hysterical. Said I'd ruined her life. I think she was gonna hit me with 'em, but she never got the chance. You know what that damn marble is like when it's wet—it's like glass. I was standing there staring at her with my mouth open, and about halfway up, her feet slipped out from under her. If she hadn't been holding those shoes maybe she could a' caught herself. As it was, she dropped 'em at the last minute—I guess that's when she tore that fingernail loose that dropped off in the car—and I heard her head smack the edge of the stair. Sounded like the crack of doom."

"Why didn't you call 911?"

Dub shook his head. "Because she was all right! She seemed fine. She slid down a couple of stairs, but by the time I reached her she was sitting up shaking herself. She'd stopped being hysterical—I guess the fall scared that out of her. I grabbed ahold of her and helped her down to the chair by the front door. There wasn't any blood. She said she'd probably have a big goose egg and how was she going to explain that to her parents. Then I went back and got her shoes, put them on her. Her feet were all muddy. She was shaking her head and staring up at me kind of bleary-eyed. I told her I was taking her to Jackson to the emergency room."

"To the hospital?"

"Yeah, she didn't want to go, but when she stood up, she said she felt kind of dizzy. I brought the car around and got her into it and we took off. I drove like a bat out of hell. She was sitting beside me with her eyes closed and her head back on the seat. I kept talking to her, but after a minute or so, she didn't answer me. I figured she'd passed out. I have never been that scared in my life, let me tell you.''

''When did you discover she was dead?''

Dub sighed deeply. ''I stopped by the levee where there weren't any trees. The moonlight was shining into the car. I leaned over and tried to get her to respond. I've seen death before, David, plenty of times. I know dead, and she was dead. Her eyes and her mouth were open, staring. She didn't have any pulse.'' He dropped his head into his hands. ''She was so cold.''

''So you picked her up, took her to the top of the levee and left her there?'' David asked. ''Why didn't you go to the hospital?''

''I couldn't, don't you see? What was I gonna tell them? This nineteen-year-old girl just fell down my front-hall steps because she's carrying my illegitimate baby? I couldn't be associated with any of this.''

''But it was all right for Jason to be associated with it?''

''I thought they'd think it was a hit-and-run, or—hell, I don't know what I was thinking except to get as far away as fast as I could. But I swear to God it never occurred to me that Jason would get blamed, or that they'd think she was murdered, for God's sake.''

''But once they did, you still didn't come forward, did you?''

''I couldn't. It had gone too far. Besides, I was sure they'd drop the charges.''

''You do live in a fantasy world where everything works out the way you want it to.''

''Hell, nothing in my life ever worked out the way I wanted it to!'' Dub said. ''I never wanted any of this. I wanted to see the world, not be some dirt farmer with a wife I didn't love and a daughter I couldn't control.'' He reached out to David and there were tears in his eyes. ''You were the only good thing to come out of all this—you and Jason. Now I've lost you both just the way I'm going to lose Long Pond.''

''Dub, we've got to fix this,'' David said.

''You believe me?''

''Yes, I believe you, but that doesn't mean anyone else will.''

''I'll go to the police. I'll tell them what happened.''

''It's too late for that. They'll say you're confessing just to save Jason.'' He leaned over and reached for the telephone. ''We've got to get Kate over here. She'll know what to do.''

''No!'' Dub roared. ''I won't go begging to some woman to save my bacon.''

''You don't have a choice any longer.''

''No!'' Dub stood and took two steps toward David. His face was suffused and dangerously red. Then the anger was replaced with bewilderment, and a sudden spasm of pain. He reached out one hand and pressed the area under his rib cage with the other. ''David?'' he choked.

Then he collapsed, full length, facedown, narrowly missing the corner of the desk.

David reached him in a stride and turned him over. Dub's face was contorted. His breath soughed in his chest.

''Oh, God, I'm dying,'' he groaned.

''Don't you dare die on me, Dub,'' David snapped. He reached up for the telephone on the desk and dialed 911.

Dub gripped his hand so hard it felt as though it would break. David grimaced, and returned the pressure. Dub's eyes were terrified, his breath came in shallow gasps. He pulled David down to him with surprising strength. ''Promise me,'' he whispered through his teeth. ''Promise me you'll never leave Long Pond.''

''Dub...''

''Promise me. Oh, God, it hurts!'' Dub's back arched. ''Please, promise me.''

David sighed. ''All right, Dub, I promise.''

''Say the words.''

''I promise I won't leave Long Pond.''

Dub closed his eyes. For a moment the pain seemed to subside. In the distance, David could hear the clang on the Athena fire truck and rescue squad.

Dub looked up. ''Power of attorney.'' Every word seemed agonizing. ''For you.''

''Don't talk.''

''Got to. Read my will. You must... Power. In safe.'' His mouth opened, his eyes rolled back in his head and he stopped breathing.

''Damn!'' David leaned over, crossed his hands over Dub's breastbone and began to count as he started CPR.

''My word, David,'' Neva said from the hall. ''What is all that... Oh, sweet heaven! Dub!''

''One, two, three, four,'' David counted. He had little breath left over. This was much harder work than he'd ever suspected. He bent down to blow into Dub's mouth. ''Let them in, Neva.''

The sirens cut off, and a moment later David heard the stomp of heavy male feet in the front hall. ''In here!'' he called.

He felt himself shoved away and other quiet, quick men took his place. ''I think he's had a heart attack,'' David said.

''Sure looks like it,'' one of the EMTs said and called over his shoulder, ''He's breathing. Let's roll.''

Two minutes later David followed them out the front door. "Where you taking him?"

"Jackson Memorial. Emergency cardiac unit."

David nodded. "I'll follow." From the gurney he saw Dub's hand wave. He forced away the oxygen mask that covered his face. David went to him. "Relax, Dub, you're going to be fine."

"Remember. You promised," Dub whispered. "Your responsibility now. Read my will."

David nodded. "Don't worry about it."

He watched the trucks roll out the driveway. He knew Dub had a living will and a power of attorney naming him executor in case of emergency. He'd better take both along with him in case he had to make decisions about Dub for the doctors.

He opened the wall safe quickly and began flipping through the blue folders of legal papers. He found the power of attorney quickly, but not Dub's living will. He took a stack of papers to the desk, all the while telling himself to calm down, relax, that Dub would be fine, and all the time growing more and more guilty. Had he caused Dub's heart attack?

He opened a folder that said will. Dub's last will and testament. Dub wanted him to read it. Because he thought he was dying? He couldn't die. David had always thought the old man would go on until the end of time. He didn't want to open Dub's will now, but he'd promised.

He opened it, scanned the legalese of the first pages and came to the main part. Jason was left one hundred thousand dollars in trust to be handed over on his twenty-fifth birthday. Everything else—Long Pond, the house, land, barns, stock—everything—went outright to David.

For a moment he was too stunned to take in what he'd read. Then he carefully refolded the will. Beneath it lay the living will. He put it and the power of attorney aside, replaced the other papers in the safe, closed and locked it just as Neva rushed back into the room.

"They're gone. Oh, sweet heaven!"

"Neva, get Jason."

"He's not here. Oh, Lord, David. Is Dub going to be all right?"

"I don't know. Jason must be still at Jimmy Viccolla's. Call him, tell him to meet us at Jackson Memorial."

"I'm coming too."

"Of course, but find Jason first. You can come with him."

She nodded.

David ran to Dub's Cadillac and drove away as fast as he dared.

Please God, he prayed silently, *let Dub be all right.* He looked around him. *I thought this was what I wanted. But now all I want is Kate. I can't chain her to this place. If I love her,* he thought as he slid the car into drive, *if I truly love her, then I have to send her away.*

He looked at the house in his rearview mirror and said aloud, "I wish to God you would burn down all over again, damn you."

CHAPTER EIGHTEEN

KATE DROVE the Navigator. Arnold sat beside her silently, his eyes focused on the window beside him. Ten minutes later Kate pulled off the road under a grove of naked oaks. A deteriorating picnic table with attached benches canted sideways a few feet in front of them. "This is where Jason said he parked," Kate said.

"We've been all over this place," Arnold said, "So have the police."

A hundred yards down the road she pulled off again to the side of the road. "Look," she said, and pointed across Arnold's chest.

Although they were still four or five miles away from Long Pond by road, it sat, as it had the first day when David showed it to her, across a single large soybean field. "Less than a mile if you don't mind walking through a muddy field."

At night with lights on the wide front porch, the house would be a beacon. Kate slipped out of the car and walked over to the field. Arnold followed. Running along the edge of the field was a strip of unplowed land perhaps five feet wide. Probaby muddy since October, the path led straight as a ruler to the front lawn of Long Pond.

"She was out here alone," Kate said. "Mad as a hornet, probably crying. Where else would she go to get a ride home?"

"But did she make it, or did something or someone stop her before she got there?"

"I'm very much afraid she made it," Kate said.

"Was Jason there?"

Kate shook her head. "He was off looking for David, remember? Neva Hardin goes home at dusk. There was only one person at home."

"But Dub never said a word about seeing her that night."

"Come on," Kate said. "We've got one more thing to check before we talk to Dub."

Five minutes later they pulled up in front of Long Pond. As they started to climb out of the car, Neva Hardin ran down the front steps. She looked frantic.

"Oh, Miz Mulholland! Do you have any idea where Jason is?"

"I think he said he was going over to Jimmy Viccolla's to help replace his father's flywheel."

"I can't get anybody to answer the phone over there."

"What's happened?" Arnold asked.

Neva turned a stricken face to him. "It's Dub! He's had a stroke or a heart attack or something! They took him off to Jackson Memorial in an ambulance thirty minutes ago." She began to shake. "Somebody's got to find Jason. That boy'll die if anything happens to Dub."

"Where's David?" Kate said. She took hold of Neva's shoulders and stooped so that she looked into the woman's eyes. "Neva?"

"He was here when it happened. Thank God he knows CPR." She looked terrified. "Oh, Lord, don't let anything happen to Dub."

"How was he when they left?" Arnold asked.

"I don't know!" Neva wailed. "David's following the ambulance. I got to go too, but I got to pick up Jason at Jimmy's first."

"You go on, Neva," Kate said, glancing at Arnold. "We'll lock up the house and go by Jimmy's for Jason. If he's not there, Jimmy will know where he is."

"Could you?"

"Go. Don't worry."

Neva pulled her keys from the pocket of her apron, and ran over to her Honda. A moment later they watched her spew gravel down the driveway.

"She forgot her purse and coat," Kate said.

"Then we'd better find them and take them to her," Arnold said grimly. "We did say we'd lock up. Come on, Kate, no time like the present."

"Arnold, this just makes it worse." She followed him up the porch stairs and into the front hall. They stopped and stared up the foot of the pink marble staircase. Arnold knelt and sat on one of the treads, then ran his hand over the edge.

"Not really sharp," he said.

"Sharp enough," Kate said. "Waneath must have been carrying her shoes. Her feet would have been wet."

"I wouldn't want to fall down this thing," Arnold said. He pulled his hand away. A pinkish streak ran faintly across his palm. "I'd have thought the way Neva keeps these stairs..."

"Marble sheds dust no matter what you do—unless you varnish it, God forbid. And it's like glass when it's wet. With her shoes in her hands, Waneath wouldn't have been able to catch herself."

"But did she fall or was she pushed?" Arnold asked. "That is the sixty-four-thousand-dollar question."

Ten minutes later as they drove into Jimmy Viccolla's yard, Arnold said, "I say we don't mention our suspicion to Jason or David until we're sure,"

"I disagree. I think we have to tell David. Not Jason.

He's got enough on his plate. What on earth are we going to do if Dub dies?''

"Might be better for him if he did," Arnold said.

"Arnold!"

"Well, it might."

"And leave us with nobody to confirm or deny anything? We need him alive and in his right mind if we're going to get the D.A. to drop the charges against Jason."

"Jason won't thank you."

"I warned him the first day that my only job was to get him off, and that if he got in the way I'd run right over him. I don't think he believed me."

"He'll believe you now. What does this do to your relationship with David?"

"I can't think about that now." She climbed out of the Navigator and picked her way through the mud puddles to the side door of Jimmy's garage.

She found Jason and Jimmy elbow deep in the innards of David's truck. Rock music blared from a pair of speakers mounted under the eaves. No wonder they couldn't hear the telephone. Apparently, they communicated by sign language, since there was no way either of them could hear the other at any level below a bellow.

Arnold went directly to the tuner and hit the power switch. The resulting silence was stunning.

"Hey!" Jimmy raised his head from the engine compartment.

"Jason?" Kate said.

"Yeah?" He stared at her a moment. "Something's happened."

"I'm afraid so."

"Is it my dad?"

Arnold stepped in. "Your grandfather's in the hospital."

"What?" Jason looked stunned, young and suddenly very frightened.

"Maybe a heart attack," Arnold continued. "We've come to take you to the hospital."

"Oh, man!" Jimmy said. "You want me to drive you?"

Jason shook his head, grabbed the rag at Jimmy's waist, wiped his hands and ran them through his hair. "Come on!" he said, and ran for the Navigator. "I'll drive."

"No way!" Kate said, following him.

He gave her a look, then slid into the back seat. In a moment they were off.

"What happened?" Jason said. He leaned over the back of Arnold's seat. "Is he gonna be all right? Oh, man! This is all my fault! He's worried about me."

"Nonsense," Arnold said. "Sit back and put on your seat belt. Kate, you have any tissues?"

"In my purse."

Arnold reached between them, found her purse, opened it, pulled out a packet of tissues and handed it over the back seat to Jason. "You have oil on the end of your nose. Wipe your face. And do you by any chance have a clean T-shirt under that filthy shirt you're wearing?"

Jason took the tissues and began to scrub at his face. Again, Kate marveled at Arnold's ability to hit the right note.

"Yeah, but I didn't stop to get my jacket," Jason said.

Kate reached over to turn up the heat. "The hospital has seen worse," she said.

"Man, can't you drive any faster?"

"You want to wind up in the emergency room beside your grandfather? Cool it, Jason, we'll get there."

"Is he gonna die?"

"Neva said he'd had a heart attack or a stroke. That's

all I know. Your father did CPR on him until the ambulance got there.''

"Dad was there?'' Jason sighed and leaned back. "It'll be all right, then. Dad'll save him.''

Kate glanced at Arnold. Fathers did carry incredible burdens. Whatever else David was to his son, he could obviously perform miracles.

"Listen,'' Jason said. "He know about you and my dad?''

"Dub?'' Kate asked.

"No. Him!'' She glanced in the rearview mirror and saw Jason point to the back of Arnold's head.

"He has a pretty good idea. Why?''

"'Cause I'm sorry about this morning when I mouthed off. I've been thinking, and my dad's right. I mean, I'm outa here once this trial thing is over, and my dad's always been lonely, even with me. I mean, I kept trying, but I never could fill him up, you know? It's like he had this empty place inside him. But, I mean, he wouldn't want to leave Long Pond and you can't leave Atlanta.''

"We're a long way from that.''

"Keep it that way,'' Arnold said softly. "For all our sakes.''

"So you and my dad do your thing, okay? I mean, you've been pretty nice to me, and you were really great with Coral Anne.''

"I hope you continue to feel that way,'' Kate said with a sinking feeling. "And don't worry, Jason. You're going to beat this thing.''

"At what cost?'' Arnold whispered.

Kate shook her head. This Christmas looked worse and worse. She had to get to David. She wanted to take him in her arms, hold him against her and tell him that everything was going to be all right.

But it wasn't. Whoever she saved—Dub or Jason—David would never be able to forgive her for condemning the other.

JASON LOPED DOWN the hospital hall toward his father. "Is Granddaddy all right?" Behind him David saw Kate walking toward them with Arnold following three paces behind.

"The doctors think it's a mild attack." His eyes sought hers. He needed to feel her against him, the warmth of her body flooding into him. But not with Jason standing there.

"A heart attack?" Jason wailed. "It's all this with Waneath. It's killing him."

David knew that was probably true, but not in the way Jason meant. Over Jason's shoulder he said to Kate. "Thanks for bringing Jason," he said. He raised his hands in a gesture of futility.

She nodded and kept her voice even. She knew, bless her. But then she'd always known when he needed her. "No problem," she said. "Jimmy's not quite through with your truck."

"Can I see him?" Jason asked.

David shook his head. "He's in surgery."

"Surgery? But I thought…"

David put a hand on Jason's shoulder. "Sit down, son," he said, and led the boy to one of the couches along the wall. Kate leaned against the door frame and watched them. "You know how Dub's been having those spells lately?"

"Yeah?"

"He's got some blockage. They're doing an emergency angioplasty to clear it out. And he's got blockage in one of the arteries in his neck. He'll have to go back into surgery to fix that too." He looked at Jason's stricken face. "Both relatively simple procedures, they tell me. His heart muscle's strong. He should be better than ever."

"You telling the truth?" Jason said.

David nodded. "I'm telling you what they told me."

"He's not going to die?"

"His chances are very good. I should have made him go to the doctor months ago, the old fool." He shook his head. "I let it slide because I didn't want to fight with him. I know how he feels about doctors."

"When can I see him?" Jason asked.

David shook his head. "I don't know. Why don't you go find Neva in the cafeteria? I sent her there because she looked ready to pass out when she got here. Get yourself something to eat, and make sure she at least has a cup of hot chocolate. Then the two of you settle down in the waiting room, okay?"

"I want to stay here."

Kate touched his shoulder. "I need to speak to your father. You can come back up in a few minutes."

David was struck by the gentleness of her tone and by the concern in her eyes. Then he was even more struck when Jason covered her hand with his and smiled up at her. "Yeah, okay."

David watched Jason wander off toward the elevator with his hands in his pockets. Suddenly he had no idea what to say to Kate. He felt trapped. He'd have to betray Dub to save Jason, or sacrifice Jason to save Dub. Unless he could come up with a new solution.

If he told Kate now what he knew, she was duty bound to use it on behalf of her client. He had to keep his mouth shut until he was certain of the best way to handle the situation.

Kate slipped into the seat beside him and took his hand. "I'm so sorry about Dub," she said.

He felt strength flow from the simple touch of her fingers. "Me, too."

Gently she pulled her hand away. "I got the results of the autopsy today," she said quietly. "I think I can clear Jason."

David felt his heart turn over. He closed his eyes for a moment. "Thank God."

"But only by accusing Dub," she continued.

David sat up straight. "What?"

She looked at him curiously. "Waneath's wound had particles of pink marble dust in it," she said. "I'm willing to bet they'll match up with the marble from the staircase at Long Pond."

David froze. Anything he said would only make the situation worse.

Kate narrowed her eyebrows at his expression. "David? What is it?"

He shook his head. "Nothing. Go on."

"Remember that first day after the bail hearing when you drove me out to Long Pond? You showed the house from across the soybean field. As the crow flies, it's less than a mile from where Jason and Waneath had their big blowup."

"So?" David said softly.

"So, she walked across the field barefoot."

"You don't know that."

"Her feet were dirty, but her shoes were clean. She went to Long Pond, David, maybe just to get Dub to drive her home. Something happened, and she died."

"That's a big jump, isn't it? Maybe Dub didn't even hear her. Didn't answer the door."

"Did you know Waneath had an abnormally thin skull?"

He shook his head.

"A blow that might give you or me a mild concussion cracked her temple like an egg."

"Dub would never hurt a woman on purpose."

David heard Arnold's quick intake of breath. That had

been a bad slip. He had to watch himself. Time. He had to buy time to think how best to serve both Dub and Jason. He needed to head Kate off, but she'd always been as tenacious as a bulldog.

"Myrlene said something to me this morning, David, something I'd never thought before. She said it was odd that the three most eligible bachelors in town were three generations of the same family—you, Jason and Dub." She shook her head. "And the *most* eligible is Dub—he's rich. Waneath told everyone she wasn't averse to marrying an older man if he was rich and socially prominent. I think it's possible she seduced him, that he was the father of her baby."

David felt the breath go out of his lungs. "Kate, it was an accident."

She sat up. "What?"

"She fell running up the steps. He was taking her to the emergency room in Jackson when he realized she was dead."

For a moment Kate simply gaped at him. Then she began to shake her head and her forehead creased. "How long have you known?"

He waved a hand. "Not long."

She stood. "When were you going to tell me? The day before Jason was to be sentenced?"

He surged to his feet. "Kate, it's not like that."

She pulled away from him and started down the corridor. "Good grief, David, I thought you'd changed, I really did. If I hadn't put all this together on my own, would you ever have told me what you knew?"

He followed her, reached for her arm. "You're Jason's lawyer. I needed a little time to decide what was best for everyone."

She shook him off and turned to face him. Her voice was

deadly quiet. "A little time? How much? *You* needed to decide. I thought you hired *me* to make those decisions, and you're supposed to give me the information I need to make them properly. I said my clients lie to me, but you're more than a client. I'm an officer of the court, David. It is my duty to give this report to the sheriff, and when I do, he's going to figure out precisely what I did, and he's going to come arrest Dub for murder."

"No!" David and Kate both spun at the howl that erupted from Jason. He ran down the hall toward them, the soft drink in the cup in his hand spilling with every step. "You can't do that!"

"Jason, listen to me," Kate began.

"My granddaddy didn't kill Wancath," he wailed.

"He told your father it was an accident, and maybe it was, but that's for the sheriff and the courts to decide."

"He's sick, he's been having spells, he didn't know what he was doing!" Jason cried.

"The autopsy goes to the sheriff," Kate said. "And he's going to want to talk to your grandfather." She avoided David's eyes. "As for me, I'm going home to Atlanta. I've done what you hired me for, David. And I've had enough Southern Gothic to last a lifetime." She walked away. David followed her.

"Kate, Kate, please wait. Listen to me."

Kate raised her hands. "You did it to me again, didn't you?" she said, and punched the down button on the elevator savagely. "I thought we were on the way to becoming a team again. You chose not to let me share your problems in New York. You're doing the same thing now. I can't live with a man who shuts me out, David, and I can't go on loving one either." The elevator doors opened. "I'll recommend a lawyer for Dub. Arnold can clear up things here. Have a really great Christmas." The doors closed and she was gone. The three of them, Jason, Arnold and David, stared after her.

"Dad?" Jason put a hand on his father's shoulder. "You can't let them arrest Granddaddy. I don't care what he did. He's an old man. You've got to stop her."

"I can't." He sighed. "Besides, she's right. That's exactly what I'm doing—locking her out, locking you and everybody else out." He leaned against the wall beside the elevator. "Trying to keep everything smooth on the surface for everyone else, fighting everybody's battles alone. Keeping my own counsel."

"That's what men are supposed to do," Jason said.

David stared at him. "Is that what I've taught you?"

"Yeah. I mean, we're supposed to take the heat, aren't we? Not let anybody see how we feel about things? Suck it up and keep going. That's what you always do. 'Cause when you let people see into you, you get creamed."

David shut his eyes. "Then I've made you into a coward," he said softly.

"A coward? Hell, no, Dad, I respect you. You're the bravest man I know."

"No, I'm a coward. So afraid of letting even the people I love most in this life see me vulnerable, see me needing help, support, love. That's what it's all about, Jason—not being strong and silent and locking everyone outside for fear if they see the real you they'll run away and leave you. I've done that all my life. My father did it, and if you're not careful, you'll do the same thing. It lost me the woman I love once, son, and I'm damned if it'll lose her for me again."

"Dad?" Jason looked at his father uncertainly, as though seeing him for the first time. "Dad, you're scaring me."

"Good. That's what growing up is about. I watched my mother damn near destroy my father the moment he let his guard down, and I swore I'd never ever let mine down in front of anyone. I'm scared too, Jason. Scared and so damn lonely for Kate that I'm sick with it. I'm not going to let her go, and if that means walking away from Long Pond, from Dub, and even from you for a little while, then that's what I'm going to do. It's all on your shoulders, son. I know you're strong enough to handle things without me.'' He turned to Arnold. ''You mind staying here with Jason? I've got to find Kate.''

''Go. You two are crazy enough to deserve each other.''

David hugged his son, and when the elevator doors behind him slid open, smiled at the boy as he slid from view.

KATE PULLED ON her gloves as she walked into the parking garage of the hospital.

She'd drop the autopsy report by the sheriff's office, pick up the rental car at the motel and drive straight through to Atlanta. Arnold could bring her clothes.

She and Alec might not have been the world's greatest lovers, but at least they'd been a team. Alec had shared his problems as well as his triumphs with her. She could no longer accept anything less, especially from the man she loved.

She caught her reflection in the side mirror as she unlocked the car. Her hair was wild and her face looked flushed.

Suddenly, the strength left her legs. She wrenched the door open and sank onto the seat.

Talk about repeating old habits! She'd accused David of doing the same thing he'd done twenty years ago. What was she doing except re-creating her same knee-jerk reaction? Had she given him a chance to explain? To justify his choices? Even to tell her how long he'd known about Dub?

No, she'd simply gotten on her high horse and run screaming from the room, just as she planned to run back to Atlanta with her tail between her legs. From the only man she had ever, *would* ever love.

A small voice from within her spoke then, "And from a man who truly loves you." Oooh, boy. Talk about responsibility. Talk about scary. Talk about vulnerability.

And what about acceptance?

Yeah, she thought, *let's talk about acceptance.* Was that why she ran? Made a mountain out of a molehill? So she wouldn't have to face the realities of loving him?

Did she love him only when he was strong and perfect and doing precisely the right things? The right things, that is, according to the gospel of Kate. Making the choices she would make? When he lived up to her idea of perfect hero?

Is that the way he loved her?

Or do I love him when he screws up big time? Does he love me when I do?

Damn straight. "Get up off your rear end, Kate Mulholland, and go back upstairs," she said.

As she stood, David came pelting down the ramp toward her.

She froze.

"Damnation, you're not leaving before we straighten this out."

"I'm not leaving, period," she said.

"What?" He frowned.

She shut the car door and leaned against it.

"I just found out today that if Dub dies I inherit Long Pond," David said.

Kate blinked. This was not the way she'd envisioned the conversation.

He continued, "You want me to hire another lawyer, fine. But if I have to hog-tie you and keep you a prisoner until this mess is cleared up, I'll damn well do it, and after that I'll walk away from Long Pond and go wherever you want to go and do whatever you want to do. I'm not losing you again, and if you don't like it, or like the fact that you don't always agree with what I decide, you'll have to adjust. Do I make myself clear?'' His chest heaved.

''I thought Long Pond meant everything to you,'' she said with more truculence than she felt. Inside, her heart began to lift.

''So did I. I love running the place, but I love you considerably more. If I have to go back to school and learn to be a landscape gardener or a computer programmer, then that's what I'll do, but I will not give you up and I won't let you give me up.''

''And Jason?''

''He's very close to being a grown man and out on his own living his own life. If Dub has to go to jail, I don't know how I'll manage to fulfill my other obligations, but if I have to commute from Atlanta, I will.'' He stared at her. ''Well, say something, dammit!''

An elderly couple walked up the ramp past them and eyed them suspiciously. For a moment she thought the man would ask if she needed help, but his wife whispered something to him and dragged him along.

''Yes, David,'' she said meekly.

He gaped at her. ''What?''

''I'm sorry I yelled at you and walked out.''

He eyed her suspiciously. ''This isn't like you.''

''Being loved is a darned sight scarier than loving. I'm terrified.''

''Being loved? You actually admit I love you? You've never done that before.''

She shook her head. ''I never believed it before.''

He reached for her, pulled her into his arms and buried

his face in her hair. Then he raised his head and kissed her, deeply, tenderly and forever.

After a moment she broke the kiss, and said breathlessly, "But if you ever keep anything from me again, I swear I will deck you."

"And then walk out on me?"

"You should be so lucky. I will not walk out, I'll get right up in your face and make your life miserable in true lawyerly fashion until you spill your guts. I'm through walking out."

"Till death do us part?"

She caught her breath. "Are you asking me to marry you again?"

He squeezed her so hard she thought she'd pass out. "On Christmas Eve with holly in your hair." He sobered an instant later. "But you'll have to put up with a commuter marriage until this business with Dub is resolved, and he can start running Long Pond again on his own."

"No way. Do you think it matters one whit to me where I practice law? In some fancy law office in Atlanta or in Jackson, Mississippi, or even in Athena? What matters is the people I represent, not the fees they pay me. I've got enough money. What I don't have is a life or a love."

"I can't let you—"

"I beg your pardon? You're doing it again, David. Knock it off."

"The logistics are a nightmare," he said ruefully.

"They certainly are. We have less than three weeks to get the charges against Jason dropped, convince the sheriff and the district attorney not to prosecute Dub on anything other than obstruction of justice for not reporting Waneath's death, get him home to Long Pond to convalesce, affiliate me with a law firm in Jackson and arrange a marriage." Her eyes widened. "Oh, Lord, and then there's Christmas!"

CHAPTER NINETEEN

CHRISTMAS EVE morning dawned clear, bright and twenty degrees colder than normal.

"Thanks for offering to pick up my mother and Arnold at the airport," Kate said to Jason over breakfast at David's kitchen counter. "But do not drive like a lunatic."

"Yeah, right." Jason grinned at her.

"My mother will go upside your head with her handbag. She has turned into a very forceful woman."

"Gee, wonder where she gets that from?" Jason said innocently. "I'm sorry my gram and granddad couldn't make it."

Kate wasn't certain she felt the same way. She knew David's father was delighted, but Mrs. Canfield? She'd have an opportunity to find out for herself when they visited in the spring. At the moment she had to admit she had heaved a small sigh of relief when they didn't want to leave home at Christmas. The town was still divided by the scandal of Dub's admission. Not having to face the Canfields was a small blessing.

"Where's my dad?" Jason asked. "And are you going to eat that last piece of toast?"

"Over at your grandfather's, and no, I am not."

"Great." Jason reached for the toast and began to drizzle honey over it in precise patterns. "How come Dad's over there?"

"Dub wanted to talk to him about something before the wedding."

"Neva says we'll have Christmas dinner about four tomorrow if that's all right," Jason said. "I mean, you going to be newlyweds and all."

"Tell her that's fine." She propped her chin on her hand. "You really okay with this marriage business?"

"Yeah. I mean, you saved all our butts. Kind of handy to have a lawyer in the family the next time I get arrested."

"Don't even think that. I didn't actually save anybody's butt. Your grandfather is going to have to do a hundred hours of community service, he's had to eat a bunch of crow with the townspeople as well as apologize to the Talleys. And he's had to pay a whopping fine."

"But he didn't have to go to jail."

"The only thing he was actually guilty of was the improper disposal of a body and failure to report an accidental death."

"He was guilty of a whole lot more than that," Jason said.

"Not according to the law." She laid her hand on Jason's sleeve. "Hard to see your idols have feet of clay, isn't it?"

"He's still my granddaddy, and I still love him. I guess this is part of growing up. Frankly, Kate, I downright hate it."

"Sure you do. It's going to take some time for the town to get over this."

"My dad didn't do anything wrong. Neither did you. Besides, Neva says the next big scandal and the Canfields will be ancient history." He sighed deeply. "Hope she's right."

"Me, too. But remember, it's Christmas, and you can't hurt Christmas. Is Coral Anne coming to the wedding tonight?"

"Yeah. Mrs. Talley hit the ceiling, but Coral Anne's tough."

"Good. Now scat. I've got the caterer and the florist to check, a bunch of presents to wrap and a hair appointment at Charlotte's. See you at seven? And do not drive my mother into a ditch."

"HERE," Dub said, and handed David a blue-covered legal document. "That Selig did this for me."

"What is it?"

"Power of attorney for my shares of Long Pond. From here on in, David, it's your show."

"Now, listen, Dub—"

"I won't be available to answer questions or get in your way."

"Just because you're working with the parks commission..."

"Nope. I'll have that done in a month. I'm feeling a little guilty about this, David. I went behind your back and did something you may not approve of."

"What now?" David asked.

"Well, since you have decided not to move to China, I stole a march on you and talked to those guys myself." He sounded proud, but a little defensive. "They want me to go to China for three months this spring—just to see if it works out. Nothing definite."

"Dub, that's wonderful!" David said, and meant it. "Maybe you'll get your chance to see the world after all."

"Yeah, that's what I was thinking. You're not mad?"

"I'm delighted. We'll miss you. Maybe I can persuade Kate to come see you."

"Whew! That's a load off my mind."

"But what'll happen to Long Pond?"

"You'll run it."

"No," David said, waving a hand above his head. "All this—the house, I mean."

"Neva'll look after it. Unless you and Kate want to move in."

"Not on your life."

"Didn't think so. I won't be gone forever. Long Pond'll be here for Jason, if he ever decides he wants to come home. If not, he can use it as a vacation house when he's not off making movies."

"It's a big responsibility," David said.

"Shoot. You been doing most of it for the past ten years anyway. And I'll expect my share of the profits. I'm not a total fool."

"No, but you're a remarkable one."

"Call this my penance. I'm also endowing a college scholarship fund in Waneath's name for a deserving graduate from Athena High. That way, if for some reason Big Bill and Mrs. Talley won't cough up to send Coral Anne to an Ivy League school the way she wants them to, I can make sure she goes. If they pay for her, then I send somebody else. Good plan?"

"Great plan, Dub."

"Had to do something to make up for what happened."

"The doctors say there's no telling how much your good sense was affected by the garbage in the arteries in your neck. According to them, you've been experiencing spells for some time, judging from the state you were in. I should have seen the signs and made you do something about it."

"I didn't want to know what was wrong with me," Dub said. "Sure didn't want to see any damn doctors. I can't joke my way out of this one. I wasn't crazy. I was responsible. And a blithering idiot. I got some things to work out, and I'd be better off getting away from Athena to do the working. Plus, there are some folks who'd rather not run into me on the street right now. Now, how's about we have us a little bourbon and branch to seal the deal?''

"SCARED?" Arnold asked. He was sprawled across the bed in his motel room, which Kate was using to dress for her wedding.

"Terrified. How's my hair?''

"What do I know? You sure you want all that green stuff in it?''

"The holly? It's tradition. I wear it in my hair at all my weddings to David Canfield.''

"If you say so.''

"Arnold, are you certain you want to move to Whitman, Tarber and McDonough with me? I still think I can get you that senior partnership in Atlanta as my last official act before I move to Jackson.''

"Wouldn't know what to do with myself without you to boss me around.'' He locked his hands behind his head. "I was never that attached to Atlanta. Besides, Pink Tarber is paying me more than you cheapskates ever did in Atlanta.''

"And all we have to do is make enough rain to pay our respective salaries. Think we can pull it off?''

"Indeed I do,'' Arnold said. "I've already got us lined up to do a malpractice suit in Birmingham the minute you come back from your honeymoon.''

"Honeymoon? David intends to teach me to drive a combine on my honeymoon.''

"I warned you. Have you pulling the plow in no time.'' He glanced at his watch. "Come on, the hour of thy doom approacheth. We're due at the church in fifteen minutes.''

"Oh, Lord, Arnold, I am so happy I may cry!''

THE SMALL EPISCOPAL church was already festooned with greenery for the Christmas midnight service. Dub, much taken with Mrs. Hillman, was playing the southern gentle-man on the front pew. Behind them sat Myrlene and Jimmie Viccolla with Myrlene's mother. David and Kate had dis-cussed the guest list and decided to keep the ceremony small and private, so the only other person invited was Coral Anne Talley.

Coral Anne looked downright pretty. She'd dropped a few pounds, and had taken Juanita's words about her hair to heart.

Jason stood beside his father. From the back of the church Kate thought again how remarkably alike they were. Two men. Jason was no longer the boy he'd been only a few weeks earlier. Like his father he had become wiser and sadder. Kate prayed the rest of life's lessons for him would be kinder.

As the music started, David looked up and caught Kate's eye. She walked down the aisle to meet him, handed her prayerbook to her mother as she passed and took her place beside him at the altar. As the priest began the age-old ceremony, David leaned over and whispered, "This time forever. Merry Christmas, my love."

HARLEQUIN SUPERROMANCE®

**From April to June 1999,
read about three women whose
New Millennium resolution is**

By the Year 2000: *Revenge?*

***The Wrong Bride* by Judith Arnold.**
Available in April 1999.
Cassie Webster loves Phillip Keene and expected to marry
him—but it turns out he's marrying someone else. So
Cassie shows up at his wedding…to prove he's got
The Wrong Bride.

***Don't Mess with Texans* by Peggy Nicholson.**
Available in May 1999.
Susannah Mack Colton is out to get revenge on her
wealthy—and nasty—ex-husband. But in the process
she gets entangled with a handsome veterinarian,
complicating *his* life, too. Because that's what happens
when you *"Mess with Texans"!*

***If He Could See Me Now* by Rebecca Winters.**
Available in June 1999.
The Rachel Maynard of today isn't the Rachel of ten
years ago. Now a lovely and accomplished woman,
she's looking for sweet revenge—and a chance to win
the love of the man who'd once rejected her.
If He Could See Me Now…

Available at your favorite retail outlet.

HARLEQUIN®
Makes any time special ™

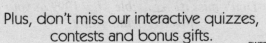

Look for a new and exciting series from Harlequin!

HARLEQUIN

Duets™

Two __new__ full-length novels in one book, from some of your favorite authors!

Starting in May, each month we'll be bringing you two new books, each book containing two brand-new stories about the lighter side of love! Double the pleasure, double the romance, for less than the cost of two regular romance titles!

Look for these two new Harlequin Duets™ titles in May 1999:

Book 1:
WITH A STETSON AND A SMILE
by Vicki Lewis Thompson
THE BRIDESMAID'S BET
by Christie Ridgway

Book 2:
KIDNAPPED? by Jacqueline Diamond
I GOT YOU, BABE by Bonnie Tucker

2 GREAT STORIES BY 2 GREAT AUTHORS FOR 1 LOW PRICE!

Don't miss it! Available May 1999 at your favorite retail outlet.

HARLEQUIN®
Makes any time special.™

Look us up on-line at: http://www.romance.net   HDGENR

COMING NEXT MONTH